THE IDES OF JUNE

THE IDES OF JUNE

A Libertus Mystery

Rosemary Rowe

This first world edition published 2016
in Great Britain and the USA by
SEVERN HOUSE PUBLISHERS LTD of
19 Cedar Road, Sutton, Surrey, England, SM2 5DA.
Trade paperback edition first published
in Great Britain and the USA 2016 by
SEVERN HOUSE PUBLISHERS LTD

British Library Cataloguing in Publication Data

Rowe, Rosemary, 1942- author.
   The ides of June.
   1. Libertus (Fictitious character : Rowe)–Fiction.
   2. Romans–Great Britain–Fiction. 3. Slaves–Fiction.
   4. Murder–Investigation–Fiction. 5. Great Britain–
   History–Roman period, 55 B.C.-449 A.D.–Fiction.
   6. Detective and mystery stories.
   I. Title
   823.9'2-dc23

ISBN-13: 978-0-7278-8591-3 (cased)
ISBN-13: 978-1-84751-694-7 (trade paper)
ISBN-13: 978-1-78010-754-7 (e-book)

All Severn House titles are printed on acid-free paper.

Severn House Publishers support the Forest Stewardship Council™ [FSC™],
the leading international forest certification organisation.
All our titles that are printed on FSC certified paper carry the FSC logo.

Typeset by Palimpsest Book Production Ltd.,
Falkirk, Stirlingshire, Scotland.
Printed and bound in Great Britain by
TJ International, Padstow, Cornwall.

To Malcolm and Jill, with fond memories of Fowey

FOREWORD

The novel is set in AD193, at a time when the mighty Roman Empire was still reeling from an almost unimaginable series of events. The increasingly crazed and profligate Commodus was dead – finally assassinated on New Year's Eve after several failed attempts – and his immediate successor, the austere and upright Helvetius Pertinax (the ex-governor of Britannia who has featured in these books as the supposed friend and patron of the fictitious Marcus Septimus) did not survive for long.

Pertinax's attempts to curb expenditure – including the cessation of the lavish banquets, gifts and entertainments for which his predecessor had been famed – did not endear him to the former beneficiaries, and when he refused to honour a bonus to the elite Praetorian Guard (the Emperor's personal protection) on the grounds that there was not enough money in the treasury, he was set upon and killed. That was a political outrage in itself, but what followed was a scandal that rocked the Empire.

Two rival candidates appeared, each claiming the Imperial purple for himself, facing each other across the citadel and each promising increasingly high bribes to the Praetorian Guards for their support – effectively an auction for the Roman Empire. As with any auction, the highest bidder won and Didius Julianus was acclaimed as Emperor. However, if Pertinax's tenure of the office had been brief, his successor's grip on power was shaky from the start.

For one thing, he quickly discovered that Pertinax was right – there was insufficient money to pay the promised bribe – so the Praetorian Guard could not be relied on for support. At the same time, new claimants had emerged. No less than three outraged supporters of the previous Emperor, each asserting that he'd been named as successor by Pertinax himself, sent immediate emissaries to Rome and had themselves severally proclaimed as rightful heir. All three were serving Provincial Governors, with substantial troops at their command: Pescennius Niger, the governor of Syria and probably the senate's favoured candidate; Septimius Severus, who had the support of the entire Danube army; and (significantly for our story) Clodius Albinus, the serving Governor of Britannia. The situation was clearly dangerous.

Didius, in Rome, continued to attempt to cling to power. At first, it seems, his instinct was to try to buy support (promising influence and promotion if not actual cash to known sympathizers with the old regime), and exiling and indicting those he could not bribe. Chroniclers vary in their accounts of how bloody and severe his measures eventually became, but there are stories of violence and assassination in the streets of Rome, and swingeing edicts against his enemies elsewhere. Allegiance to Didius – never strong – continued to ebb inexorably away. Wealthy citizens began to flee, seeking the safety of their country homes, while his increasingly desperate attempts to treat and compromise as a rival army neared the capital were undermined when even his own ambassadors defected.

This is the background of unrest against which the action of the book is set, although I have taken some liberties with historical probabilities – choosing details from (sometimes questionable) near-contemporary accounts to suit the narrative.

It is frankly doubtful that the news from Rome would arrive in Glevum as quickly as the story suggests, but when Commodus died a claim was made that the news had 'reached all corners of the Empire within half a moon', and throughout these novels the same time-scale is assumed. (It is slightly more feasible, at this season of the year, as the mountain roads would be passable!) This convention means that by the Ides of June – which fall on the thirteenth, rather than the fifteenth, as June was one of the short months in the Roman calendar – news of what happened on the Kalends would be imminent.

Also, it is distinctly possible, despite the suggestion to the contrary in this tale, that Didius did not directly order the violence and murders which took place in Rome – indeed, the reports may be exaggerated tales, invented by later critics to discredit him. (When Didius fell, as he inevitably did, he is rumoured to have asked his executioner, 'Why? Whom did I kill?') Nor is there evidence that the order from Clodius Albinus summoning the Britannic legions to march in his support was actually ever issued (for reasons which emerge in the narrative) though it was clearly planned. However, for the purposes of the story, both of these events are assumed to have occurred.

The Britannia to which this Clodius had been appointed governor was the most remote and northerly of all Roman provinces: still occupied by Roman legions, criss-crossed by Roman roads, and subject to Roman laws and taxes. Latin was the language of the educated: people – especially in the newly founded towns – were adopting Roman dress and habits, and citizenship, with the precious social and legal rights which it conferred, was the aspiration of almost everyone. However, Celtic life and customs continued to exist, most especially in country areas, and many poorer families (like the trappers in this tale) living in native settlements well off the major roads, might have little contact with Roman ways at all, except for essential trade and business purposes.

These major roads were military routes, built by soldiers for the army's use, but they had transformed communication within a century. Travel between towns (themselves a Roman concept) was still difficult, of course, but paved roads made long distances possible, as the journey outlined in the book suggests. Travellers were obliged to leave the carriageway and take to the verges if the army passed, but otherwise were free to use the roads, though with brutal penalties for highway robbery. Trade flourished, and soon civilian inns and hostelries appeared, offering refreshment and accommodation on the way.

These 'casual' inns were hardly welcoming; one was likely to share a bed with fellow travellers, let alone a room, and bedding (difficult to clean) might not be changed for months. The food was basic, there were bugs, and sanitary arrangements were rudimentary at best. But fleas, filth and overcrowding were the least of the hazards one might face.

Many establishments were notorious drinking-dens, frequented by thieves and prostitutes, where rape, robbery and even murder were not unknown. (The innkeeper who lodged the Holy Family in the stable, may have been acting in their interests.)

Of course there were exceptions – as suggested in the text – especially in country areas, but respectable citizens avoided such places whenever possible, preferring the official military inns. However, the army *mansio* (like the respectable private guest houses in towns and the accommodation offered at some shrines) did not cater for casual passing trade, requiring a letter of recommendation under seal before it would admit civilian travellers. However, as with the characters in this book, obtaining such a permit was not always practical.

The centres of population which were linked by these main roads, varied in size and status and sometimes purpose, too. Glevum (modern Gloucester) was an important place, thriving with shipping, trade and industry. Its historic basis as a *colonia* for retired legionaries gave it special privileges: all freemen born within its walls were citizens by right. Most inhabitants of Glevum, however, were not citizens at all. Many were freemen born outside the walls, scratching a precarious living from a trade. Hundreds more were slaves – mere chattels of their masters, to be bought and sold with no more rights or status than any other domestic animal. Some slaves led pitiable lives, but others were highly regarded by their owners and might be treated well, though female slaves were available for their master's pleasure at all times and any resultant offspring might be sold or killed (perfectly legally – infants were not considered to be possessed of souls as yet). However, a slave in a kindly household, ensured of food and clothes, might have a more enviable lot than many a poor freeman starving in a squalid hut, and – as in this story – desperate families some-times sold their children into servitude, at least partly to ensure that they survived.

Aquae Sulis (modern Bath) was a different sort of town. Recent research suggests that it was not a town at first, but simply a large walled temple complex built around the spring. The road led past it to a strategic river-crossing further on, controlled by an army guard-post, which attracted a few tradesmen to supply their needs. As the shrine became more famous and more visitors arrived (hot water rising directly from the earth must have seemed miraculous), a straggle of habitations arose along this road, followed by small businesses and stalls, until they occupied the entire area and flourished into a busy market-town – and that is the interpretation favoured in this tale.

Power, in town and country, was vested almost entirely in men. Although individual women might inherit large estates, and many wielded considerable influence within the house, they were excluded from public office and a woman (of any age) was deemed a child in law, requiring a man to speak for her and manage her affairs – a father, husband, or a legal 'guardian'. Widows might fare better, if they were named as heirs, but those whose husbands did not leave a will might find themselves under the protection of some distant relative, or forced into remarriage with a husband found for them, either by their guardian or by order of the courts.

Marriage and motherhood were the only realistic goals for well-bred women, although tradesmen's wives and daughters often worked beside their men and in the poorest households everybody toiled. One occupation, however, was available – reasonably well-paid and respectable enough – to those of lower rank. Rich women often put their infants out to nurse – meaning that some poorer mother with a baby of her own would breast-feed a highborn child till it was old enough to wean, often taking it into her own family meanwhile. The role was sought-after, not merely because it afforded welcome income, but because breastfeeding was thought to have contraceptive powers. (Only the really wealthy, like Marcus's wife in the story, could afford a full-time wet-nurse living in the home.) Part of the content of this book hinges on the difference between the life and expectations of a woman of high rank and those of her humbler sisters, who might be citizens, but who lacked the wealth and status to merit privilege.

The rest of the Romano-British background to this book has been derived from a number of (sometimes contradictory) pictorial and written sources as well as artefacts. However,

although I have done my best to create an accurate picture of
the times, this remains a work of fiction and there is no claim
to total academic authenticity. Didius Julianus and (most)
events in Rome are historically attested, as is the existence
and basic geography of the two British towns. The rest is the
product of my imagination.

Relata refero. Ne Iupiter quidem omnibus placet. I only tell
you what I heard. Jove himself can't please everyone.

ONE

Something was seriously wrong. I should have guessed as much when Marcus's messenger arrived at my round-house to summon me to the villa 'without delay, please, citizen'. There's usually a problem if my patron wants me suddenly – but actually I was not surprised that he had called for me today.

It was the Ides of June, an officially unlucky day, when all the courts and most of the Glevum businesses are shut – which is why I was at home, of course, instead of at my workshop in the town – and on such occasions Marcus does sometimes want me to run errands of some kind. (I am not a follower of the Roman gods, preferring the more ancient deities of rock and tree and stream, and though I don't shirk the rites required by the state, I don't share the Roman horror of doing things on 'inauspicious days'.) But as soon as I was shown into the villa *atrium*, I realized that this time it was something of real significance.

For one thing, Marcus was already waiting there. Generally, he leaves his visitors to linger for a while before he deigns to come – even when, like me, he has invited them! This gives the guest due opportunity to admire the opulent appointments of the house, the rich murals and handsome furnishings, while partaking of the refreshments which courtesy requires and reflecting on his host's superiority of rank. Marcus Septimus Aurelius is one of the most important people in all Britannia, reputed to be related to the imperial Aurelian house, and the lower the caller's status, the longer he will wait.

So I was ready for a considerable pause; intending to amuse myself, as usual, by staring at the mosaic in the floor. It is not my handiwork, I am glad to say, as parts of it are rather crudely laid. However, it was in the house when Marcus purchased it and he has never chosen to have it altered or improved. ('It's not just a pavement,' he once testily explained, 'it's Neptune and the creatures of the sea. If I were still in Rome, I'd have a proper pool – an open *impluvium* catching water from the roof – but that's not practical in damp Britannia, and this mosaic is the next best thing!') So there it stays, an affront to the pavement-maker's art, and I was expecting another half an hour of gazing at its distorted fish and crooked seahorses, while nibbling on a plate of dates and figs and waiting for my patron to appear.

However, today there were no sugared fruits for me. His Excellence was not even sitting on the gilded stool which had been set for him, but was on his feet and pacing to and fro, clearly in a state of great anxiety. He whirled around to greet me as soon as I arrived and curtly dismissed the slave-boy who had shown me in.

'Leave us, page. And don't stand lingering outside the room. Go wait at the outer entrance, until I call for you!' The pageboy scuttled off, but Marcus did not smile. 'So there you are, Libertus!' he exclaimed, striding over and extending a ringed hand for me to kiss. 'I've been expecting you!'

Meaning that I should have been here long ago, of course. 'Excellence, I came as soon as possible. I was working on my palings when the message came. I only paused to put my toga on!' I pressed my lips against the seal-ring as I spoke, dropping to one painful knee in the customary bow.

Marcus snatched his hand away and gestured me to rise. 'Oh get up, Libertus! There's no time to waste on social niceties!'

This outburst worried me still more. My patron has always been a stickler for appropriate respect and if I had not knelt, I would have angered him. This matter must be even more serious than I'd guessed. 'Something has arisen, Excellence?' I prompted, heaving my aged bones upright again.

He glanced around the room, as if to make certain that we were quite alone. 'I suppose it's safe to speak? That page is out of earshot, by this time?'

More curious than ever! Of course, the current staff were all recently acquired, but Marcus is so used to having servants everywhere that he generally thinks of slaves as pieces of domestic furniture and talks as freely as if they were not there.

(I've had occasion several times to point out tactfully that they are sentient creatures with ears and eyes and tongues – adding that I might claim to know since I was once a slave myself.) So this sudden circumspection was distinctly troubling.

I looked at my patron more closely, with alarm. I had only seen Marcus once before since he had come back from his ill-starred trip to Rome the previous month, and I had noted then how strained and worn he looked. However, I had put this down to the rigours of the journey and the unhappy events which had caused him to abandon it midway. The assassination of a personal friend and patron is bound to cause distress – the more so when the friend in question is the Emperor. And as for coming home to find that all one's personal household slaves are dead! Anyone might be forgiven for looking anxious and distraught.

But new slaves had since been purchased, or transferred from his other properties elsewhere, and by now there had been ample time for him to rest – yet Marcus was looking more strained than before. He was as smart as ever in his coloured *synthesis* – the combination robe and toga he always wore indoors – but otherwise the change in him was quite remarkable. The fair curls were touched with unexpected grey, his face was pale and his usual expression of handsome arrogance had quite deserted him.

'The loss of the Emperor Pertinax has been a blow to you?' I murmured. If so, I thought, I understood his grief. I had been honoured to meet Pertinax myself, when he was governor of this province, and his severe but upright honesty had impressed me very much. 'And the nature of his successor must have pained you too.' The promotion of Didius Julianus to the imperial throne, simply as a result of offering the biggest bribe for it, had been a shock to everybody in the Empire.

Marcus shook his head. 'If that were only all!' he muttered bitterly. 'The truth is, Libertus, I don't know where to turn! I think I am in danger.'

'Danger, Excellence?'

'All known associates of Pertinax are in some danger now. First, I had a messenger from my relatives in Rome – and they report that they are in despair. Far from being disappointed that I didn't visit them, they tell me I was wise to turn back when I did. Those who supported Pertinax are being hounded everywhere, stripped of office and beggared by fines for imaginary offences. The capital's in uproar, my old friend, and those who can afford to are getting out of town.'

'People are leaving for their country seats?' I hazarded.

He answered with a nod. 'And that's not half of it. Those same supporters held senior positions in the state, so the whole Empire is falling into disarray. Jove knows how it will end. You know that there are other claimants to the purple, I suppose?'

I nodded. Several patricians of senatorial rank, particularly those posted to provincial posts, had formally refused to acknowledge Didius, and had set up counterclaims. 'I heard as much,' I answered, truthfully. 'I understand the local garrison commander's much concerned.'

Marcus snorted. 'Concerned! It's more than that. The armies throughout the Empire are in revolt against the accession of that upstart to the throne.' He put one hand on my shoulder and bent towards me, lowering his voice. 'Let's hope that they succeed. Didius is denouncing people everywhere.'

I could see why Marcus was so troubled now. He'd been a close friend of Pertinax for years – and if there were denunciations here, my patron would be among the very first to fall! 'You don't think that will happen in Britannia? Surely we're too far away from Rome?' I could not believe that Marcus Septimus, one of the richest and most powerful men in all Britannia, might find himself disgraced and stripped of all that he possessed. The idea was too shocking to be entertained.

Marcus turned away and ran his fingers through his tousled curls. 'I don't know what to think. Didius has already lost the favour of the Praetorian Guard, I hear. Pertinax was right. There wasn't any money in the imperial purse, so Didius can't pay the guard the bribe he promised them. So it's just a matter of how long he can survive. If he doesn't flee the capital, my guess is that he will not live another moon. But a moon is long enough when one is fearing for one's life. Though if he clings to power – as my family think he will – we can expect the news at any moment that the guard have toppled him, and dragged his body through the city on a hook. In which case I may survive this trouble yet.'

'So, if he falls, who will be Emperor, do you think?' If it was hard to imagine that my patron might be ruined, it was harder still to comprehend that the famed Praetorians – the Emperor's personal bodyguard and the absolute elite of Roman soldiery – could turn assassin and sell the Empire for a bag of gold. 'The senator who offers the guard the biggest bribe?'

'It will be whoever brings the strongest army, I suspect. There are already three claimants to the throne, all of them provincial governors.'

'So all of them have troops at their command?'

'Exactly. And this is not merely theoretical. They've each sent a so-called "ambassador" to Rome, to proclaim them in the forum as the one true Emperor.'

'Proclaimed, perhaps. But who would dare to march on Rome?'

He turned to that gilded chair at last and sat down heavily, gesturing that I should take the small stool at his feet. 'From what my family report, they are already doing so. Septimius Severus is marching on the capital with the backing of his troops from Africa – if he's victorious, there's some hope for me. He was a friend of Pertinax, himself. But Pescennius Niger – supported by his legions from the eastern provinces – is favoured by certain of the senators. I'm much less certain of what he would do. Didius has tried to treat with both of them, but his messengers defect so he's reduced to trying to improve defences around Rome.'

'You think that there'll be an actual battle? Roman against Roman?' I was horrified.

'More than that. There's going to be a war. In fact it has begun. Quite apart from what Didius has done, these claimants are creating their own terror in the streets. They have agents kidnapping each other's family and friends, and putting their rivals' supporters to the sword.' He shook his head.

'So you fear for your property and family in Rome?'

He looked at me as though I'd taken leave of all my wits. 'Not at all. I told you, they have fled. I fear for my property and family, here!' he said.

'But war won't reach us in Britannia, surely?' I cried. 'Imperial edicts, I can understand. But war?' This was the most far-flung of all the provinces, and the last to feel the effects of what went on in Rome.

Marcus sprang impatiently to his feet again – meaning of course that I had to do the same. 'We're going to lose the local garrison – or almost all of it. I told you there were three contenders to the throne. The third is our own Provincial Governor, Clodius Albinus. He is calling on the loyalty of the army here – and in Hispania, where he served before. And he has a case, of sorts, through lineage. Better than Didius, in any case. He intends to take the local troops and march on Rome himself.'

'So we would have no governor in the province? But there will still be laws,' I said.

He whirled around. 'And who will enforce them? The army will be occupied elsewhere. The legion here is moving in support of Albinus – I had a message from the commandant today – and without the garrison to back them up, the town watch is practically powerless.' He began that restless pacing up and down again. 'Without the legions, the populace is like a herd of pigs without a swineherd to keep control of them. Brute force will be the only argument.'

'But the civil authorities . . .?' I murmured, doubtfully.

'What authorities? Each of the claimants will attempt to kill the other two, and until someone emerges, there will be no Emperor.' He had walked away from me, and was staring at the family altar as he spoke and I noticed that there'd been a recent, feathered sacrifice. 'Can you imagine what that is going to mean? No one to appeal to in the last resort. No imperial warrant, no troops to keep the peace. The Empire will be rudderless, and that's a recipe for crime and discontent. I'd almost rather have Didius survive. Better a weak or vengeful Emperor than nobody at all.'

'Someone will emerge as Emperor in the end,' I muttered, doubtfully.

'And then the new reprisals will begin, here in Britannia as much as anywhere. Just as Didius is attempting now, to wipe out his predecessor's friends.' He looked at me. 'Fresh decrees arrive by every courier, so the commander says. I said I was in danger. Now you understand. He doesn't say so outright, naturally, but the commandant is clearly warning me that once the legion's gone, he won't be in a position to protect me, any more. I wouldn't be surprised if there's already rumour in the town.'

I frowned at him. 'I was in the colonia yesterday,' I said. 'People were muted – they're still mourning Pertinax – but there was no sign of any discontent. All the shops and businesses were open, just as usual, and the ordinary courts were operational. There was a public flogging and a crucifixion of a thief, but no rumours of savage imperial edicts – far less any signs of such things being carried out.'

He gave a bitter laugh. 'But they exist all right. I suspect that I've already been named in some of them.'

I stared at him. 'Dear gods! You mean . . .?'

He gave a bitter laugh. 'I see you understand. However, I think the commander has been hesitant to act. As he says, news takes a little while to reach us in the provinces. For all we know, the Emperor Didius is already dead and *damnatio* declared, in which case his imperial edicts would be of no account. But once the commandant has gone the *curia* here may take a different view. It's impossible to tell. Perhaps I should thank Jupiter that I've escaped so far.'

'So what do you propose to do?'

He went over and sat down on the stool again. 'Glevum is still peaceful from what you say of it – and I confess that comes as a relief. Very soon, I shall have to go into town myself. I own that so far I haven't shown my face since I came back from my travels – but I am a magistrate, I cannot simply fail to come to court. However, I must be prepared for what may come. I've drawn up an official document, naming a legal guardian for my wife and family if anything should happen and I face banishment.'

'That would be wise, I suppose.' It would be nice, for Julia, I thought to have a rich man to take care of her. Though the office of guardian would be no slight affair. If Marcus was officially proscribed, all his possessions would be forfeit to the imperial purse and he would be exiled from the Empire

– probably to some desolate rocky island, sustained by only fish and rainwater, far from the comforts of the Roman world. 'Who are you appointing?'

He frowned at me as though I should have guessed. 'Why you, of course, Libertus.'

I was thunderstruck. 'Me? But I'm a humble tradesman.' I didn't add that I had difficulty feeding my own household, now and then.

'You are a Roman citizen, you are intelligent, discreet, you know the family and you have my trust. Also, you are of no particular account, so the Emperor Didius will not have heard of you. And if nothing happens to me, I can destroy the deed without insulting you. You seem to me the perfect candidate. I presume that you do not refuse the role?'

He knew I dared not do so, though I dearly wished I could – fond as I am of Julia and her little boy and girl. 'Of course not, Excellence.'

'Then that is settled and there's no more to be said. Of course I'll give you money if I'm forced to flee, and if I'm ever pardoned – as might occur if Septimius Severus succeeds as Emperor – then I'll return and try to build my life again.'

I was still reeling from the magnitude of this. 'And that is why you asked me here today?'

He gave me a shifty look. 'Not entirely.' He wiped a hand across his brow. 'Look, Libertus, I won't prevaricate. Imperial edicts are not my only fear. I had another letter earlier today.' He slid his hand into his upper folds and produced a battered writing tablet, the two halves loosely tied together with a piece of thong. He handed it to me. 'I haven't told my wife about it, and the servants merely know that it arrived – but when you read it, you will see why I'm distressed.'

I looked at the tablet. There was a message crudely scratched into the wax:

> This is your only warning – the next time I will strike.
> You have no Emperor patron to protect you now – and
> the garrison is leaving so your friend the commander
> can't be any help. Run to him, if you choose – it won't
> do any good. He may send a guard for you, but it can't

stay for long. I can wait and I will find my chance. I plan to see you suffer, and your wife and children too – just as my family suffered at your hands. What shall it be? Fire, or strangling? Or shall I drown you all? I have not decided yet – but the next time you hear from me will be your last. I pray Dis that the knowledge costs you sleep.

TWO

I snapped the tablet shut. 'This is an outrage! You have detained the messenger, I suppose?'

Marcus had two telltale spots of anger in his cheeks, but when he spoke his voice was icy calm. 'It was not delivered, it was thrown across the wall – and the gatekeeper retrieved it and brought it in to me.'

'This gatekeeper?' I echoed. 'He's new here, isn't he? I suppose his word can be relied on?' It all seemed so unlikely that my first thought was to doubt.

'His can, I believe,' Marcus said bleakly. 'I brought him here from the Corinium house; he's worked for me for years. If it had been one of the newer men, I could not be so sure. It's a dreadful thing, Libertus, to get a threat like this and find yourself surrounded by slaves you do not know. I knew I could trust my previous household unreservedly, but any one of these that I recently acquired could be working secretly for whoever wrote that note.'

I nodded. Marcus rarely went into the slave-market himself; he had the dealer choose the best available, then bring those to the villa so he could select from them. It would be easy for an enemy to offer the trader an outstanding slave or two, and so have spies installed into the household here. No wonder Marcus had been nervous of the page. 'And you have no idea who this letter writer is?' I said. 'The gatekeeper saw nothing?'

'Nobody at all. He simply saw an object come across the wall and went and picked it up. He saw it was a writing-block and brought it straight to me. By that time, whoever threw it had run off down the lane, and though I sent a rider after him there was no sign of anyone. Probably escaped into the woods and hid.'

'So you have no means of finding who the sender was? Is it someone simply crazed? Or does some plaintiff really think he's been unjustly used?'

That was rather daring of me – and unreasonable too – because as a magistrate my patron is conspicuously fair. I have never known him take a bribe and he isn't swayed – as many are – by the wealth of an accused or the number of noisy supporters hired to make a protest at a trial. However, once or twice he has made a judgement more expedient than wholly scrupulous (usually to avoid reprisals from the Emperor Commodus) and there had already been one act of vengeance by someone he had found against in court – the one that had cost him a household full of slaves.

Perhaps that's why my patron did not take offence at my remark. 'Who knows?' he said despondently. 'I hear so many cases – and the letter gives no details of what grievance is involved. The note is badly written but it's in military script – the kind that any educated person can produce – not that of an amanuensis who could perhaps be traced. The writer does not intend me to work out who he is.'

'But it's someone literate? Which suggests a citizen.'

My patron made a face. 'It would have to be a citizen, for me to hear his case. Non-citizens are dealt with by the lesser magistrates.'

'And the whole family was affected, so the message said. So it's likely to be someone that you exiled, don't you think?' I am no expert on Roman law, but even I knew something about serious punishment. The state has several unpleasant methods of execution, depending on the crime, and non-citizens are often made to suffer them; but unless there is treason against the Emperor, the worst sentence for a citizen is usually banishment and confiscation of property – exactly the fate that Marcus was now fearing for himself. 'If this man was exiled,' I went on doggedly, 'he must have been reprieved, since he's clearly back again. Pertinax issued many pardons during his short reign, but there can't be many men now in Glevum to whom that could apply.'

'You're only assuming that it was exile, anyway!' Marcus dismissed my careful deduction with a wave. 'There are a dozen possibilities. There's the retired centurion I stripped of civil rank because he married his neighbour's slave without first freeing her – he was furious, of course. So was the grain officer I fined so heavily for adding sawdust to the sacks. Or the tax collector that I sentenced to the mines for falsifying records and keeping money for himself! Or even someone whose case I refused to hear at all – a judge has to decide what is permissible.' He sighed.

I could think of nothing sensible to say.

'It could be an exaggerated grievance, anyway.' Marcus took the writing-tablet back again, bound it together and put it carefully away. 'But you can see why I am concerned about this threat – it could not have come at a worse time for me. Because the wretch is right, of course. I have been under imperial patronage for years and suddenly I am left without recourse. Well, it's clear what I must do.'

'Act as your family have done in Rome and move away to safety somewhere else?' I asked. 'Obviously this country house is no escape. Your townhouse in Corinium, possibly? It would not be safe to use the Glevum flat, I suppose.'

He shook his head. 'I'm not talking about me. I don't propose to flee. That would be cowardly. And against my duty as a magistrate. The Empire has need of what legal officers it has, now more than ever. Justice must be done and law must be upheld as long as possible. I shall attend the court.'

'Despite the threat of edicts from the Emperor?'

'Because of them, perhaps. It's harder to capture a lion than a mouse – I have support among the populace, and arresting me is likely to enrage the mob. Of course the curia would not be swayed by that alone, but they can't be certain what the long-term future is. When Didius is overthrown – as I'm convinced he will be soon – his successor might punish them for laying hands on me. And they're aware of that. So I shall stay and maintain my duties in court, though – given the letter from this maniac – I shan't take the risk of constant travelling all the way out here. I'll move into the town apartment.'

I nodded. 'Where you have your enormous doorkeeper as a bodyguard?' I had met the man in question once or twice – a giant bear-like fellow, twice the size of any other gatekeeper I have ever seen and with appalling breath. The smell alone would fell a would-be assassin in his tracks. 'That would be wise, I think. But he can't be everywhere – come to court with you, and protect your flat as well.'

'I am aware of that,' Marcus said soberly. 'I'll keep armed slaves about me – as a magistrate I'm entitled to have *lictors* guarding me, though I have never used them up till now – and I'll engage a food-taster, as well. I'll make sure that no member of the public comes to me, without a search for hidden knives and daggers – in the court, or out. I shall have the best protection I can buy. But after that I'll have to take my chance.'

I shook my head. 'Are you quite sure, Excellence? Would it not be wiser to move right away from Glevum as soon as possible? With this new Emperor in power, you will have public enemies as well as private ones.'

He cut me off. 'I am a Roman, a patrician, and my duty keeps me here. It is my wife and family that I worry for. And that's where you come in. Your first duty as their legal guardian.'

I was astounded. How could an aging Celtic pavement-maker be of help? 'You wish me to assist? By purchasing some guard-slaves in the slave-market perhaps? So that the transaction is not generally observed?'

Marcus shook his head. 'More than that. I want you to smuggle my wife and family away and hide them safely until the risk is past. And as fast as possible. I'll give you a sealed letter of authority until I get the warrant witnessed properly.'

I gazed at him. 'Where do you suggest?'

'I'll leave that up to you. It is quite impossible for me to organize, there are always people watching what I do and where I go. It's easier for you. Find a way to get them out of the villa unobserved, take them somewhere and keep them hidden till I send for them again.'

Getting a woman, a small boy and a babe in arms out of the villa and secreting them elsewhere without attracting anyone's attention to the fact? It was impossible. There would be clothes and food and parcels of necessities. And – since we were talking about patricians here – no doubt there would also be a retinue of slaves. 'But how can I do that?' I allowed myself to say.

He misinterpreted – or he affected to. 'I'll give you gold,

of course – there'll be no problem there – but ensure that
no one knows where you are going or sees you leave here
with my family. Obviously it isn't safe to stay here at the
house. You have seen the letter. Someone may choose to storm
the walls or set the house on fire. So get them out, but guard
them on the road: it would be too easy to seize and kill them
there. Take them somewhere where they can't be harmed.
Once you've got them settled you can send and let me know,
though you'll have to contrive some way of doing that – I
fear that, following these messages, there may well be spies
already, watching every move.'

'In that case, they will have seen me come today,' I pointed
out.

Marcus chose to wave this irrelevance away. 'Oh, I'll send
you with a letter to the garrison – they'll assume you've come
for that. The letter-writer will expect that I'll report the threat
– though obviously, as he says, there's nothing much the
commandant can do. Even if he left a guard here it could not
be permanent, and all my enemy would have to do is wait.
And, between ourselves, I'd be unwise to ask, in case the
Emperor Didius has issued a decree declaring me a public
enemy – I don't want to be arrested by my own bodyguard!
I'm better off providing protection for myself.'

'So why send me to the garrison at all?' It is a long way
to Glevum at that time of day, and I had jobs to do at home.

'I want to bid the commandant farewell, in any case, and
that's innocuous enough – so you can show the message, if
by any chance you're intercepted on the way.' He reached
across and patted me warmly on the arm, as though this were
a comfort, rather than a recognition that I might be set upon.
'They'll recognize the tablet as having come from me.'

I nodded. Marcus's wax-tablet holders were famously ornate,
and no doubt he'd use his seal.

'In the meantime, you work out a scheme. And as soon as
possible – my family's not safe here.' He gave me a smile.
'Thank you, Libertus. I feel much relieved.'

He always flattered when he wanted me for something
difficult. I could not let it pass. 'I'm sorry, Excellence. I'm
not sure I can help. I'll try to think of how it might be done

of course – but I fear it may be near-impossible.' I didn't
mention the obvious, that if I undertook this task, my own life
was likely to be in danger too.

'Oh, you'll think of something, Libertus, my old friend. I
rely on you for that.' He gave me the smile again. He knew
as well as I did that I had no choice. He might be in mortal
danger and out of favour now, but he was still a powerful
man – and it was not wise to cross him when he wanted
something done.

I bowed, in silent acknowledgement of this.

'Then, I'll go and write this letter to the commandant. I'll
send a servant in here with some figs for you, meanwhile.'
And he was gone, leaving me to stare at the pavement after
all, cursing the Fates who had allowed me to get involved
in this.

THREE

The message, when it finally appeared, was not written on my patron's fancy writing-block, it was written on the one which had contained the threat. Marcus had symbolically obliterated it by warming up the wax and scratching over it. It was not what I'd expected, and I was sure it was not wise – there was now no proof of what the original had said. But it was clearly too late now. He hadn't even attached his seal to it, merely tied it with the fraying cords which were affixed.

It was delivered to me by a pretty little page – one of my patron's recent purchases – whom I'd not seen before and who had nothing whatever to report.

'No further message?'

The servant shook his head. 'Master says that you'll know what to do with it.'

I gazed at the wax tablet. Could it tell me anything? It had been handsome, once, with carving on the frame – clearly the possession of a wealthy man. I had seen such things before, imported at some cost for private customers, who might in fact buy several at a time. It might be possible to trace who'd purchased it, if the original importer could be found, though it was clearly very old and worn. Besides, the recipient of a message, where there is no reply, is often expected to keep the tablet as a gift – as Marcus had effectively just done, himself – so this one might have changed hands several times by now, or even been collected from a rubbish pile.

My thoughts were interrupted by the page. 'Citizen, if you are ready to depart, your attendant is already awaiting you outside,' the boy said, sweetly, pulling back the inner door. 'I'll show you out to him. And then, if you'll excuse me, I have other tasks to do. My master is expecting dinner guests tonight.'

I paused mid-pace and turned to stare at him. 'The household is expecting visitors?' Any one of which could be the letter-writer, I thought bitterly. How like Marcus not to think of that – or mention it to me.

The boy gazed innocently back at me. Clearly he was not in his master's confidence and saw no threat at all. And I knew Marcus was anxious to behave as if everything was normal in the house. So how should I proceed? I chose my words with care.

'Tell your owner to be careful whom he invites here from now on,' I said.

The boy looked startled. 'Citizen! I would not dare to speak to him like that.'

'Tell him it's a message from Libertus.' His face was still doubtful and I pressed the point. 'Warn him from me that the times are dangerous. After all, the Emperor Pertinax is dead. Your master may have hidden enemies.'

A disbelieving smile curved the pretty lips. 'Oh, these are ancient friends. Councillor Varius Quintus Flavius and his brother Claudius.'

I nodded. I slightly knew the councillor concerned – handsome, charming and ruthless as a bull. 'A long-standing invitation?' It occurred to me that Marcus had ruled against him once in a legal wrangle pertaining to some land. Yet apparently it had not crossed my patron's mind that the man might be the author of the note. 'I did not know His Excellence had been in touch with anyone in the colonia as yet.'

The page was already opening the outer door. 'He did not contact Varius, citizen. Varius sent to him. He sent a messenger requesting an urgent audience – something about hoping to speed up a hearing in the courts – but the master was still weary from his travelling and didn't want to go into the town, so he invited Varius and his brother to dine here next day.'

'But they did not come?' That was disquieting. A sign that Marcus's status had declined.

'There was a sudden sickness in the house and they sent again to say they could not come that night, so His Excellence renewed the invitation for today. It gave them time for the malady to pass and if they really wanted him, they would ignore the Ides, he said. Besides, he's decided that he wants

them to be witnesses of some document that he is drawing up
– he has to have Roman citizens for that. I thought that's why
he might have wanted you.'

'I would not have been suitable at all,' I said. It sounded
deprecating but it was the truth – since the document was
almost certainly the one he'd told me of and I could not be a
witness since it appointed me. 'Nonetheless,' I went on firmly,
'since he has guests tonight, please pass my message on. Tell
him – from me – to keep armed slaves around him at all times
and advise him, in particular, not to partake of any gifts of
food or wine. Not without employing a slave as food-taster.'

'If you say so, citizen,' the pageboy said, in a tone which
made me doubt that he would do so, even now. 'And now – if
you permit, my master is waiting for me to help him change
and wash his feet before he eats.' And nothing, he implied,
must keep Marcus from his food. 'This way, citizen.' He
gestured me firmly towards the entrance court.

I longed to speak to Marcus and warn him of my fears, but
there was nothing I could do. I sighed and allowed the page
to usher me outside. I collected my own servant, who was
waiting in the lane. 'Home!' I told him, and together we set
off down the wooded lane. 'I've got to go to Glevum, but the
way leads past our gate.' Besides, I would have to tell my
wife where I was going.

How one event can change an atmosphere! Only a little
earlier – on the way to Marcus's – I had revelled in the beauty
of the stony lane dappled with sunlight through the bright green
leaves and the summer forest, still and silent as a sleeping
slave. Now all at once, the woods seemed menacing. I was
convinced that there were unseen eyes trained on me from the
trees and the undergrowth seemed full of rustlings. I was glad
that I had brought an attendant slave with me, though I'd only
done so for convention's sake. Such things – like the clumsy
toga that I wore – were expected when calling on His Excellency.

It was little Tenuis who was escorting me today. As the
newest and youngest of my household he had been the easiest
to spare from other chores and he was intensely proud of being
chosen for the task, stalking along in his new tunic like a
midget Emperor and swaggering mightily. He could not have

been more than five or six years old, at most, so naturally I didn't tell him anything about my interview – time enough to worry him if anything occurred. Instead, I encouraged him to talk.

The child had been a land-slave before he came to me, and had not been trained in household protocol. So, although he'd now learned to wait respectfully till he was spoken to, once he'd started talking he was hard to stop. Perversely, that was what I was now relying on. If there was anyone loitering nearby, his piping voice would make it clear that I was not alone. (Not that Tenuis would be of any help in fighting off attack, but he was small and slippery as an eel. If nothing else, he could scuttle off and fetch rescue from the house.) So I asked the boy how they'd received him at the villa we'd just left (where he'd once been an outside servant of no account at all) and he prattled cheerfully.

'Oh they treated me with more respect than you'd believe, master – though only because I now belong to you. Do you know they even offered me some buttermilk and a piece of new-baked bread . . .'

I listened to his burblings with only half an ear while I scanned the forest for any signs of the watchers that I feared were hiding there. I was beginning to conclude that my qualms weren't justified when, just as we rounded the corner towards the enclosure where my roundhouse lay, I glimpsed a darting movement in the trees. Animal or human? I could not be sure, but suspicion was enough. I decided in that instant that – since I was forced to go to town – the safest method was to ride there on my mule. Arlina is not the fastest animal alive, but she moves more quickly than I can walk myself – and can deliver a fearsome kick, besides.

I had travelled the road to Glevum many hundred times but suddenly the prospect seemed a daunting one. The track ran for miles through unfrequented woods, and I was acutely conscious, all at once, of how few people ever went that way and of how narrow, steep and treacherous the path can be in parts: ideal for an ambush, if such a thing were planned. And it was already well past noon. If I was to go to the colonia, I must do so soon – it was possible that at the garrison I would

be forced to wait some time. The daytime hours are longer at
this time of the year but today, of all days, I did not want to
be returning in the dusk!

So, as soon as I got home I went inside ready to announce
that I was leaving instantly, but I found my assembled family
sitting round the fire. Gwellia, my wife, was fussing over the
new infant in its mother's arms while my adopted son, Junio,
and his two-year-old boy tucked into the fresh oatcakes that
had been baked for them.

'Ah, Father, there you are at last. Come and see your pretty
little grandson,' Cilla, the new mother, called out to me at
once. 'We've saved some oatcakes for you and there's fresh
bread and cheese.'

I shook my head. 'I'm afraid I cannot stay. I'm obliged to
take a message to the garrison at once.'

Gwellia frowned. 'Could not your patron have excused you
that today?'

'It's urgent business but it should not take too long.' I hoped
I sounded more convincing than I felt. 'It's just a message to
the commandant.'

'Poor Father. Forced to go to Glevum, and on the Ides as
well. I can just imagine it,' Cilla said, and added, in a wonderful
imitation of my patron's voice, 'Just a small commission for
you, my old friend!'

Everybody laughed. She was famous for her mimicry – and
knew Marcus well, of course. She had been a slave-girl at the
villa once, just as Junio had been a slave of mine. (When I
freed him and adopted him, he'd gained my rank, of course,
and she'd become a citizen when she married him.)

Today, however, her clowning did not make me smile. 'It's
a serious matter. I will try to hurry back. I'll take my toga off
and ride the mule to town.'

Gwellia made a little face at me. 'Trust Marcus to find an
errand which must be done at once, so you don't have time
to eat. I'll wrap some oatcakes for you, to stave off hunger-
pangs.' It was typical of Gwellia to be concerned for me. Of
course, she had no notion that there might be a threat, and I
certainly wasn't going to worry her with that – especially in
front of our young visitors.

However, while she was busy wrapping the food in a clean cloth and Tenuis was saddling up my animal, I stepped out to the round hut where I kept my tools and took the unusual precaution of sliding a knife into my belt – a very sharp one which I used for pruning trees. My intention was to hide it underneath my cape: carrying a potential weapon in a public place is a serious offence for civilians like myself.

Unfortunately Gwellia had followed me outside, and caught me in the act. 'What are you doing, husband?' she exclaimed. Her face was horrified. 'Dear gods! A knife! What's Marcus said to you? I knew that there was something that you weren't telling us. Are there Druid rebels in the woods again?'

I shook my head. 'Not that I know of,' I said truthfully – though I was less honest when I added, 'but it's the Ides of June – and there are bears about. The general omens are so dreadful nowadays, I felt that some protection would be wise.'

She gave me a look that told me she was not convinced. 'Don't get yourself arrested. If anyone sees you carrying that blade in town, there would be Dis to pay. You won't even have the automatic protection of a toga! Are you sure you shouldn't wear it after all?'

She had a point of course – the garment marks a Roman citizen and usually offers some protection from arbitrary arrest – but I shook my head. 'It is not a suitable garment in which to ride a mule for miles in difficult terrain. Besides, if I did encounter any savage beasts a toga would be nothing but an encumbrance.' I sounded pompous, even to myself, and Gwellia frowned at me.

'That's nonsense and you know it. There's something else afoot. I don't like this at all. Surely your patron could wait an hour or two and let you deliver his famous note tomorrow, when the shops are open and you're in town anyway?' She saw me shake my head and said impatiently, 'And I wish at least you'd tell me why you feel you need a knife! You've never worried about meeting bears before – has there been someone savaged recently?'

I decided I could tell her a little of the truth – though not about the threat to Marcus, and possibly myself. 'The fact is, wife, the times are dangerous. Marcus says the garrison is planning to move on – in support of our provincial governor, who does not accept the reign of Didius and wants to claim the purple for himself.'

Gwellia looked appalled. 'But surely that is treason? The Emperor will send his troops from Rome and decimate the ranks.'

'Only if they lose!' I tried to turn the matter to a jest. 'Marcus seems to think the present situation cannot last in any case.' I confided what my patron had told me about the chaotic situation in the capital and the two pretenders set to march on Rome.

'That sounds like civil war! Thank all the gods that we live far away!'

I nodded. 'Though even in Britannia we may not escape. Marcus had a message from the garrison commander today, saying that he intends to march his legion to Londinium at once. They won't set off this afternoon, because it is the Ides, but it could be as soon as tomorrow possibly: so if this reply is going to reach him there's no time to lose. Though you're not to mention this to anybody else.'

'I see.' She glanced towards the knife which I had thrust into my belt. 'And that? You're not going to join the fighting personally, I suppose?'

I shook my head. 'But once the army's gone – and it seems they'll only leave a small detachment here, at most – who knows what one might encounter on the roads? Marcus thinks it's an invitation to criminals and thieves.'

Gwellia sighed. 'He may be right. Then you must take a slave with you – I know you did not plan to, but husband, I insist. I only wish that Minimus was here, he's bigger and would be a better guard, but I sent him to the spring for water and Kurso, the kitchen slave, has gone out with the goats – so it will have to be young Tenuis, I suppose. Better a small slave than nobody at all.'

I made a face at her. I wasn't keen to take the boy this time – he hated being on the mule and was afraid of crowds. 'He's far too young and little to be of any help. He isn't strong enough to stop a chicken in its tracks! What use would he be, if anything occurred?'

'He's quick and nimble.' Gwellia could look and sound determined when she tried. 'He could run for help – and two people are always safer on the paths than one.'

That was so exactly what I had thought myself, on the way back from the villa, that I could not help but smile.

She seized on that at once and said triumphantly, 'So that's decided. Just as well I've put sufficient oatcakes in for two!' She thrust the bag at me. 'And I wish you'd take your toga – though I don't suppose you will. Otherwise they might not let you inside the garrison.'

I shook my head. 'If Marcus is correct about the legion moving on, nobody's going to let me see the commandant in person, anyway. All I need to do is hand in the writing-block and wait for a reply. But I will take Tenuis, if you insist – though I'm sure there is no need.'

'I wish I could believe you, since you insist on carrying that knife. Don't shake your head like that. I know you far too well. I'm sure there's something else you're not telling me.' She turned away, avoiding my embrace and led the way to the enclosure gate, where Tenuis was already waiting with the mule. The boy stepped forward to hand the reins to me, but Gwellia shook her head. 'You're going with your master, Tenuis. I'll tend our guests myself.'

Tenuis glanced nervously at me. Both of us would rather that he'd stayed at home, but I nodded glumly. 'You will come with me.' And since he was a slave there could be no argument.

Gwellia said gruffly, 'Just get home safely, that is all I ask.' She turned away and went back to the house, not even pausing to wave us on our way.

Perhaps Marcus was right, I thought gloomily as I climbed onto Arlina's back and settled an unwilling Tenuis up in front of me. Ordinary ordered life was breaking down. Here was I – a generally peaceable and law-abiding man – riding to Glevum on an ill-omened day, clutching a slave who didn't want to come, refusing to confide in my beloved wife, and defying the authorities by carrying a blade. No wonder Gwellia was affronted and upset.

I resolved that when I got back home I'd tell her everything – supposing that I did get back unharmed! Gwellia was resourceful and intelligent. She might have some suggestions as to how I could best smuggle that young family away – though I could imagine what she would say about that assignment when she knew!

But it was too late for regrets. I turned my attention to urging on the mule.

FOUR

I t was an awkward journey, with Tenuis sitting with his eyes
tight shut but babbling like a brook to quell his nervous-
ness. He was mercifully oblivious of my own anxiety and
how my heart quickened every time we passed another traveller
on the road – even an aged woman gathering honey fungus
from the trees and a goatherd ushering home his charges were
enough to make me jump. But that was nothing to the nervous
care with which I gazed around when the track was sinisterly
empty.

Because now I was sure that someone was trailing us. Several
times there were suspicious rustlings close by and once, in
the steepest, darkest portion of the track, I saw a flash of blue
among the trees which could not possibly have been an animal
– but by the time I'd turned my head to look again there was
no sign of anything.

I could not bear the tension any more. I glanced around.
There were no other travellers about, so – quite deliberately
– I braved the law. I dropped the rein, took out the knife and,
reaching overhead, ostentatiously cut myself a switch, making
quite sure my vicious blade was visible to anyone who might
be watching us.

Tenuis had his eyes shut, so he didn't see, but I'm sure I
was observed because there was a sudden crackle in amongst
the trees and then a total hush. I loitered for a moment – still
brandishing the knife – then rode deliberately slowly down
the path. But the rustling had abruptly ceased and there was
no further evidence of movement in the woods. It seemed our
unseen escort had been scared away.

I hoped so, anyway. Sending up a silent prayer to all the
ancient gods, I put the knife away and urged Arlina on, using
the fresh switch to persuade her to a faster pace.

Of course, because my nerves were stretched to breaking
point, the forest seemed suddenly full of people dressed in

blue. First we passed a fowler in a woad-dyed cloak squatting by the path, emptying his traps of birds; then a barefoot goose-boy came shepherding his flock, wearing a torn blue tunic far too large for him; then someone's fleet-footed private messenger went loping past, though none of them gave us even a passing glance. But each occasion made the tension worse. It was almost an anticlimax – though an immense relief – when we reached the junction with the major road without further incident.

The military road that leads up to the South Gate of the town is much frequented by traffic of all kinds, so I felt much safer after we left the forest track. Not that there were many travellers today. Few people came to town on officially inauspicious days like this, but there was still a pedestrian or two – a woman with a bundle of kindling on her back, and a man with a handcart full of watercress – and their presence made me feel a good deal more secure.

Besides, as we approached the gateway to the town, I saw that there was still a soldier on duty at the arch, though I'd wondered if there would be, with the legion on the move. But there he was, a burly dark-skinned fellow with a spear – an auxiliary, judging by his uniform and helmet – with an expression of disdainful boredom on his face. When we arrived he scarcely glanced at us, just nodded us straight through – though he stopped and questioned the farmer with the watercress.

Tenuis, however, held back nervously. 'What about Arlina?' He nodded at the mule.

'You can bring her with you – animals are permitted in the town – it's only horse-drawn vehicles that can't come in by day.' By law the military has precedence on all roads everywhere – other travellers must step aside to let them pass – and in legionary towns, like Glevum, carts and wagons aren't allowed inside the walls till after dusk, when they are less likely to obstruct the movement of soldiers and supplies.

Tenuis nodded nervously and did as he was told, but he was clearly anxious, so when we'd reached the corner by the military inn, just a yard or two within the walls, I left him there to hold the animal while I hurried the short distance further to the fort.

I bustled to the gate in the enclosing walls, preparing a little speech of introduction to the guard. I meant what I had said to Gwellia, earlier. Without a toga, at a time like this, I hardly expected to be ushered in to see the commandant, though with Marcus's distinctive seal on the writing-block I did anticipate that I'd be shown inside to wait for a reply, like any patrician's messenger. But today was different. I was not permitted even to produce the words that I'd rehearsed.

'Greetings to his Worthiness the Commandant. I am—' But the sentry cut me off.

'You have a message? I will deal with that!' He seized the writing-block from me, looked at it wordlessly and disappeared within, leaving me standing like an idiot outside. (I didn't dare to glance at Tenuis – the same thing had happened to me once before and he'd been there to see it that time, too!)

I waited. And waited. The man did not return. It was most unusual! I'd never known a sentry leave his post before – even for a moment – and now there was a lot of shouting coming from within.

I peered around the gate. Not much of the enclosure could be seen from here but it was clear why the sentry had thought it safe to leave his post. There were soldiers everywhere. The legion really was preparing to depart. Military ox-carts were lined up on the central road that ran through the fortress, and even from my limited vantage point, I could see that groups of soldiers were busy loading them – Ides of June or not! They'd formed a human chain with crates and packages, under the eye of an officious *optio* who was obviously responsible for all the bellowing.

'Now that's enough on there! You two, fetch a rope and get that load secured, and look quick about it, you lazy sons of dogs!' He was barking at a pair of burly young recruits. 'The rest of you can go and move your kit outside, and get your sleeping room swept out! You won't have time tomorrow if we're leaving at first light. And see you do it properly, like that unit over there.'

I followed his pointing finger and saw another group of men outside the barrack block, bringing out the personal equipment – mattocks, shovels, blankets, cooking pans – that soldiers always carry when they are moving camp, and placing it on the ground nearby in tidy piles. Another orderly was bellowing at them.

I was leaning forward to get a better view, when a hand on my shoulder made me literally jump. I froze, not daring to turn round. The hand – on the periphery of my sight – was covered with a plethora of rings, and the arm emerged from a drape of toga with an impressive purple stripe. A curial magistrate, by the look of it. Varius, perhaps? I still wondered if he might have been the writer of that note.

The very thought had turned me into stone, but as my brain began to work again I realized – with relief – that these fingers were too plump and the hairs upon them far too dark and thick for Varius. He was tall and blond and lean, conspicuously handsome and aware of it – so he always had his barber-slave shave all his body-hair, as he liked to demonstrate in ball games at the public baths. But if it wasn't Varius, whoever could it be? Was this a magisterial arrest? Had someone reported that illegal weapon at my belt?

My mind was still racing when a voice spoke in my ear. 'Citizen Libertus!' The hand propelled me round to face the speaker and I gulped.

'Councillor!' I muttered, certain now that different trouble lay in store.

I was looking into the plump, pink face of Porteus Tertius, a patrician member of the town curia with whom I'd had dealings several times. He had sometimes dined with Marcus and I'd seen him there, but he was not a man I cared for. Quite apart from his unattractive appearance (he was pompous and portly, with acne on his face) he had conspired to have me arrested, once. That had been on a wholly baseless charge, but if he knew about that knife he would have proper grounds this time.

He had no cause to love me, either, I was aware of that. Not long ago, he had lost much of his fortune on a commercial deal – tricked into it by a fellow councillor. I did no more than find the culprit out, but Porteus was inclined to blame me for the whole event – and the consequent loss of a dowry for his ugly daughter too.

'Councillor!' I said again, ready to burble some excuse.

He cut me off. 'Pavement-maker!' To my amazement he seemed quite affable. 'What brings you to the fort?'

'My patron's business, worthy councillor,' I fawned, not quite certain that I dared believe my luck. However, Porteus was famous for enjoying flattery and I knew how to grovel. It seemed worth a try.

It appeared to be effective. He blinked his pink-rimmed eyes at me and gave me a thin smile. 'Ah, your patron, naturally! I had heard that he was back. And how is His Excellency? I'm sure he's sorely grieved that Pertinax is dead.'

I remembered what had been said about the new Emperor's decrees. Was Porteus looking for a careless word from me? I tried to find a neutral form of words. 'The whole Empire was shocked to hear about his fate.'

Porteus moved a little closer, giving off faint wafts of musk and spikenard. 'But it must affect your patron in particular,' he murmured in my ear. 'He would certainly have risen to eminence at the imperial court if the Emperor had lived.' He waited for a moment, and when I did not reply, he added, 'I was sorry to hear that was not to be the case.'

I shot him a doubtful look, but he almost seemed sincere. Perhaps he really was. If Marcus had moved to Rome as adviser to his former friend, as he'd intended to, Glevum would have needed a senior magistrate – and Porteus had no doubt hoped to be a candidate for that. So he might well regret that Marcus had returned. He'd made several attempts to rise to eminence before. Not content with being a mere town councillor, he had also spent a fortune a year or two ago attempting to gain the nomination as Imperial Priest, though without success. The more recent losses – the ones he blamed me for – had therefore been a double blow to him, and the experience had left him an embittered man.

Now, however, he seemed determined to be agreeable. He gave me the smile again. 'And now the garrison is leaving. That will be a loss for Marcus, too. He was very friendly with the commandant, I think?'

Was this a veiled threat about what the curia would do without the legions here? Or the simple gloating that it

appeared to be? I produced a civil smile. 'Indeed. He has sent
me specially with a message of farewell.'

A strange look crossed Porteus's acned face. 'Merely a
message of farewell! I see. I wondered if he . . .?' He trailed
off suddenly, his plump cheeks turning pink. 'It wasn't that
he . . .?' He moved a little closer, overwhelming me with
scent. He was renowned for it; I remembered a rumour that
he rubbed his slaves with perfumed oils, to mask the smells
of animals and sweat and urine-pots that might reach his town
apartment from the marketplace. The effect was overpowering
and I flinched away, but he grasped me firmly by the sleeve.
He glanced around as if the soldiers in the fort might hear. 'It
wasn't by any chance because he had received a threat?' This
time the whisper was hardly audible. 'I saw you send a writing-
tablet in.'

'A threat?' I glanced at him, sharply. 'What gave you that
idea?' And then, seeing that Porteus's cheeks were turning
pinker still, I realized what should have been obvious at once.
Of course, he had been coming to the garrison himself. With
a message for the commandant, perhaps? There was a leather
container dangling at his waist, just big enough to take a
writing-block. I took a gamble. 'You got a letter, too?'

He nodded sheepishly, and slipped his hand into the bag
and brought out what it contained. The item was indeed a
writing-block, so strikingly similar to the one I'd brought
myself that – almost without thinking – I seized it from his
hand. The rudeness was compounded when it fell open at my
touch.

'You have been warned,' was all the writing said. I recognized the script.

'This is a second message!' I exclaimed. I looked at Porteus.

Taking it from him, without permission, had been inexcus-
able, but far from chiding me he almost seemed relieved. 'So
Marcus did receive one?' He glanced towards the fort. 'And
he's applied to the garrison for aid? I was wondering about
doing that myself. But I'm not sure they're likely to be of any
help. They circulated a message only yesterday, to all the
members of the curia, saying that the army is about to leave
the town. So even if they did consent to send a guard, which

I doubt they would – a man is expected to provide his own protection, in a general way – they could not keep it up for very long.'

'So whoever wrote the letters only has to wait?' I was looking at him keenly, noticing the way the acne scars showed white against the pinkness of his piglike face.

'Obviously your message was very similar to mine,' he muttered, sheepishly.

'Have you any notion who might have written it?'

'Someone with a grudge.' He looked at me sideways. 'There's always somebody who blames the magistrate if things go badly for him in the court – I've heard your patron say that many times.'

'It's what he said to me,' I assented, thoughtfully. 'But is this a grudge against the two of you alone? Or have all the members of the curia received a threat?'

That would put a different complexion on everything, in fact. Not all the magistrates could possibly have been involved in the same trial – even the most serious cases were heard by two or three at most, usually with Marcus as the senior man. So if all the members of the council had received a letter too, that made the whole thing much less personal – and might, indeed, be simple posturing.

Porteus, though, shook his head decisively. 'No one else!'

'You've asked them?'

'I've made a point of visiting as many as I could.' He was still huddling up against the fortress wall and talking in an undertone. 'Though I haven't managed to speak to all of them quite yet.'

'So when did the first message get to you?'

The pink face flushed again. 'Just this morning, a little after dawn. It was thrown through an open window of my apartment, here in town. Of course I was alarmed. I went to all the curia members I could find. I didn't ask them outright, just enquired tactfully, whether – with the omens as they are – anything unsettling had occurred today.'

'And they did not think the enquiry was odd?'

'I pretended that it was connected with the Ides.' He preened with satisfaction at his own cleverness. 'While Marcus was away, many of his duties were transferred to me, including dealing with the public augurers – and I claimed that this enquiry came from them. But none of the council members had anything to say. Some of them had tales about portents of bad luck – altar flames at household shrines that wouldn't light, or stepping through a door the wrong foot first – but when I mentioned messages, they just looked blankly at me. It was clear that no one had any notion what I meant.'

'And when did you get this?' I handed back the open writing-block, with an apologetic bow.

'Awaiting me when I got home again. Delivered in the same way, by the look of it. I can't imagine who the writer is.' He put the tablet in the bag and drew the string again.

'You and Marcus are the two recipients. That might make the writer easier to catch,' I pointed out. 'Not everyone would have a grudge against you both, specifically. What exactly did the earlier message say?'

'Oh, I imagine it was much the same as yours.' His ringed hand made a vague gesture in the air. 'Violent threats against my life and family – I have a daughter, as perhaps you know. "The next time that you hear from me will be the last" – I think that was the phrase.'

'And now that time has come?'

He seemed to take a moment to work out what I meant, then nodded vigorously. 'If I had a house away from Glevum I would move to it at once. Will Marcus take his household to Corinium, do you think?'

I shook my head. 'My patron sees it as his duty to remain—' I broke off as he touched my arm again and gestured down the path. The sentry was returning, at a run.

'Here comes your answer from the commandant, by the look of it. I'll leave you to your message, citizen,' Porteus said. 'Otherwise the soldier will give me precedence.' And to my surprise – Porteus is famous for insisting on his rights – he backed away politely as the fellow hurried up.

The soldier beckoned me. He did not have my writing-tablet, I observed, nor any other kind of written message in his hand. 'No reply?' I asked, astonished. Marcus's rank should have required a quick scratched note, at least.

'Only a verbal message, I'm afraid. The commandant sends his greetings to your patron,' the man said, full of self-importance. 'And apologies. He will send a personal reply to Marcus Septimus in due course – a proper written one – but at the moment he is fully occupied. There is army business to be dealt with urgently, as you can no doubt see. So take that message to His Excellence.' He nodded curtly at me and took up his post again, striking a pose with feet apart and leaning on his spear, while ostentatiously looking past me down the street, where Porteus was hovering.

He saw the purple stripe and his manner changed at once. 'Councillor, did you have business at the fort?' he called out. 'A thousand apologies for causing you to wait. I was dealing with this wretch. How can we be of any service to you, citizen?'

Such is the privilege of rank, I thought, sincerely wishing I had listened to my wife and brought my toga with me. But I had not done so, and I had clearly been dismissed.

FIVE

I stomped back in the direction of Tenuis and the mule, not in the sunniest of moods. But before I'd got halfway, I heard my name again.

'Citizen Libertus, a word before you go!'

I turned, to realize that Porteus was hastening after me. 'Why, Worthiness!' I must have sounded as astonished as I felt. 'Were you not shown inside the garrison, either?' From the gate-guard's manner when he saw the councillor, I had expected that the patrician would be ushered in at once and given an audience with a junior officer, even if he couldn't see the commandant himself.

Porteus shook his well-barbered locks at me. 'I changed my mind about attempting it. It's obvious the garrison is fully occupied and it is pointless trying to contact the commandant today.' He made a deprecating face. 'If your patron is not treated with appropriate respect, what use is there in my attempting to seek an interview?'

It was false modesty, of course. Porteus came from an ancient Roman family and so, despite his present comparative want of wealth or civic rank, regarded himself fundamentally as the equal of anyone at all – even Marcus, who is immensely rich. But I knew when sycophancy was required. 'But you were there in person, councillor – not represented by a mere tradesman like myself. And you didn't even send your message in, I see?'

He looked quite startled at the question, until I gestured to the bag, which still quite clearly contained the writing-block. 'Oh, I see. I wondered how you knew. You are famous for your perception, citizen, and it's clear that your reputation is deserved. You're quite correct of course. I didn't send my message to the commandant.' He glanced at me sideways, and turned a little pink. 'What you said about your patron's reaction to these threats . . . it gave me cause to reconsider what I ought to do myself.'

'In what way, Worthiness?'

Perhaps this courteous title was rather a mistake. 'If Marcus Septimus intends to stay here, then I must do the same!' Porteus had been decidedly friendly up to now, but suddenly he adopted an astringent formal tone. 'I too am a Roman citizen of high patrician blood. I cannot have it said that I showed cowardice, by running to the army for protection from a threat, when he has not.'

'Spoken like a true Roman,' I said, as genially as I could. 'Marcus will be flattered that his conduct has been an exemplar for your own.'

Porteus gave me that sideways glance again and dropped his voice to the confidential murmur of before. 'I suppose I can rely on what you're telling me? I should not like to stay and then find that he had fled, or arranged a permanent military escort for himself. You are sure he only wrote to bid the commandant farewell?'

I shrugged. 'I did not see the letter, naturally, but that is what he told me, and I'm sure it's true.' I could speak with confidence. My patron had his own reasons for not seeking army help – the fear that an overzealous soldier might arrest him, on the basis of an impending imperial decree – but obviously I didn't say as much to Porteus, who was still looking dubiously at me. 'Besides, you have the evidence of what just happened here,' I urged. 'You saw that I received no answer from the fort. If somebody of Marcus's rank had asked for military protection – rather than merely sending a farewell – courtesy would have demanded some sort of a reply, even if only in the negative. Especially when the commander is a personal friend.'

Porteus seemed persuaded, although unwillingly. He nodded slowly. 'I suppose I should have come to that conclusion for myself,' he conceded, with a frown.

'So perhaps you should consider sending in your message, after all,' I said sweetly. 'You are a man of civic stature. If you ask for help, it may be that you will get an answer, where I did not.'

He turned the frown on me. 'But how could I do that? Beg for a guard when your patron makes a point of asking none?

I would just invite his public scorn and risk my reputation as an honourable and courageous man.'

Porteus had no such reputation that I knew about; if anything, he was known as suspicious, fussy and not averse to bribery or dubious schemes for gain – but it did not seem appropriate to point this out. Instead I nodded. 'Then you will carry on the business of the courts as usual, just as my patron does? He will be glad to know. He fears that normal law and order is likely to break down now there is no strong leadership from Rome – once the army does not have a presence here.'

He swallowed, as if the prospect did not please him very much, but then he raised his white-scarred chin and attempted to look resolute. 'Of course I will continue to attend the courts. I would not have dreamt of doing otherwise,' he declared, with a sincerity which would not have convinced an idiot.

'And I may tell my patron so?'

He looked abashed. 'I suppose so – if you must. Though—' he dropped his voice and placed his ringed hand on my shoulder once again – 'on second thoughts . . . perhaps . . . I'd be grateful if you didn't mention that you saw me here at all. I thought I was the only one to have received a threat, you see. But now that I am sure that there are of two of us . . .' he trailed off.

I saw perfectly. Porteus did not want His Excellency to think that he was weak for planning to ask assistance from the garrison. 'The second threat diminishes the risk?' I suggested, in an attempt at tact. 'I had thought the same myself. It is clearly more difficult to kill two men than one.'

But I had piqued his Roman pride. 'It's not a question of diminished risk! I'm sure this letter-writer means exactly what he says!' Porteus had turned an angry shade of puce. 'Left to myself, I would have fled the town – and advised your patron that he should do the same. However, since he has resolved that he will stay, I can hardly do less without dishonouring my name. I shall continue to come to the forum every day – just as long as Marcus does so too.'

I muttered something about their being safe in the basilica, at least.

Porteus shook his head. 'You might imagine so, but I am

not so sure. It is a public place. This killer could attack at any time. I shall employ a bigger bodyguard and keep an armed escort about me at all times.'

It was exactly what Marcus had resolved himself, and I was about to say so when Porteus spoke again. 'And I may look into trying to rent a country house – for occasions like today when the courts don't operate. The one I'm building is barely half-complete.'

It was difficult to know how to reply to this. Everyone in Glevum knew the story of the house. Porteus was only building it against his will.

It had come about like this. Porteus had owned a pleasant villa on the other side of town, but had been forced to sell it when he got into debt – perversely, over the construction of this house he didn't want. He had been persuaded that he was acting for somebody abroad and – working on their commission as he thought – had made lavish purchases, tons of imported marble and expensive wood and stone. He had even supplied the site for the new house himself, believing that he'd sold a tract of woodland for an attractive price, and had his servants clear the ground in readiness and at his own expense. It was all to be paid for when the man arrived from Gaul – but the whole instruction proved to be a hoax. Porteus had spent a fortune he could ill afford and (since no so-called 'client' could be produced in court) there was no redress in law.

He'd suffered a huge loss as a result of the affair and it was widely rumoured that he would have to sell this new villa, too, as soon as it was built, to pay off his remaining creditors. And this was the fraud which I had helped unveil, revealing how gullible and foolish he had been. So it was hard to think of anything tactful I could say.

'I'm sure it will be splendid when it's finished,' I furnished – after a long pause.

Porteus gave an embarrassed little cough. 'You don't suppose your patron would consider letting his?' He raised a pale eyebrow at me. 'He does have that townhouse in Corinium after all.'

So that was why he'd raised the subject of country houses! Hoping he could rent my patron's as a hiding place! I could have pointed out that it was nothing of the kind – whoever had written that threatening letter had delivered it out there, so clearly knew what its location was – but surely Porteus could have worked that out himself?

I was about to say so, but I changed my mind. It was not my place to state the obvious. And since my patron was intending to move to his flat in town, he might be interested in leasing out the villa for a while. It would no doubt command a considerable rent, and if Porteus was so foolish as to want to come, I did not want to dissuade him and deprive my patron of a lucrative let.

But there was one point which I felt compelled to make. 'I can hardly ask him, Worthiness,' I said respectfully, 'if I am not to tell him that I saw you here. You will have to ask direct. Send him a message – or approach him when you see him at the courts, since it seems that you will both be serving there. Though even that might mean revealing that you'd had a letter too – and that you're aware that he'd had threats as well.' I could see that Porteus was puzzled, so I spelt it out. 'Why otherwise would you suppose that he would want to let the house?'

Porteus had turned scarlet and looked discomfited. 'Of course. You're quite right, citizen. I hadn't thought it through. I'll go away and work out what's best to do – in the meantime, better not mention to Marcus that we spoke.' He was clearly embarrassed at making himself look foolish once again and was suddenly anxious to be somewhere else. 'And now, if you'll excuse me, I must take my leave. I am half-expected to take *prandium* with friends, and I see my slaves have come for me.'

He waved a pudgy hand towards the outer arch, where a couple of athletic youths in lavish uniforms – their lilac capes and azure tunics were made of finest wool, embroidered with gold thread and trimmed with silver cord – had bustled up and were talking to the soldier at the gate, while four litter-bearers loitered nervously nearby with a curtained carrying-chair.

'You're lucky to have found a public litter, on the Ides,' I said. 'There are not many bearers who ply for trade today.'

'But my servants have clearly found one, citizen. Perhaps

it is the privilege of rank,' he said, all pompousness again. He raised his voice. 'Over here, chair-bearers! To me! At once! The day is drawing on – if you don't hurry I won't be offered lunch. What are you waiting for?'

He gestured to his servants who came over at a run, followed by the litter. The bearers put the chair down and he got into it.

'Go well then, citizen,' he said, extending his ringed fingers for me to take and bow over. 'I'll think about whether to approach your patron about the house or not. Otherwise keep this conversation to yourself. You never know who might be listening.' He seemed oblivious of his attendants and the boys who held the chair – another man who did not think that slaves could see and hear! He withdrew his hand and shouted to the bearers, 'To the house of Varius Quintus, by the public baths!' He settled back and pulled the curtains shut.

The litter-carriers raised the chair and set off down the street, with Porteus's attendants running close beside. I watched them go, astonished.

Varius Quintus! There was that name again. Was it coincidence? Had Porteus been invited to the house? If so, the invitation was distinctly odd, given that it was already very late and Varius was expected to feast elsewhere that night. And Porteus also had received the threat, it seemed. But I'd had no chance to warn him to be specially on his guard – any more than I'd had a chance to tell His Excellence. I shrugged. Well, if anything happened to Porteus, it would simplify my task.

I hurried back to Tenuis, who'd been waiting patiently. 'Who was that person with the purple stripe?' he murmured, much impressed. 'Someone most important by the look of it!'

'He likes to think so, anyway!' I could not help but grin.

'And in a hurry!' Tenuis observed.

'Gone off in hopes of being offered some prandium,' I said. 'But he'll be disappointed, if I'm any judge. Quintus is due to dine with Marcus later on, and I doubt he'll be lunching on much more than bread and cheese. Marcus is famous for his sumptuous dinner feasts. But it's time for us to snatch a little nourishment ourselves.'

Tenuis's eyes lit up with pleasure at the thought. He was

always keen to eat, probably because he'd half-starved when he was young. 'Shall we go over to your workshop then?'

I wasn't really anxious to delay at all; I wanted to hurry back to Gwellia, though doubtless our visitors would be long gone by now – but my wife would be affronted if we did not eat what she'd taken such pains to provide. I shook my head.

'Not the workshop. It's locked up for the Ides, the fire is out and the water jug's not filled – and it is right on the other side of town. There's no point in dragging Arlina all that way. There's a fountain at a crossroads not very far from here; let's go down there to eat.' It seemed appropriate: that fountain was one which Porteus had donated to the town, as part of a programme of ostentatious public works when he was first campaigning to join the curia.

Tenuis, however, looked a little shocked. Eating in the street was a thing that poorer people did.

'We can sit there on the stone trough to eat our food and get a drink of water in our hands to wash it down,' I told him heartily. 'I'll lead the way, since you are not familiar with the town.'

Tenuis, needing no further encouragement, urged Arlina into a walk again.

Our fountain was down a little alley to our right, where four streets met to make a little square. The shops which lined the route were shut and shuttered now, so it took no time at all – none of the usual hawkers and traders plucking at your sleeves, trying to tempt you with the piles of goods heaped up on the pavements, or laid out on tabletops outside the shop. One hot-soup shop was open and full of customers while, from the crowded flats above, a smell of smoke and burned meat seeped down into the street. (People were obviously cooking in their homes – at some risk of conflagration and against the law, since none of these premises had provision for a fire!)

At the public fountain we found a little queue of slaves and a few free-women with their water jugs – people need water, even on the Ides – but there was none of the usual jostling, and no one hindered us. We tied Arlina up and found a space, sat down on the stone edge of the drinking-trough, and ate our oatcakes there. It did not take us long.

I had just finished, and was stooping to scoop some water up – intending to drink it out of my cupped hands – when Tenuis leaned over and tugged my tunic sleeve.

'There's the litter, master! It's that rich man again.'

I looked up. It did appear to be the carrying chair I'd seen before; I thought I recognized the bearer at the front. However, most of these hired devices look very much the same, especially with the green-brown curtains drawn, and this one was coming from the direction of the fort and travelling at a run, so I dismissed the notion and prepared to go back to my drink.

However, as they approached the fountain the carriers slowed down, and someone began twitching the curtains from within – presumably so the occupant could take a quick peek out. There was a high, barked order – which might have been 'That's him!' – and the litter ambled to a stop.

I frowned. Had Porteus changed his mind and followed me? Had he discovered some news of Varius? Or was it simply that he'd been disappointed of his hoped-for lunch – as I'd predicted – and happened to be passing on the way to somewhere else? It couldn't be his own apartment, because that didn't lie this way. So what had made him go back to the gate? Whatever the reason, it seemed he wanted me. All things considered, this was disquieting.

I let the water run out through my fingers and got slowly to my feet, ready to confront Porteus when he emerged. But to my surprise, as I approached, the curtains were pulled back and revealed the occupant to be a female form – and a very diminuitive female form, at that. Ancient too, from the aged hand which now appeared from beneath the woollen cape. 'You there, in the cloak and tunic – the one without a jug!' The voice was weak and quavering but still somehow contrived to sound imperious. 'Is that your animal?' She waved one skinny arm to indicate the mule.

She was making no attempt to get down from the chair, so I went across to her, drawing curious glances from the watchers at the trough. 'Madam?' I murmured, trying to peer through the veil without success.

This was a wealthy Roman by the look of it, though she seemed to be travelling without an attendant slave of any kind.

The hands, weighed down with jewels and jet, were wrinkled and shrunken as an old dried pea – giving the impression of a living skeleton – though of course the face and hair were covered by that veil, as appropriate for an honourable matron in the street. Otherwise she was rather unbecomingly attired, in a hooded palla of pale violet hue, which hung half-opened on her skinny form, revealing a dark-blue grecian robe underneath and exposing a surprising length of scraggy neck. These garments had clearly been expensive once, but now they showed signs of fading, stains and wear.

'Young man, I asked a question! Is that your animal?'

I was so bemused at the description – I am nearing sixty years of age and nobody has called me 'young' for many years – that I could only nod.

'Then you must be Libertus, the man I'm looking for.'

It was a question. I could only nod again.

She made a tutting sound. 'Then I was misinformed. I was told that you were heading out of town, so I've made a wasted journey to the gate. But the sentry advised me that he'd seen you come this way – he said you had the mule and little slave with you. Mercifully I have found you now. I have an errand for you. Though I can't instruct you here—' she gestured contemptuously at the queue for water – 'too many idle servants and plebians listening in. This is a private matter, not for general ears. Follow the litter. I will see you at the gate. See to it, bearers!'

And without another word she pulled the curtains to, and the conveyance went lurching off again, round the little square and back in the direction from which it had just come.

SIX

I was still staring after the departing litter, marvelling at its unlikely occupant, when I felt a timid tug on the corner of my cloak. I turned to find Tenuis looking up at me, with a bemused expression on his little face.

'Who was that, master?'

'I've no idea,' I told him, truthfully.

'Yet she seemed to know your name?'

'I can't imagine how. I haven't glimpsed her face, of course, but I'm perfectly certain that I've not seen her before.'

'You wouldn't forget her in a hurry, would you master? I've never seen a woman with a neck so long and thin. She looked like a goose – and she snapped like one, as well.'

I grinned, despite myself, then carefully composed my face again. Gwellia was always telling me that I encouraged the slave-boys to make irreverent remarks. 'A forceful lady, certainly, and clearly of some rank. So one must be respectful.' I tried to sound severe.

'So are you going to do this errand for her, master?' he enquired. 'She obviously expects you to leap to her command. But you are not a slave!' He glanced at me doubtfully. 'Or were you hoping it was something I could do?'

I shook my head. Such a thought had not occurred to me – and after what I'd learned at Marcus's I certainly did not want to be without my servant-boy today. 'We'll do it together, if we do it at all,' I said, and saw that he was genuinely reassured. Obviously her manner had alarmed him – it had almost frightened me! 'But that depends on what the errand is,' I added. 'I confess that I am tempted to find out – if only because she's made me curious. How could she know me? Or know that I was here?'

'And I expect you'd like to discover who she is, as well?'

'Of course!' I raised a brow at him. 'Well, there is only one way to discover that! We've got to go back through the southern gate in any case. No doubt she is waiting there impatiently by now – though she can wait a little longer while I have my little drink.' I cupped my hands and scooped up the water that I'd failed to have before, then shook the excess from my fingers and gestured to the mule. 'You untie Arlina and bring her along. We'll go and see if we can find the litter at the gate.'

It would have been hard to miss it – as we saw when we arrived. It was drawn up immediately inside the central arch, blocking the roadway and forcing the few pedestrians to skirt it as they passed. The guard on duty was observing this, but had not interfered, so it simply stood there with the curtains firmly drawn and the bearers standing nervously nearby.

This was perhaps because the chair was now accompanied, too, by a tall, thin, balding manservant of advancing age, who had obviously just got there at a run, since he was red-faced, out of breath, and perspiring visibly. He was dressed in an elaborate ochre tunic which marked him as the slave of some-body of rank, though it was now damp with sweat and clinging to his chest, revealing the slave-disc that he wore around his neck. His whole form was heaving and his lined face was puce, but when he saw us he stepped up to the chair and tapped twice on the frame.

'Mis-mis-mistress. The pa-pa-pavement-maker with the mule is here.'

'Very well, Hebestus,' said the thin voice from within. 'Pull the curtains back and stand aside so I can talk to him.'

Hebestus did as he was bidden and the woman turned to me, thrusting back the palla-hood impatiently. She had already pushed her travelling veil aside in a way most Roman matrons would have shuddered at – showing her hair and face in public to a man to whom she'd not been introduced! And it was such a face! I had not met her anywhere before, of that I was now sure.

She was quite the oldest woman that I had ever seen, beady-eyed and pale as wood-ash but sharp-beaked as a bird. Once she had probably been beautiful, but now her skin was stretched like fragile parchment over bony cheeks and her brow was crisscrossed with a thousand little lines; though

perhaps the most striking thing about her was her hair. It was
thin and patchy, with the pink scalp showing through, but far
from being decorously white, it was dyed to a conspicuously
vivid henna hue, and arranged in meagre ringlets and a fringe
of wispy curls.

I found that I was staring; the effect was so bizarre.

'Ah, pavement-maker, there you are at last!' The crone –
that was the only word for her – gave me a thin smile. (The
wrinkled lips were grotesquely touched with red – doubtless
the same ochre and alkanet paste used by my patron's lovely
wife, though here the result was wholly different!) Mercifully,
she appeared to have a few remaining teeth. 'You have been
so long, I feared that you'd gone home another way – though
your roundhouse lies in this direction, I believe?'

I did not return the smile. 'Lady citizen, you have the
advantage over me. You clearly know my name and trade –
and even where I live. Whom do I have the honour of addressing
in my turn?'

She looked affronted, as if I had been impudent, but after
a moment she did deign to reply. 'Since it bears upon your
errand, I suppose there is no harm in telling you. My name
is Eliana Tertia and I am a relative of Varius Quintus – the
sister of his grandmother, in fact. You've heard of Varius
Quintus, I suppose?'

I had more than heard of him, I thought, but all I did was
bow. 'Indeed! He is to dine with my patron, Marcus Septimus,
this very night, in fact.'

She shook her head. 'I fear that's not to be. My great-nephew
has been taken ill again – and this time his whole household
have succumbed to it.'

'Ill?' Whatever I expected, it had not been this. Could it be
genuine, or was it just a ruse – a way of worrying my patron
a little more, perhaps. 'Are you quite sure?' I said.

One claw hand made an impatient gesture in the air. 'Are
you hard of hearing? Ill is what I said. It happened overnight.
By this morning it was clear that I – and this fool Hebestus
who is attending me – were the only healthy people remaining
in the house. That's why I was forced to come out after you:
we had no slave to send.'

It seemed my doubts of Varius had been unjustified. 'But how did you know who I was? Or that I was in town? I don't believe we've ever met before?'

She gave a cackling laugh, more like a goose than ever. 'Oh, we had a visitor, a frightful man who had been half-invited to come for prandium, or so at least he claims – though he was impolitely late, in any case. One of Varius's councillor acquaintances, I think. Naturally I had to send him home unfed, but he told us that he'd seen you in the town and said you'd be the perfect person to take a message back, as you lived not far from Marcus. My plan had been to find an urchin in the town, and send him with a letter, but this man was quite insistent that I sent you instead. Seemed particularly smug at having thought of it and being able to advise me what to do.'

'Councillor Porteus?' I enquired, although I was in little doubt – the picture that she painted could only be of him.

She made a dismissive gesture with her skinny jewelled hand. 'I believe that was the name. I didn't know the man – I have not been long in town. But his arrival was quite fortuitous. I don't know Glevum well, and neither does my slave – I have only been here half a moon – so I had no idea where this Marcus person lives.'

'So how were you going to send a messenger?'

She looked at me as if I were an irritating child. 'I understand that Marcus is an important man, so I was relying on his villa being well-known hereabouts. What worried me far more was where I'd find a messenger, but the arrival of the litter solved all that for me. I was watching from the window-space as it drew up outside and I knew the bearers would have some idea where urchins congregate. So I went out to greet the visitor at once, and made sure that he did not dismiss the carriers. And then, of course, he said that you were here, so I came to look for you instead.'

'But how did Porteus come to mention me? Or Marcus, come to that?' I seemed to be asking questions endlessly, but this was getting odder all the time. 'Obviously he did not know about the prospective feast tonight, or he would not have called on Varius expecting prandium.' I certainly hadn't mentioned it to Porteus, and it seemed that Varius hadn't spoken to the visitor at all.

She shook her head impatiently. 'I told him, naturally, when I explained what I wanted to use the litter for.'

'And commandeered his bearers and his chair?' I tried not to sound amused.

'Obviously, pavement-maker! What would you expect? It's perfectly proper for a man to walk about the town – but it would not be appropriate for me, a Roman matron of advancing years. Any honourable citizen would have thought of it himself! And so I told him, when he did not offer me the chair. I had to be quite sharp with him before he would dismount, but when he learned my errand he changed his attitude and told me you were here. He even mentioned that you had a mule with you.' She waved a lofty hand at Arlina. 'So – since it could hardly incommode you to do this little task on our behalf – I set off after you. I assume that your Porteus – is that his name? – went home.'

So the portly, self-important councillor had been shamed into a walk by this formidable lady! The image made me smile. I was beginning to warm to Eliana Tertia and her eccentric ways. 'Then I am glad that he agreed to yield the chair to you. And I will take your message, gladly.'

She did not seem particularly gratified. 'Good. That frightful man was certain that you would. In fact, he seemed to think you'd find the news significant – though I can't imagine what he meant by that. You can't be an associate of my great-nephew, I'm sure. He does not socialize with tradesmen – and I'm told that's what you are.'

'A craftsman and a citizen,' I said. 'And I have met Varius Quintus once or twice, though mostly at my patron's villa, certainly. But I think I understand what Porteus had in mind – he wished me to warn Marcus that there's sickness in the town.' I spoke with care, but it occurred to me suddenly that it might be more than that. Did Porteus think that there was something sinister afoot?

Perhaps, in fact, I should have thought of that myself. Here was another magistrate at risk, and one who'd worked with Marcus several times. Far from Varius being the author of the

note, had he been the recipient of one? Porteus had clearly
not had the chance to ask him earlier, when he was making
those covert enquiries about 'unusual events'! So was it
possible this 'illness' was really poisoning? Had the threatener
struck? That prompted my next question. 'Is Varius very sick?'

'Bad enough, and so are all the others in the house. It
was violent and sudden, though doubtless it will pass – as
it did the last time. Most likely simply something that he ate
or drank – again. Young people have no stamina these days.
Infected meat, I expect. Or perhaps it was the water. I don't
trust these city wells.' She gave a cackling laugh. 'If, like me,
you live on bread and cheese you don't tend to suffer from
such maladies. But your patron lives a long way outside the
walls, I hear. I don't think he needs to be concerned that he'll
succumb to anything similar himself.'

I thanked her and nodded, though I was not so sure. From
the description, this could indeed be poisoning and it had
extended to the whole of Varius's house – just as the threatening letters had foretold. I could see exactly why Porteus
was alarmed – and why he had consented to give up his litter
and send word to me.

'And how will you manage, lady, with this sickness in
the house?' I asked. 'From what you say there are no staff
to help.'

'Concerned about my welfare? That's very kind of you! I'm
not accustomed to such civility. Especially from strangers in
the street.' The beady eyes looked sharply up at me, convincing
me – if I had needed further proof – that this was a lady of
some intelligence. 'Though you are a Roman citizen, you say?
I had not realized that – and you can hardly blame me for not
guessing from your dress. So I apologize if I have been abrupt.
But there's no need for your anxiety – I don't eat the fancy
food that's served to Varius. It's much too rich for me. I brought
my own provisions with me when I came.'

I must have looked astonished – which in fact I was. It is
not usual for a visitor to bring supplies with them. 'But
surely—'

Eliana Tertia interrupted me. 'I am old and not accustomed
to such luxuries – and, in any case, since I was forced to close

up my own house at last, and throw myself upon my great-nephew, I was hardly likely to leave things there to rot!' She saw my startled look. 'I am a recent widow, citizen – my husband was crippled in a fire and I lost both my sons – and now the whole estate will pass to different heirs.'

'I should have thought you capable of running it yourself,' I said. 'You seem a woman of some character.'

The pale cheeks flushed and the eyes grew very bright. 'There speaks a man who does not understand the world. There was no provision entitling me to stay, indeed there was no will at all, so custom passed me to my great-nephew's *potestas* – as my nearest living male relative – and Varius decided I should leave the farm. At first I was grieving so much that I did not care, and by the time I took an interest there was no way that I could even sue to rent the place. And no money to do so, if I did.'

'So Varius is now running the estate? I presume that he has temporary management while you're in his potestas, even if he does not formally inherit until the courts have ratified his claim as nearest male of kin?'

'It's all too recent and Varius has been ill. In any case, he isn't interested. I don't believe he cares a fig for it. He just intends to sell. Anyway the place is in decline. My steward was cheating, of that I'm almost sure – the fields were neglected and half the crops had failed, yet he amassed sufficient to pay his slave-price from the heirs – while I was left with almost nothing to my name. But without a formal guardian who would act for me, there was no recourse in law.'

'Varius would not prosecute this thief?' I enquired – too eagerly. 'Or did the court decide it would not hear the case?' I asked, in case my patron was involved in any way. If the magistrates had declined to bother with a trial, Varius might lead me to the letter-writer after all.

But I was disappointed. The red lips parted in a bitter smile. 'Varius was too busy with his civic duties here and, as I say, he was not interested. The sums involved were far too small, he said, and pursuing a freed slave was beneath our family's dignity. What he would do is offer me a home – for which I should be grateful, I suppose.'

There was no reply to this and I did not offer one.

'I tried to fight the move as long as possible,' she went on, bitterly. 'I would have preferred to stay there while I lived – but in the end there was nothing I could do. I sold the few remaining slaves I had – except for Hebestus who's been with me since a boy – packed my poor possessions and, as you see, I came to Varius. Just in time, since he and Claudius were sick, and without us two to tend them . . .!' She pursed her wrinkled lips. 'And now, it seems, we'll have to do it all again.'

'And what would have happened to you, if Varius had died?' I was still pursuing anything which touched upon the law.

'Ah, that's a question, citizen. It all depends on whether he has made a will or not. He has no offspring so I might have rights as a surviving heir – although I can't be sure of that.'

'And Claudius?'

Eliana shrugged. 'I have no claim on him. Claudius is no blood-relative of mine. Varius's father took a second wife – after my niece died in giving birth to Varius – and Claudius was born just six moons afterwards. My sister almost broke her heart, losing her only daughter in that way, so we had no contact with the family for a while. But Varius did come to visit us – the first time when my sons were still alive, just about the time we had the fire – to tell us that his father and step-mother had been gathered to the gods. He even stayed to help us fight the fire – carrying water and beating at the flames, himself – though by that time it had too fierce a hold. And after the fire he called back several times to see what he could do.'

'That was good of him!' Varius was rising in my estimation all the time. 'Especially if a distance was involved.'

'The estate is on the road to Aquae Sulis, citizen,' she said, dismissively. 'With a good horse one might reach it comfortably in a day. But once I made it clear to Varius that I didn't want to move and I would nurse my husband to the end, he didn't come again – though we have been in touch by letter ever since.' She stopped short suddenly and looked at me. 'But why in Jove's name am I telling you all this? It cannot be of any interest to you.'

But the mention of letters had prompted a new thought.

'And Varius never mentioned that he might have enemies? No one has threatened him?'

'Enemies?' Her voice went squeaky with astonishment and she sat bolt upright. 'Whatever do you mean? What makes you think that Varius would have enemies?'

'I fear this sickness may not be an accident,' I said. I realized that she was staring at me, horrified. I took a risk. 'More than one town councillor has received a threat,' I went on. 'That's why Porteus thought my patron ought to know at once.'

She sank back in her seat. 'I see.' And then she frowned. 'But Claudius is not a councillor.'

'The threats are made against the whole household, in each case, not just the head of it. Revenge for something that the master is alleged to have done – some injustice or injury. The letter-writer does not specify.'

She thought for a moment. 'That alters everything. How many people have received such threats?'

'I cannot tell you that. I don't know all the details myself.' I spat discreetly on my hand and rubbed my ear with it – the age-old method of averting the ill-luck which might result from telling an untruth. (Or failing to tell the whole truth, in this case, like the fact that Marcus had received a threat himself.) 'My patron is the senior magistrate. He is taking an interest in the facts and trying to discover who is responsible.' I looked at her. 'Of course, it's not for everyone to know – we wouldn't want to start a panic in the town. But you're not aware of Varius receiving threatening messages?'

Her bright brown eyes looked boldly into mine. 'Varius would not have told me if he had. He's not a man to tell a woman anything – much less an old and ugly woman like myself. He didn't even let me know that he was ill some days ago – though I was on the way and we were exchanging messages.' She started, suddenly. 'You don't suppose that was another poisoning attempt that failed?'

'Or a warning, possibly,' I said, though up to now I hadn't thought of it. But I could see that it would fit. 'Anything to make the victim terrified. But this time the killer might actually have struck.'

'Well, if it's possible that someone's poisoned Varius, I had better go to the temple and get the priests to offer a dove or something to the gods. Or even have a votive tablet made and nailed up at the shrine. And find a proper *medicus*, perhaps. Claudius was asking me to do that earlier, groaning that he thought he was about to die, but I thought he was exaggerating and I did not take the suggestion seriously, I fear. Where would I find a medicus in any case?'

'I don't know anyone who keeps a private doctor these days,' I said. 'Marcus had one, briefly – a proper Greek-trained fellow – but he didn't last for long, and it's not the fashion that it used to be.'

'But in a town as big as Glevum I assume that there's a public one available somewhere?' Eliana's bright eyes looked anxiously at me. 'There'll be a cost, of course, but I'm sure that Varius has money in the house – though I shall have to locate it if I'm to pay the fee.'

I gave her directions to the doctor's residence. 'But remember that you may not find him there, since it is the Ides,' I said. (I did not add that I did not rate his skills – the man is an advocate of cabbage soup and 'rocking' carriage rides. He boasts in public of his many cures but, as far as I'm aware, he's never produced the slightest proof.) 'But he has a new apprentice who will probably be there. He's watched the medicus at work, and may be able to assist by now.'

Eliana must have thought I sounded dubious. 'Better than nothing. I will go and try at once.'

'I could recommend a wise woman who is good with herbs,' I said. 'Though she lives in the forest a little way from here.'

She shook her red-dyed locks. 'The medicus, I think. If Varius is really poisoned, then it's probably too late, but I don't want people saying that I did not try to help. If he dies I shall feel responsible, in any case. I assumed this sickness was something that would pass.' She shrugged her skinny shoulders and pulled up her hood again. 'And now I can't remember the directions you just gave – please tell the bearers where they are to go.' She gestured to the litter-slaves, who were lounging by the wall, under the eye of the sentry at the gate.

It was a strange request, but I went to speak to them. They

hastened to their posts. As they did so she gestured to her ancient slave and whispered – like an actor in the theatre – so loudly that I'm sure the gate-guard could hear.

'Hebestus, give this man the tip that we arranged. He turns out to be a citizen, but he's a tradesman too, so I don't imagine that he'll take offence. Then follow me again. The street of the silversmiths at the further end – you heard what he just said. Ask for the home of the medicus if you are in any doubt. And be quick about it.'

And with that she pulled the curtains closed again. The slaves sprang forward to seize the carrying shafts and before I could even call 'farewell', they had picked up the chair as though it had no weight in it at all, raised it to their shoulders and gone loping off with it.

SEVEN

'Citizen?' A throaty voice spoke softly in my ear. I turned to find the slave, Hebestus, standing at my side. He had recovered some of his composure by this time and was breathing almost normally, though his face was still unnaturally red. 'My mistress spoke about a tip, but she's only given me two *quadrans* – I hope that is enough. We hadn't realized that you were a man of any rank.'

I had to smile at her frugality. Two quadrans – that was only half an *as* – barely enough to buy a bunch of rotting turnips or a small loaf of yesterday's stale bread. I shook my head. 'I don't require your money. I was going home anyway – but if you want to repay me, you can talk to me. Tell me a little about Varius and his house. You're Eliana's private servant, I believe?'

He nodded cheerfully – so cheerfully that I suspected that the 'tip' was likely to find its way into his freedom fund. 'An unusual lady, but one I'm proud to serve. I was her child-page when she was first a bride. Her life has not been easy, but she has struggled on alone when many weaker people would have resigned themselves, or blamed it on the ill-will of the Fates and given up.'

'You say she was alone. But she had a husband until recently?' I said.

Hebestus made a deprecating face. 'She did indeed – and a good master he was, too, in his time – but he was a cripple and confined to bed for years before he died. A well-born citizen, of course, but even when young he preferred the country life and never aspired to public office. Perhaps he should have done. He was a fine and honest man – he would have made a splendid councillor.'

'So there was considerable property?' I said. There is a minimum qualification for election to the curia.

Hebestus nodded. 'At one time, certainly, but he'd put all

the gold he had into the estate, he told my mistress that when she first married him. For years it was a profitable enterprise as well – woodlands, a large farm and even a small vineyard, though that never prospered much. But then there was a dreadful fire and that changed everything. Happened just at harvest and all the crops were burnt, and half the woodlands with it. Both the sons were killed in fighting it – charred so that only a few scraps of bone were ever found – and my master was so injured that he never walked or spoke again. Eliana nursed him faithfully until the day he died, but the estate fell into ruin . . .'

'She told me the chief steward had been cheating her,' I said. 'Though Varius would not stoop to taking him to court.'

He looked around him doubtfully as if afraid the sentry at the gate would hear. 'It's not for me to say so, but I'd been warning her for years. He was a sullen fellow and neglected everything. In the end there were hardly any crops and fewer animals – barely enough to keep the household going – so how he made his slave-price is a mystery to me. If he was stealing profits, I don't know what they were!' He shrugged. 'But that's all over now, and I'm very glad of it. My mistress is much safer where she is . . .' He broke off, suddenly. 'Though that wasn't what you asked, forgive me, citizen. The answer is, I am Eliana's slave – the only one she brought to Glevum in the end, though Varius wanted her to sell me on as well.'

'She has no female attendant, then?' I was immensely shocked. No Roman matron should be without a maid.

Hebestus laughed. 'Varius has provided a handmaiden of course. Though, like the other servants in the house, the girl has fallen sick. So at the moment, there is only me!'

I looked at his worn, flushed face and said, 'You interest me, Hebestus. If there is such widespread sickness in the house, I'm wondering why you did not succumb yourself? Eliana says she lives on bread and cheese, but I imagine you get slave-rations like everybody else – from Varius's kitchen?'

He looked surprised at this, as if he hadn't thought of it. 'I do, in general.'

'Which means there's something that you do not share with them?'

'Only the water. My mistress does not trust the public wells
– she insists on buying it from a man who sells it from a
barrel on a handcart on the street. She believes that's better
than the town supply.'

'And is it?' My mind was racing furiously, of course.

'I doubt it, citizen – but she believes it is. "Fresh water
from the country" is his cry, and she always sends me down
to buy some when he comes. I don't think Varius knows – he'd
be offended if he did – but, if I read your thoughts aright, it
may be fortunate for us. You think the water from the town
supply has made the household ill? It might be so, I haven't
tasted it.'

I looked sharply at him. 'How did that occur?'

'My mistress brought some watered wine with her – though
it's not a good vintage and is rather sour.' He gave a little
laugh. 'The last that was ever produced on the estate. She
offered it to all the household, but they don't like the taste and
Varius insisted that I should use it up. I don't mind because
I'm used to it. The water from the barrel tastes a good deal
worse than that!'

'So you have drunk that – a little anyway?'

He made a face again. 'One sip was quite enough – I've
stuck to the sour wine ever since, though it's almost finished
now.'

'And your mistress?'

'She's been drinking it as well – in between that dreadful
water that she buys. She could have had the better vintage that
Varius serves, of course, but she doesn't care for waste – and
she never dines with the others anyway. She claims the food's
too rich. But citizen, excuse me, if you won't accept the
quadrans, could you let me go? My mistress will be waiting.'

'And she can be sharp when crossed?'

He gave me a grateful look. 'I've already had a chiding for
not keeping up. I was supposed to be following the litter earlier.
I tried to run as quickly as I could, but I didn't get here to
the gate till after she was gone.'

'But you somehow managed to catch up with her again?'

'I didn't, citizen. She caught up with me.' He gave a rueful
smile. 'I was just asking the sentry which way she had gone

and when I looked where he was pointing I saw the litter coming back. The mistress wasn't pleased with me at all – she doesn't seem to realize that I'm getting old and can't run quickly like the bearers do. But she'd told me to keep a lookout for a tradesman with a mule – and then I saw you and the rest I think you know. So, if you will excuse me?'

I dismissed him with a nod. There were a hundred things that I would like to have enquired, but Hebestus was looking anxious so I let him go. But I'd learned one thing from this interview, I thought: if Varius had been poisoned, it was probably the wine. His house was next door to the public baths so almost certainly drew water from the town supply – and that served the fountain, which I could answer for, since I'd myself just drunk a little with no ill-effects! I'd have to warn Marcus to be careful what he ate and drank, and appoint that poison-taster as soon as possible.

I turned back to Tenuis who was waiting by the arch, still holding Arlina by the leading-rope. 'Come on,' I said. 'It's time for us to go. There's not only the verbal answer from the garrison, but I have been entrusted with a different message now, which I must take to Marcus straight away. And my women will be waiting – so let's be on our way.'

I took Arlina from him, clambered on her back (with the aid of a convenient low pediment nearby), then pulled Tenuis up to sit in front of me again. He looked so woebegone I felt quite sorry for the boy, but there was no help for it. I did not want to tarry in the woods, with him simply walking by my side. However reluctant, he would have to ride the mule.

The sentry had been watching these preparations with a grin, and as we trotted through the gate he winked at me, 'Go well, citizen – and be careful on the roads. Just take care that nobody important sees that knife.'

I glanced down and realized that the hilt was visible – perhaps I had dislodged my cloak in climbing up. I gulped, but he was smiling, so I rearranged my garments guiltily and was about to trot away, when he suddenly reached out a hand and took hold of the reins, bringing Arlina to a stop again.

Dear Jupiter! I had been arrested after all – so what would

happen now? At best I could expect to be thrown into the jail
– at worst, without the protection of my toga, even more
unpleasant things might lie in wait for me. I closed my eyes
in horror, sending up a mental prayer to my ancestral gods.

But when I opened them again, the sentry was still there,
holding the bridle and grinning like a circus-goer whose team
has won the palm. 'I have some questions for you, townsman.'

'I'm a citizen,' I burbled, though without much hope that I
would be believed. 'Ask any of the civic councillors – they
know my patron well.'

He nodded. 'So I understand. I overheard the lady in the
carriage say as much. And, quite clearly, you have important
friends. Some relative of Varius Quintus, so the bearers claimed?
Did I overhear that there's been a poisoning?'

Despite the circumstances, I did not answer this. Obviously
the sentry had been listening in. That would not be difficult
– Eliana's voice was quavering and shrill, but it carried easily
and she had no notion of moderating it.

The soldier tugged the rein impatiently. 'Oh come now,
citizen – if that is what you are. I'm doing you a favour by
letting you go free, and now I want a little information in
return. So now I'm asking – is that rumour true?'

'What's your interest?' I said, and realized that I had
confirmed the story by my words.

He gazed into my face. 'I heard it earlier, from a passer-by,
but I didn't trust the man, he's only a water-seller and a well-
known cheat – he fills his barrel from the public fount and
sells it to the rich and credulous, claiming that it's purer and
from a country well. But if what he said was accurate, for
once, I'd like to be the one to tell the commandant the news.'
He grinned again. 'And I see it is, so thank you, citizen. They
are offering a bonus at the fort for any news of incipient trouble
in the town. Favour for favour.' He let go of the rein.

I breathed out heavily, hardly able to believe that I'd escaped.
But the soldier seemed to have lost all interest in me now and
had turned to talk to a fellow with an empty hand-cart and a
spade who had been waiting patiently outside the gate for us
to let him pass. He was doubtless going into the town to clear
the stinking midden-heaps and take the reeking, rotting slime

to fertilize his fields. I felt that I was carrying home unpleasant things, myself.

I dug my heels into Arlina's ribs and made good our escape before the soldier changed his mind, almost glad when we were in the shelter of the trees – though conscious that there might be other threats awaiting us. But nothing happened: no one came jumping out at us and no one barred our way. No glimpses of colour among the leaves this time and no rustling in the bushes by the path, though I could not relax until we were out of the gloomy forest and trotting down the open lane past my son's roundhouse and towards my own.

As we did so, someone called my name. I started, but when I turned my head I saw a familiar figure waving from behind the palisaded fence. It was Junio's wife Cilla, with the infant in her arms and behind her Junio walking with the older boy – it was obvious that they were just returning home.

I shouted a greeting in return and brought Arlina to a halt. 'I'm sorry to have missed your visit,' I called out, in genuine disappointment.

In answer, Cilla brought the infant closer to the fence, so I let my slave-boy slither to the ground. 'Tenuis, go and tell your mistress I am here and safe, but that I am going straight on to Marcus's with a message. Don't come back, I will journey on alone – though just for a moment, I would like to stop and see the child.'

He scurried off, while Cilla held the infant up for me to admire. 'There is your grand-dad, Titus. Give him a big smile,' she said, whereupon the baby burst into tears at once. She laughed. 'I'm sorry, Father, he is hungry, I expect. I'd better go and feed him straight away. Don't worry, we'll come again to visit you the next time you're at home – probably the next ill-omened day! But if you've really got a message for your patron, you'd better hurry on. Mother won't be pleased, though – she's been concerned all day, and she'll scold you for not coming home at once.'

'Why do you think I sent Tenuis on ahead, instead of calling in to tell Gwellia myself?' I grinned at her.

But Cilla did not smile. 'I mean it, Father. She is really anxious – more so than usual. You know what she is like!'

She hitched the child on her hip and mimicked the voice and posture of my wife. '"Your father's up to something and I don't know what – but I'm almost sure that it is dangerous. I shan't be easy in my mind till he gets home. And it's all the fault of Marcus – I wish he'd stayed in Rome!" That's what she said, though she probably wouldn't thank me for repeating it!'

Cilla had imitated Gwellia so well, it almost made me laugh, though I was not surprised. Her gift for mimicry had been of use to me before – helping to identify a suspect in a crime. I said, 'I'll go and calm her fears as soon as possible. But I really must deliver this urgent message first.'

'Urgent message?' Junio and his toddling son had joined us at the fence. Cilla took the small boy's hand and made him wave to me, then took him and the wailing infant inside to be fed. Junio came a little closer to the palisade. 'From the commandant, I suppose? Are you free to talk? It must be a verbal answer since I see no scroll and seal. News of the army's movements, I presume?'

I shook my head. 'You might imagine something of the kind, but all he did was send his greetings back and promise a proper written message later on. The real tidings that I bring are from Marcus's prospective dinner guests tonight.'

'Marcus is having another of his feasts? He's only just come back from travelling! I didn't know he'd even ventured into town as yet.'

'I don't believe he has. This is his way of avoiding doing so. Varius Quintus wanted to see him privately and was invited here to dine. And it's not the first time either – he was expected once before, but wasn't well enough to come. And now he and his brother have been taken ill again, and all their household with them, so they cannot come tonight.'

Junio made a face. 'Then you won't be looking forward to the interview with Marcus. When there's bad news he always blames the person bringing it!'

'I'm aware of that,' I said. 'But this was very sudden, and Marcus needs to know before the kitchen spends more time on preparation for the feast.'

In truth, that was the least of my concerns. Never mind the non-appearance of the dinner guests, Marcus might be in mortal danger as we spoke. Furthermore I was a client and confidante of Marcus's myself, and – judging by the poisoning of Claudius – that might put me and mine in jeopardy as well. But I didn't want to worry Junio with that, just yet. 'Best if I tell him as soon as possible,' I said.

Junio nodded and turned as if to leave, then seemed to change his mind. 'But how do you come to be the messenger for Varius, anyway? Especially if he's ill. You did not go and call on him, I suppose?'

'I was commissioned by an aged relative of his,' I replied, grinning at the recollection, though I was inwardly anxious to be off. 'A fearsome lady. I met her in the town.'

'A helpful accident!' He raised a brow at me.

'No accident at all. Someone had told her to come and seek me out.' I felt my smile fading and I stopped and stared at him. I'd failed to think of any way of smuggling Julia away, though I'd puzzled over it all the afternoon, but suddenly . . . Roman matrons' veils and Cilla's mimicry . . .

'Dear Gods! Of course! There is a way in which it could be done. Pardon me, Junio, I must go and speak to Marcus urgently! He is in secret danger, which might touch all of us. But it might yet be thwarted – with a little help from you and your good wife.'

'Of course, we'll help in any way we can. But don't keep your patron waiting. You must not delay. Explain to us tomorrow.'

I shook my head. 'It cannot wait till then. I'll come up to your roundhouse when the children are asleep.' I smacked Arlina's rump and shocked her to a trot, then called over my shoulder to my bewildered son, 'If Marcus will agree to this, we'll have to act at once!'

And I urged Arlina on towards my patron's house as fast as her reluctant legs would carry me.

EIGHT

nevitably, because I was anxious to speak to Marcus now, this time when I got to the villa I was made to wait – and when my patron finally arrived he was already dressed for dinner in a fresh blue synthesis. He bustled in, smelling of sweet oils, while his face was freshly-scraped and very pink around the jaw, suggesting that a barber-slave had been at work. He was accompanied by the pretty page I'd spoken to before, and was clearly not best pleased that I had interrupted him.

'Libertus!' He came over, offering a ringed and perfumed hand for me to kiss. 'I hope this is important. I am expecting dinner guests – two important members of the curia . . .' He waited while I knelt and pressed my lips against the seal. No impatience with the courtesies this time! 'If the commander's sent a message, you could have left it at the gate.'

I got painfully upright. 'There is no letter from the garrison. The commander sends his greetings, that is all. He says he'll write to you.'

He looked at me sharply. 'Then surely you could have simply said so to my slaves?'

'This is not about the garrison,' I said, darting a warning glance towards the page. 'But I do have important information to impart – related to the matter we spoke of earlier.'

'I see.' His manner changed at once. 'I knew I could rely on you to find a stratagem. But you've been rather quicker than I thought and I fear it's not convenient to speak of this just now. Even if Varius consulted the sundial in town, it will be difficult for him to judge the hour – so he and his brother may arrive at any time, and I can hardly abandon my invited guests to come and talk to you.' He softened this social dismissal with a smile. 'A man of such importance needs time and privacy – and whatever your suggestion, we can't do anything today. Come back tomorrow and we'll discuss it then.'

'But Excellence . . .' I hadn't dared to interrupt my patron till now, but he had paused for breath.

He waved my words aside, impatiently. 'Best wait until the morning. They will be gone by then. I imagine that Varius will have hired transport of some kind – I don't think he keeps a private gig in town. So, provided I see his slaves and horses are well fed and offer him lighted torches when he goes, I won't have to ask them to remain here for the night, though Julia thinks I should. After we have feasted they won't want to tarry long: it's a long dark journey back to town at any time of year, even if you have slaves to guard you on the way. So I shan't be late to bed. Call back in the morning, about the second hour – and then we can discuss things properly.'

I smiled ruefully. By the second hour of daylight, I am halfway to Glevum in the ordinary way. It would not occur to Marcus that I had a business to attend to and might have work to do.

He saw the smile and took it for assent. 'Then it's agreed,' he said dismissively, before I had managed to form a single word. 'My page will see you out.' He made a gesture to his slave to usher me away.

I stood my ground. 'I fear not, Excellence.' He was clearly horrified at this breach of normal etiquette, but I went on nonetheless. 'I'm sorry, but I must beg you to stay and hear me out. In the first place, I bring urgent news about those dinner guests, and there are other things besides.' Marcus was still looking blankly at me, so I said again – jerking my chin towards the page, 'Private matters, which it is absolutely vital that I tell you straight away.'

'Ah!' A look of cunning comprehension crossed his face. 'Then perhaps we'll take a little stroll into the courtyard, you and I. If this really is important, I will spare the time for that.' He turned towards the page. 'Slave, you won't be wanted for a while. I'll leave you here in case the guests arrive.'

I shook my head. 'They won't be coming, patron. That – at least partly – is what I've come to say.'

'Not coming?' He was outraged. 'This is most discourteous. Once is unfortunate, twice is impolite. What is the excuse this time?'

'They have been taken sick.'

Marcus looked petulant. 'Not again!' he muttered. 'If they had not recovered fully, they should have sent and let me know. My kitchen slaves have been preparing special food for days.'

'This was quite sudden and violent, Excellence, as I understand.' I tried to keep my voice dispassionate. 'It happened just today – and all the household have been stricken down with it. It was quite impossible for anyone to tell you earlier.'

'I see!' My patron adopted his most judicious face. 'Most likely something in the water, then. I remember there was trouble with the town-supply before. They say some animal – a rat, perhaps – crawled into it and died, and lots of people who drank nearby were very sick for days. Probably this is something similar.'

'Possibly, though I'm inclined to think that it was something else.' I raised my brows and swivelled my eyes to indicate the little slave-boy who was politely gazing at the painted frieze above our heads, but obviously listening eagerly to everything we said. 'What's certain is that Varius and Claudius cannot come. Perhaps you should inform your kitchens straight away.'

Marcus followed the direction of my glance. 'Ah!' he said, again. My patron can take a hint if it is broad enough. 'A sensible suggestion, my old friend,' he said in a falsely hearty tone of voice. 'Slave, go tell the kitchens that the guests will not be here and that I will dine in private with my wife. And don't stand there staring, go and do it now.'

The page-boy bowed himself away and hurried off. Marcus turned to me.

'Into the courtyard garden, then, where we cannot be heard? We can't be too careful, with these new slaves around – I can't be certain about their loyalties.' He led the way into the peristyle. There were a pair of kitchen-boys out there, gathering herbs and scented petals for the feast, but Marcus barked an order and they went scurrying off.

The courtyard garden is divided into quarters by a pair of crossing paths, with a fountain in the centre, but there are niches all around. My patron led me to a secluded little arbour to one side, where there was a little statue and a bench. 'Now then, Libertus, what is this about? You feel there's something strange about Varius being taken ill, I can see that – though I can't imagine why. Unless you think that he's deliberately insulting me, perhaps?' He sat down and motioned me to do the same. 'It's possible, I suppose. I did find against him once.' He stopped and stared at me. 'You don't suppose he is the one who wrote that threatening note?'

'On the contrary, Excellence,' I said, sitting as he had invited me to do. 'That did occur to me, but now I fear he may have had one of his own.'

Marcus whirled round to face me on the bench, so quickly that his fashionable coloured clothing fluttered round him like a bird. He looked immensely shocked. 'Someone has told you that he received a threat?'

'Not precisely that. But I've heard about the nature of this malady. Sudden sickness, violent cramps and constant vomiting?' I said. 'What does that suggest to you? I don't agree it's likely that the water is to blame – his home's provided from the general aquifer. That feeds the public fountains, from which I drank myself – and I'm entirely fit, as you can see. So what other possibilities occur to you?'

He stared at me. 'You can't mean poison, surely?'

I did not answer him. He could draw the conclusions for himself.

He did. 'But who on earth would want to . . .?' he exclaimed, so loudly that I put my finger to my lips, fearing that the slaves would hear him from the kitchen-block.

'That is the vital question, isn't it! Because it isn't simply Varius who's sick. It's his whole household, by the sound of it.'

'Meaning, what exactly?' He twirled the seal-ring on his finger. Marcus tends to fidget when he is disturbed.

I swallowed. Could he really not see what I was hinting at? 'Doesn't it remind you of that message you received?' I murmured. 'With talk of killing everybody in the house?'

Marcus was beginning to understand. 'So perhaps he's had a letter, as you say.' He shook his head. 'But Varius isn't a senior magistrate. He's a very junior one.'

I held my hands up in a signal that he should not rush on

too fast. 'I'm only guessing that he got a threat. But he is a councillor and magistrate, of sorts – and I'm fairly certain that there are others too, who have received communications rather like your own . . .' I said no more. Porteus had asked me to respect his confidence and though I didn't like the man, I'd given him my word. 'I heard a whisper when I was in town.'

Marcus looked shaken. 'So there are several letters? All anonymous, I suppose?' He tore off a bay leaf from a bush nearby and began to toy with it, twisting it between his fingers and sniffing at the scent, as if the herb might drive away ill-luck. He hardly seemed aware that he was doing it. 'And you say Varius got one?'

'That's my guess,' I answered. 'I didn't speak to Varius – he was too ill to leave his bed. And this poisoning might be mere coincidence – but I should not like to stake a quadrans on it being so.'

'And his earlier sickness?'

'Just a warning, perhaps – and this one may be, too, since it seems that Varius is still alive. But I can't believe it's unconnected. What do you suppose?'

He threw the leaf away. 'You're sure that Varius Quintus is genuinely ill? I keep thinking of the time he did not get my vote. You don't think it's a rumour that he's put about, in order to deflect suspicion from himself? Where did you hear the news?'

'I got it from his great-aunt who is living at the house. She seemed convinced enough. Convinced enough to call a professional medicus, in fact.'

'Really!' Marcus looked startled. 'Then he really must be sick! A medicus is an expensive luxury – most people only use one as a last resort. She must be very anxious, to have thought of it.'

'And equally anxious to let you know that Varius couldn't come. That's why she asked me to be the messenger. So here I am. She's the sister of his grandmother, apparently. Not a woman you can easily refuse.'

Marcus's tense expression dissolved into a smile. 'The redoubtable Eliana? She certainly is not.'

'You know the lady, then?'

'Not exactly that. I met her once, a good few years ago. She came to petition me to speak for her – some fuss about a contract which she felt had not been met, and her husband was too ill to come to court – but I couldn't really help her, there were no documents or proper witnesses. But, as you say, you don't forget her easily.' He frowned. 'What is she doing in Glevum, anyway? Did you say that she was living in the house – I thought she had her own estate elsewhere?'

'The husband's dead,' I told him, 'so she's moved in with Varius now – though rather under protest, I believe.'

Marcus smiled again. 'I can imagine that she would not make a gracious guest. Tough as a centurion! She would have made a splendid male! Still, it's generous of Varius to offer her a home – he's no direct descendent, so he's not obliged by law. However, he's a fairly wealthy man, and can no doubt afford to keep her in some style.'

'She doesn't like it,' I observed. 'Though she's done her best to thank him, in her way. She nursed him through the other bout of sickness that he had – it appears she got there shortly after he fell ill.'

'I hope she's grateful for his generosity.' He picked another leaf of bay and crushed it carefully. 'And she should thank the gods that she escaped this poisoning – if you are right, and that is what it was. At her age it would probably have killed her.' He stopped and frowned at me. 'You don't think she . . .?'

I shook my head. 'I think she owes her fortunate escape to age and stubbornness. She declines to eat with Varius himself – declares the food too rich and subsists on bread and cheese. It's a kind of protest against being there, of course – but it's one of the things that makes me sure that this is poisoning, and not just a sudden illness which struck the household down. If it were some contagion – like an infectious plague – the old and weak would be affected first . . .' I broke off as the pretty page came bursting through the door out of the atrium. He gazed around the courtyard till he caught sight of us, and then came scurrying over and fell down upon his knees.

'Your pardon, Master!'

Marcus was frowning with displeasure. 'I thought I made it clear I was not to be disturbed?'

The page looked up at his owner, with pleading eyes. 'Master, I know. I told the steward so, but he insisted that I came. This is a matter of some urgency, he says. A mounted messenger has just arrived from town. He brings important tidings and demands an audience.'

Marcus scowled but turned to say to me, 'This will be the promised message from the commandant, I expect. I'd better have him in. We can resume this conversation afterwards.' He nodded to the page. 'Very well, you are excused. We'll see this courier. Bring him through. I will receive him here.'

The page sprang to his feet and hurried off, relieved.

'Patron,' I said, meekly, 'this may be private. This message is obviously intended for your ears alone. Do you wish me to withdraw?'

He shook his head. 'The fort should have had the courtesy to send a message back with you,' he said. 'I decline to—' He broke off, in surprise. 'Why, who is this? This is no military courier! This is a common servant!'

I looked up and saw the flustered slave he was referring to – a tall, thin aging person whose ochre hems were clearly visible beneath the dark brown travelling cloak and whose flushed cheeks and breathless haste I recognized at once. 'I know him, Excellence,' I said. 'This is Hebestus, Eliana's private slave.'

'Then we'd better hear him, I suppose!' Marcus said, rising magisterially to his feet.

I stood up too, as courtesy required.

Hebestus ventured nearer, bowed to Marcus, and then turned eagerly to me. 'Citizen, I wondered if I would find you here. I hoped to overtake you on the road. My mistress bade me hire a horse and ride—'

'You are a horseman?' I was incredulous. It did not seem a likely skill for a skinny, aging slave.

'I learned to ride when I was still a page. Among my other functions I was used as messenger, so I'm not unfamiliar with a horse – though I've not ridden one for many years.'

I exchanged a glance with Marcus. 'So why didn't your mistress send the message here with you, instead of me – or with an urchin, as she intended to?'

'And leave herself without attendants in a town she didn't know?' Hebestus made a little face at me. 'That's not Eliana's way. Besides, she counts the quadrans, citizen – as you may have observed. Hiring a horse costs money. An urchin's time comes cheap.'

I nodded. 'And my services cost nothing?'

'Exactly, citizen. But this time she decided that speed was paramount. Unfortunately, though, I didn't know the way and had to stop and ask directions several times. But here I am, and I bring sober tidings, I'm afraid.'

Marcus interrupted this exchange. 'Then pray deliver them.' He was stony-faced.

Hebestus seemed to realize that he had been impolite. It was my fault, of course. He should have delivered his message directly to our host – and I should never have deflected him. He made a deeper bow to Marcus. 'Your pardon, Excellence. I did not mean to be discourteous. I am sent to tell you that Varius is dead—!'

My patron interrupted him again. 'Dead?' he echoed, as he turned to me. His face was deathly white.

The old slave nodded. 'I fear so, Excellence. Dead by the time we got back to the house. My mistress felt that you should know at once. And the medicus declares that there's no hope for Claudius. The vomiting and seizures are getting so severe he can't even swallow poppy juice to try to dull the pain.'

His Excellence said nothing. He was looking stunned. I realized the truth that had struck him suddenly – his household might be next. I could see beads of perspiration forming on his brow.

But he was a Roman, trained to keep emotion to himself. He managed to maintain his outward poise and his voice was carefully steady as he asked, 'And the others living in the house?' His patrician forebears would have been proud of him.

Hebestus was clearly oblivious of the effect of his account. 'Apart from Varius and his brother, no one of any consequence is ill. There's just the household staff – though most of them are close to death as well, and all of them are sick. But they are fortunate. At my mistress's insistence, the doctor's with them now, cupping the strongest and least affected ones. He says that if he does that straight away, and manages to force salted water down their throats – to cleanse the toxins out – one or two are likely to survive.'

'And what will happen to your mistress?' I enquired. 'Now that her host is dead? Is she entitled to stay on in the house?'

Hebestus shrugged. 'I really do not know – and I don't think she cares. She'll stay there for the funeral, I suppose. Someone will have to organize the rites: no doubt it will be me. But after that, I really could not say. Perhaps she'll find somebody to plead for her and apply to go back to the estate. I don't know what happens, now the presumptive heir is dead.'

'It will depend upon the provisions of his will,' my patron said, suddenly imperious in his role as magistrate. 'I think I remember that he drew one up last year, and asked various council members to be witnesses – though I wasn't one of them.'

I nodded. Most councillors made wills (sometimes several versions) as a way to gain support, by promising favours after they are dead. Each version must be formally revoked and the new one sworn before seven witnesses, all Roman citizens, and after the funeral the final document is read aloud on the steps of the basilica – in their presence – after which it is binding under law. Was it significant that Varius had not chosen Marcus for the role?

My patron, though, was following a different train of thought. 'Of course it may be that Claudius inherits everything – in which case much depends on what *his* will might say, supposing that he has one. But Eliana was a woman of some family. She will have brought a dowry to her husband when she wed, and that will revert to her now Varius is dead, so she will not be destitute. Indeed, if there's no provision in his will, the court can appoint another legal guardian – or even find a husband for her – to see that she's provided for, in return for the use of any capital she has.'

I looked doubtfully at him. 'Would that be wise?' I said, thinking of Eliana's happiness.

He misunderstood my meaning. 'Well, she's old and diffi-cult, of course. But there are lots of men who'd have her if the dowry's big enough, so once the mourning period for her first spouse is fulfilled that arrangement could take place at once. That's probably the best. If there is any problem I will speak for her myself. I could not help her last time, but I can do this for her.'

Hebestus made a despairing gesture with his hands. 'If she lives as long as that. I'm afraid that my poor mistress has sustained a dreadful shock. She didn't realize that this sickness was so serious, she was making mock of it, and it has shaken her. She blames herself for not sending for assistance earlier.' He looked into my eyes and I saw that his were misting with real tears. 'Citizens, she has taken to her room, and gone into full mourning, refusing meat or drink – even the medicus could not persuade her to take anything at all, not even poppy juice to help her sleep. I fear she plans to starve herself to death.'

Marcus tutted. 'I know that widows sometimes do so out of grief – and all honour to them if they do – but if Eliana planned to do that, she should have done it when her husband died, not waited until now. Though I own I am surprised. She does not seem the sort of woman who would give up gracefully!'

Hebestus shook his head. 'You have not seen her, Excellence. When she heard what happened from the medicus, I swear she aged a dozen years before my eyes. All the spirit has gone out of her. I think perhaps it struck her how good Varius had been, and how ungratefully she'd treated him. She actually told me that she'd lived quite long enough, she'd outlived her usefulness and now she hoped the Fates would come and take her next.'

It was so unlike the woman I had met that for a moment I could think of no reply. It was my patron who spoke first.

'Oh, that is nonsense, and you may tell her so from me. Varius was taken ill before, and I hear she nursed him through that beautifully – why should she suppose that this was any different? And when she realized that he was really ill, she sent for proper help, instead of attempting to give him herbs, herself. What more could she have done?'

Hebestus exchanged a knowing look with me but he simply bowed. 'I will take your message to her, Excellence. Though I'm not convinced that it will comfort her. After the death of my master so very recently, I think the Fates have dealt her one blow too many and too soon.' He bowed again. 'But, with your permission, citizens, I will get back to her. I'm just a humble manservant, but now I'm all she has.'

Marcus nodded and the man withdrew, accompanied by the page. My patron turned to me. 'So, Libertus, you were right to be concerned. There is even more urgency than I supposed. The writer of the letters means exactly what he says – the whole of this household will be under threat – is under threat, right now. We don't have time to get that warrant witnessed after all. I'll write you a sealed letter and that will have to do. It's absolutely vital that you get Julia and the children safely out of here as soon as possible.'

I nodded. 'I have a plan of sorts, but you may not care for it.'

He gripped my shoulder so hard that it hurt. 'I will agree to anything, provided they are safe.' He shook his head. 'Writhing in poisoned agony? I can't have that for them. Tell me what it is that you propose.'

So I told him. He didn't like it, as I feared, but we brought in Julia and she saw the sense of it. It took our combined persuasion, but in the end he did agree.

NINE

W hen I got back to the roundhouse, it was to find my wife tight-lipped. 'Well, so here you are at last!' she grumbled, waving to Tenuis to take my cloak from me and pull a stool up closer to the fire. 'Your soup is halfway spoiled. Sit down and you can tell me what exactly has been happening all day! I've been worried half to death about you, ever since I saw that knife!' She thrust a bowl of steaming soup into my hands.

I ate it greedily, wiping the bowl out with a hunk of bread.

'Well?' she demanded, hands upon her hips, as I washed down my simple supper with cool water from the stream. 'Are you going to tell me?'

'In just a moment!' I replied. 'I promised Junio I'd go and call on him. I'm sorry Gwellia, but we're all involved in this – so if you're ready we will go there now, and I can tell the story properly – and only once.' I scrambled to my feet and kissed her on the brow, but she was still sulking and she turned away to dip a brand into the fire and summon Minimus to light us on our way.

Junio was watching for us at his door, and Cilla had warmed some mead to welcome us. So, as the children slept, I sat in the flickering firelight, sipped the warming brew and told my little family the story of the day – or at least about the threatening letters, the suspicious deaths in Glevum and what I now proposed.

Cilla's first reaction was one of simple shock. 'Threatening Marcus, who is famed for being just!' she exclaimed. 'Who would have dreamed it!' She shook her head. 'And my dear ex-mistress and those poor babies, too. Think of them poisoned! It would grieve the gods. No wonder she's agreed to pack for Corinium at once. Of course we must help them!' She looked into my eyes. Her own were sparkling and I could see that the adventure quite appealed to her. 'Just tell me what to do.'

My wife, however, was not at all impressed. She put her
mead cup down. 'But openly sending a carriage to the Corinium
house? You must be quite mad. They'll be spied on all the
way.'

'Marcus will provide a mounted guard, though, I suppose?'
Junio put in thoughtfully and I realized that I could rely on
his support. 'And Julia can be briefed on what to do when she
arrives. She only has to call in here as she departs.'

'And you don't think that in itself would be remarkable?
Especially to this armed escort you're so sure about!' Gwellia
retorted.

'Not really, Mother!' Junio said, peaceably. 'Everyone
knows how fond you are of those two little ones, and if they
are leaving here for an extended stay, it would be mere courtesy to call in and say goodbye.'

'And it would take our children out of danger too – threats
against Marcus's household could endanger us as well.' I knew
that this would sway her more than anything.

Gwellia looked at me. 'You really think so, husband?' It
was clear this had just occurred to her.

I nodded. 'We all may be in danger – as long as we stay
here. That's why I am anxious that we leave, as well, and go
a different way. I have a good enough excuse – Marcus has
asked me to investigate where the lady Eliana stands in rela-
tion to her previous estate. I intend to take Julia and her
offspring there – it is uninhabited, and will make a hiding-place
– though no one is to know that, outside of this house – while
Cilla and our children go to Corinium. I shall not be missed,
in any case – I am often absent from the workshop when
there's a pavement to be laid. But I'll make sure that everyone
in Glevum hears that Julia's left the town.'

Gwellia stared. 'And how will you do that?'

'Mention it to the tanner's wife, who lives next door to our
workshop!' Junio cried, sipping the last of the delicious mead.
'One word to her and half the town will know.'

I nodded. 'And it will be common knowledge that I've hired
a travelling carriage, too. Marcus offered to lend me his, of
course, but arranging one in public ensures that it is known.
If I hire a cart as well, that will occasion no remark.'

'And you're not afraid the letter-writer will watch and trace where we have gone? Or follow Cilla and the children to Corinium?'

I was more anxious about that than I cared to say, but I had weighed the odds. 'He's more likely to stay here and strike at Marcus,' I replied. 'That is his real intention, it appears. He seems to operate in Glevum, if the death of Varius is any guide – and in any case he cannot follow both of us at once. Of course it's possible that he will send some servant after Julia's coach, but once Corinium is reached she and her children will have disappeared. He'll enquire for them in vain.'

'And the staff there won't betray us?' Gwellia frowned at me. 'You think they can be trusted?'

'Better than the villa, in a lot of ways – most of them have been with Julia for years and they would die for her.' Cilla could hardly be argued with, since she had actually worked there, when she was a slave. 'I'm certain they can be relied upon to do exactly what's required – especially if they get instructions under Marcus's seal.' She had risen and was refilling mead cups as she spoke.

Gwellia nodded, grudgingly. 'But it seems to me the journey is a risky enterprise. The roads are likely to be dangerous once the legion's gone – husband, you said as much yourself. So there may be brigands, quite apart from wolves and bears. Even with a mounted guard I think it's hazardous. I'm worried for our grandchildren, and Cilla too, of course.'

'Marcus said the same,' I answered. 'But I persuaded him. I pointed out that if we move at once, the legion will be marching down that very road, towards Londinium – which guarantees the safety of other travellers, though it may involve delays.'

Marching troops have precedence on any thoroughfare; all carts, pedestrians and carriages are legally required to move onto the margins and wait for them to pass. However, the presence of soldiers anywhere nearby would certainly deter attack since the penalty for ambush on the public road is crucifixion – and is rigorously applied.

'And the road south is the one you propose that we shall take?'

I did not answer that. I just said, 'What alternative is there? Stay at the villa and wait until this letter-writer strikes – as it seems he has already done with Varius?'

'Poor Varius!' Cilla murmured, sitting down again. 'I served him once or twice, when he was a guest at Marcus's. He seemed a charming man, though interested in power, like all councillors. Imagine him dying slowly in such agony! Let's hope his killer's brought to justice before the funeral, so at least his ghost can rest in peace.' She spat on her finger and rubbed it on her ear. (The mention of unquiet spirits is supposed to bring ill-luck.)

Gwellia had not finished arguing. She shook her head. 'But Varius was murdered in the town, where his apartment is above a shop and crowds of people are passing all the time. It's not so easy at the villa when there are high walls all around, and both the gates are guarded, day and night by enormous slaves with clubs. Strangers would be noticed instantly.'

'That's why rich men have gatekeepers,' I said. 'But even that is no defence. That letter that Marcus got today was thrown across the wall, and no one saw the person who delivered it. Not even the enormous gatekeepers with clubs!'

'Then there can't have been a proper look-out at the time . . .' she began, but Junio chimed in.

'One can hardly blame the duty gate-guard, Mother, if he didn't notice anything amiss. There are always people going up and down the lane. Even visiting the villa, come to that – bringing deliveries of wine and oil.'

'To say nothing of the special traders, selling silks or slaves, or the itinerants who come and sharpen knives or put new handles on broken iron pots,' his wife agreed. 'There were always people like that coming to the house.'

'Or – the gods preserve us – citizens invited for a feast,' I said. My wife was still frowning, so I spelt it out. 'Any of those callers could be a killer in disguise. Yet obviously the gatekeeper would let them in. There might even be accomplices already in the house. Marcus is very nervous about his new slaves. He fears that one of them might be in enemy employ. But a murderer does not even have to get inside the walls. It wouldn't be difficult to tamper, for instance, with imported wine before it is ever delivered to the house. As Varius has found.'

Junio raised his cup to Gwellia. 'So, Mother, what are we to do?' he asked. 'Wait until someone smuggles poison in, or scales the villa walls and stabs them in their beds, then throws in fiery pitch torches and sets fire to the house? And ours as well, perhaps?'

Gwellia made a gesture of despair. 'Of course not. I suppose it must be done.' She took my mead cup from me and held her hands in mine. 'Husband, I think your scheme is reckless, but I have no better one. Cilla and Junio agree with you, it seems, and so must I. I've no appetite for leaving our dear house, myself. But strange times require strange actions. I will do my part.'

'But under protest, still?' I looked steadily at her.

She looked into my eyes. 'I am your wife, Libertus, you can rely on me. If we are forced to this, then I'll do all I can to help. So, since that's now agreed on, Cilla, let me see the boys. It may be some time before I get another chance.' She got up from her stool and together the two women went over to the bed, where the toddler was sleeping, tucked up at the foot, and the infant was babbling gently in the wicker crib that Cilla had woven for her firstborn, years ago. Gwellia picked the baby up and crooned to him.

I knew that this was her way of hiding that she was close to tears so I left the women to their female pursuits and talked to Junio beside the embers of the fire.

'When do you propose that this expedition should begin?' he said, kneeling to stir the red coals around the baking pot, under which Cilla had already set tomorrow's bread to bake. 'Not tomorrow morning, surely?'

I shook my head, waving away the aromatic smoke which coiled around our heads and wafting it towards the smoke-hole in the roof. 'Not as soon as that – I will need to find a cart for us and Marcus's family will require a travelling-coach. The armed guard is not a problem – Marcus hasn't yet sold on the guard he had when he was travelling. So there are just the carts to find, and Marcus's name and seal should make that possible. I aim that Julia's party should set off by noon, and we soon afterwards.'

Junio brushed his hands and squatted on his stool again. 'And Julia can be ready to depart by then?'

I grinned. 'The villa slaves are working on packing overnight – they were already filling boxes when I left. Though she won't need much luggage, the house is fully stocked – and she won't have it with her anyway, but it is just for show.'

'So the whole villa's alert to what is happening?' he said.

'They think she's leaving for Corinium,' I answered. 'It is one of the things that I'm relying on. If this unknown enemy does have a spy in place, he'll report to his master that the family have fled. And the spy will not be with them. There is already staff at the Corinium house and with reasonable horses it should be possible to get there before dark. It's agreed that Julia will only take her nurse.'

'Nourissa? The wet-nurse? I remember her. That is a splendid choice. I believe she'd die for Julia, if the need arose.' Junio's face was thoughtful in the dim glow of the fire. 'Then it seems the plan is workable. Mother is right, the roads are dangerous, but tomorrow will be safer than any other day – the presence of the legions will see to that. Let's hope that you can find a carrying-coach in time.'

'I'm taking a letter from Marcus into town, at first light, myself. There should be no problem – he still has influence, at least until the current Emperor pronounces otherwise. And he's given me a handsome sum to pay the hiring-firm. I'll negotiate, of course.' I meant it. I'd had to dissuade my patron from writing, under seal, that he was prepared to offer any fee they asked. 'But he's desperate to get Julia safely out of town. This business with Varius has really frightened him.'

Gwellia had come over and had been listening. 'So you will go to Glevum in the morning, just as you always do?' she demanded, standing over us with the swaddled baby in her arms.

I looked up at her. 'Of course. It must seem that things are just as usual. Ideally, I'd open up the workshop for an hour or two – to give the gossips something they can talk about – but I am not convinced there will be time for that. I'll just call in and tell the tanner's wife what I intend.'

'I'll do that for you, Father,' Junio said. 'Don't shake your head like that. I won't be coming with you on your journey south. You will need someone here to keep an eye on things. And to send you word if there are further deaths.' He looked into my eyes and shook his head at me – warning me not to voice my thoughts and alarm the womenfolk.

I nodded. I did not have to tell him that the next death might be his – he was as aware of it as I was. 'What will you do instead?'

'Keep the workshop open. Use my ears and eyes.'

'Then try to find out if Varius had known enemies,' I murmured seizing the moment. Gwellia and Cilla had turned away and were laying the now sleeping infant on the bed. 'There's a land-steward of his great-aunt's that I'd like to hear about – how he bought his freedom when his master died. There seems to be a mystery as to how he got the funds.'

'And you can't ask him that, if you are going to the estate?'

'I understand that he has left the property by now. He had no love for it. The man was negligent. And all the other slaves were sold. But – here's the thing – there was some question of a court case against him at one time.'

'So he might be the letter-writer, do you think?' Junio looked puzzled. 'I can't imagine it. If an action had been brought against a man like that, it wouldn't be Marcus who considered it. A steward would only warrant some low official at a public hearing in the open air. In a draughty courtyard somewhere, more than like.'

'I know,' I said. 'That's what I thought myself. And where would such a person learn to write? But I must be alert to every possibili—' I broke off as the women came back to join us at the fire.

'Possibilities?' Gwellia sounded sharp. 'You think it's possible that something will go wrong? I wish you weren't going back to Glevum through those woods, again. I knew there was something sinister when you chose to arm yourself.'

Cilla took the lighted taper and set it down nearby. 'But you'll be back tomorrow, Father, in time to keep an eye on this departure, I presume?'

I nodded. 'I can't avoid this visit to the hiring stables but I'll take the mule and I should be back by noon. I'll send the carriage straight to Julia and make them bring the other cart and driver to our roundhouse here. I'd like us to set off ourselves as soon as possible after the Corinium party have gone.'

'Then I'll have to go and set some oatcakes on to bake, or we'll go hungry on the way. We'd better say goodnight.' Gwellia's abruptness disguised her fears, I knew. I called Minimus from the slaves' sleeping hut outside, while Junio took a new pitch-torch from a hook beside the door and held it in the embers till it spurted fire.

I put my cloak on, held the torch aloft and, accompanied by my wife and serving-boy, walked the short distance to our roundhouse. Tenuis and Kurso had kept the fire aglow, so Gwellia set the baking in the ashes and then we went to bed. However, for once, she did not turn to me – and my own mind was so troubled that I hardly slept that night.

TEN

There was indeed no problem hiring a travelling coach next day although, despite my airy assertions of confidence the night before, I had secretly feared that it would be hard to find anything suitable at such short notice. But I got up at dawn and rushed at once to town – through the silent forest and unfrequented ways – to reach my favourite hiring stables as early as I dared. I was rewarded for my efforts: at the mention of a letter from Marcus Septimus, a large covered carriage was instantly brought out.

'There you are, citizen, as fine a *raeda* as you'll hire anywhere – big enough to take a family and their luggage too, provided they're not carrying too much. Cover and curtains all provided, and we even have shutters they can put up against the dust – if they don't mind it being rather dark inside. Ideal for His Excellency's purposes! You're very fortunate that it's available, it's greatly in demand.' The stable owner – a swarthy wall-eyed fellow in a sweat-stained tunic and a pair of clumsy rawhide boots tied round his legs with thongs, had come out to deal with me himself. 'Call it two days' hiring to get there and back, and I'll include a fine *raedarius* to drive it, too – the customer to provide him food and drink and find him accommodation overnight.' He named a price, which would have frightened me, if I did not have a purseful of Marcus's gold coins suspended from my belt. 'What do you say, citizen, do we have a deal?'

It was an ancient dusty vehicle but it would obviously serve, and we were in a hurry. All the same I haggled (failure to do so would have been remarkable) and after a little the price had almost halved. But I did not seal the contract – yet. 'And suppose I want to hire a sturdy *plaustrum* too – do you know where I could obtain one?'

He squinted at me, with his good eye. 'Cart, and an ox to pull it – and a driver too? For the servants and the extra baggage, I suppose? Let me see. I think I know where I could get hold of one for you – sturdy, with a wicker frame on top, complete with covered seats and everything. That would be useful on a long trip, if it rains.' He cocked his head at me. 'For two days again?'

I shook my head. 'This might take slightly longer. Say a half a moon – including the time it takes to bring it back again. And I don't think we need a driver for the cart. Oxen are fairly docile – I'm sure, between us, we could manage it ourselves.'

He named a smaller sum.

'That's too much for an ox-cart,' I declared. I shook my head. 'If it's so expensive, I might have to change my mind.' I glanced at him sideways. 'Or perhaps I'll look elsewhere. There are other hiring-stables by the western gate.'

The stable-owner looked at me and stroked his grizzled chin. I could see him calculating how much he dared to ask, without losing the whole contract – exactly as I'd hoped. 'Since this is for His Excellence, I'll tell you what I'll do. You agree to take both vehicles and I'll charge you just the two days for the cart – provided you bring it back before the Kalends of next month. But, I'll want full payment in advance and there'll be a fine of fifty *asses* if it's a moment late.'

I nodded. I could see the risks but it was my patron's gold, not mine and I needed urgent transport. 'On condition that I get them both delivered before noon this very day, the raeda to the villa of His Excellence and the ox-cart to my round-house, which is close nearby. Your driver will find it – anyone will tell you where my patron lives.'

'Done, citizen.' He gave a piercing whistle through his teeth, and a younger man – apart from the squint, the double of himself – came hurrying from the interior and out into the yard. The stable-owner nodded. 'Brother, you're a witness to the price agreed!' He spat upon his hand and we exchanged the formula, which in itself forms a binding contract under law. 'Scratch a record on that piece of broken slate inside the door.'

The brother hurried off to do so, grinning, and I knew that, even now, I'd paid too much.

The owner saw me frowning. 'Have to make a living, citizen.

And the record helps us both. Shows how long the raeda is spoken for.' He nodded at the coach. 'We'll have that swept and ready for you almost straightaway – just as soon as we have yoked the horses on – but I'll have to send out elsewhere for the cart. Give me a half an hour, citizen, say until the sun is over that oak tree over there, and you can take them both away with you,' he said.

I shook my head. 'I've got a servant and a mule with me, and business in the town. Send the carriage out to Marcus as soon as possible and make sure that the ox-cart gets to my house by noon. That was the agreement.' I counted out the coins.

The fellow tested each by biting them, then slipped them in the leather pouch he wore around his waist. 'So you won't be riding out there in the raeda then? Or the ox-cart, perhaps? Your servant could have ridden the mule back home for you. I should have thought you'd welcome the comfort and protection from the rain.' He spoke as though it were my welfare he was thinking of, and not the fact that he'd have to provide a driver for the second cart, who would then require payment for walking idly back to town.

'Unfortunately not,' I said, though, to tell the truth, I would have welcomed the protection of a cart – not necessarily only from the rain. The poisoning of Varius had really frightened me. I'd not enjoyed my journey into Glevum earlier. It was even more jumpy than the day before, except that this time my companion was my much-loved Minimus, who actually delighted in riding on the mule. (I did not like to put him at such risk, but he was likely to be a lot more use than Tenuis if forced to my defence. Not only was he bigger – though not yet fully grown – but I knew from past experience that, in a fight, he was both brave and cunning as well as being as swift and slippery as a fish. I hoped by all the ancient gods, it would not come to that.)

The stable-owner cut across my thoughts. 'Then, if you'll forgive us, citizen, we must get to work. I'll have to clean this raeda and my brother – ah, there he is . . .' He raised his voice to shout. 'Brother, go and tell Jummilius that we want his cart again – and persuade him to get it over here as soon as possible.'

The other man scowled but scuttled off at once and the speaker turned to me. 'I'll find a man to drive it out to you if Jummilius cannot spare the time himself. Never fear, we'll get it there by noon.'

'Hiring transport, citizen?' From somewhere behind me came a voice I recognized.

'Porteus?' I whirled round in surprise, amazed to see the portly councillor hurrying towards me across the stable-yard, incongruous in his magisterial purple stripe. 'What are you doing here?' It was discourteous of me, but I spoke before I thought. This was not a place that people of his rank would usually frequent – they would send a messenger, as Marcus had sent me.

My directness flustered Porteus so much that he did not rebuke me for impertinence. 'I happened to be passing by,' he muttered hastily.

I gave him a wry look. 'Really, councillor?' I did not credit for an instant that he'd been simply 'passing by'. The stables were a long way from his place of residence, and not on his likely route to anywhere. I guessed that he'd heard about the fate of Varius and was here intending to hire transport so he could flee the town – despite his protestations yesterday. Well, if he wanted a raeda now, I thought, he'd have to look elsewhere.

Porteus's face flushed pink beneath the acne spots 'Well, not in person, naturally . . .' He nodded at the gateway to the yard, where I saw the young attendants that I'd seen yesterday. 'It was one of my servants who was in the street nearby. He thought he'd seen you here and he brought word to me so I hurried down to see if it was true.'

'I see.' That made a lot more sense. Once Porteus had heard that I was here of course he'd come himself – hoping to learn that Marcus was about to flee, so he could do so too. Well. I'd have to disappoint him on that score. Perhaps he'd even planned to hire a travelling-carriage, too, as soon as his suspicions were confirmed.

The owner of the stables clearly thought the same. 'Can I help you, Worthiness?' he simpered, sidling up to us. He had been goggling at my companion's impressive purple stripe and

all but rubbing his work-hardened hands in glee at the prospect
of another handsome deal. 'You want a carriage, sir? I don't
have another raeda, but I can find a cart or gig.'

But the hoped-for client gestured him imperiously away.
'Not now, fellow.' The owner shambled off and Porteus turned
to me. 'So you are hiring the raeda, I perceive. I assume it's
for your patron, rather than yourself?' He sounded mightily
relieved at this apparent evidence of Marcus leaving town.

I was wishing heartily that the councillor would go away,
I was on an urgent errand and he was delaying me, but I could
not risk insulting a person of his rank. I said, with courtesy,
'Not exactly, Worthiness. His Excellence still intends to stay.
I am sent to hire the carriage for his wife – he thinks she
would be safer somewhere else.' I watched the pudgy face fall
mournfully and I felt an unexpected burst of sympathy. I did
not like the man, but nobody deserves to get threats against
his life. 'But councillor, if you have plans to leave the town
yourself, don't let me deter you.'

'Plans, citizen? What makes you think that I have plans?'
He had adopted his prickly, pompous tone again and my
empathy vanished as quickly as it came.

'Your slave!' Some demon of mischief prompted me to say.
'You must have sent him here. He would scarcely be passing
these gates by accident. Were you thinking of hiring something
for yourself?'

He flushed, like a child discovered stealing fruit. 'Only to
visit your patron, possibly. Nothing of importance.'

It was a lie, of course, and a transparent one. I laid a trap
for him. 'To ask about the villa, as you suggested yesterday?'
I hinted, wickedly.

He seized on the excuse I'd offered him, with evident relief.
'Exactly, citizen.'

I gave him a sweet smile. 'In that case, councillor, you are
most fortunate. The *raedarius* is going to drive there any
minute now. The carriage will be empty. I'm sure he could
take you – especially if you offer him a tip.'

He retreated so instantly that it was comical. 'But how
would I get back to Glevum afterwards? Besides, I've not
decided if I'll ask your patron yet. I've been thinking more

about it, pavement-maker, since we spoke and it strikes me that perhaps his villa isn't safe. The threatening letter-writer must have found out where it is, or he could not have thrown the message in across the wall.' He sounded proud of this deduction, though I should have thought an idiot might have worked it out.

'Then it might be safer to stay here in town and invest in a hefty doorkeeper, like the one that Marcus keeps to guard his Glevum flat,' I said. 'Though that did not save Varius or Claudius, it appears.'

He whirled around as if he were a whipping-top. 'You think that business was connected with the threats? Oh, dear gods!' He sounded genuinely shocked. 'I thought that Varius had drunk bad water from the well or eaten something rotten which had made him ill. Is that not more likely? The sickness has affected the whole household, not just the head of it.'

'Exactly as the threatener promised!' I pointed out. 'I'm almost certain that it was deliberate. A member of the council, like yourself – suddenly poisoned when there are these threats about? I can't believe it's mere coincidence.'

'Dear Jupiter!' He seized my arm. 'So, whom do you suspect?'

I shook my head. 'Anyone who had the opportunity. Clearly it is someone who knows the area, and the names and where-abouts of senior councillors.' I looked at him. 'You don't know whether Varius received a letter too? I know that you were making enquiries among the curia and I understand you called there yesterday?'

'But I did not go in!' Porteus squeezed my forearm till it hurt. 'I'd hoped to lunch with him, that's all, but when I got there I was turned away. Some old woman told me he was ill and took my litter off to look for you. I didn't speak to him. Ask Varius when he's in better health, he'll tell you just the same.'

I disengaged myself. 'Varius cannot tell us anything,' I said. 'He's dead. You didn't know?' I stared at Porteus. 'You hadn't heard the news?'

'Dead?' He had turned paler than a corpse himself. 'But . . .? That isn't possible . . . Varius Quintus . . . I'd no idea. I can't believe . . . Oh mighty Dis!' He tailed off, wordlessly.

'Not only Varius but his half-brother too, and most of their household servants from what I hear of it. The old woman's steward brought Marcus word last night. There must be a connection with the threats. So you can see why I'm interested to know if Varius received a letter yesterday. But it appears that you can't help me?'

'Dear Jupiter! This is appalling news.' The shock had visibly affected him. He was perspiring with fear. 'I swear, Libertus, I know nothing about what happened to Varius at all. Ask the old woman if you doubt my word. I did not even cross the threshold yesterday.' He grabbed my arm again.

I moved it from his grasp. 'Then perhaps you're fortunate. If you had lunched with him . . .'

He froze. Porteus was not quick of thought, but I saw the light of genuine panic in his eyes. 'What are you trying to tell me, citizen?' he murmured, as if he could not bear to accept the obvious.

I spelt it out for him. 'If you had dined with Varius Quintus you would have drunk his wine. In that case you might well be dead yourself. And not just dead, but dead in agony. So, take this as a warning, councillor. You see what it implies? The man who wrote the letters is not uttering mere threats, he clearly means exactly what he says.'

'You think that I'm in danger?'

'If I am right about these letters, then I am sure you are.'

'And you don't know who wrote them?' He sounded desperate. 'Have you any clues?'

'Not as yet,' I said. 'Though we're looking into it.'

'But you already have suspicions?'

I could not say as much. 'I hope to make some progress in the next few days,' I said. 'In the meantime, Worthiness, take especial care.' I glanced around to see that we could not be overheard. 'If you wish to flee the town, I am sure that His Excellence would understand the reason why.'

He looked tempted for a moment and then he shook his head. 'I shall not run away. I can hardly do so, after what's been said.' He shook his head. 'But . . . on the other hand, what fate awaits me here? Libertus, if you were in my place, what would you do?'

'Remain in town and try to find out who poisoned Varius,'

I said. 'A simple threat is difficult to trace, but murder's different. Someone has committed a terrible offence, with motive, means and opportunity – there must be witnesses, at least, to prove who *didn't* do it. That narrows down the field. And, incidentally, once it's known a search is on, and we are on our guard, it makes it much more difficult for the man to strike again.'

He nodded. 'You're right,' he said. 'I won't feel safe until the killer's caught. Thank you, pavement-maker, for your excellent advice.' He clutched my sleeve again. 'In fact, you have given me a new idea. Marcus is always praising you for solving mysteries. I tell you what I'll do. I'll offer a reward. A hundred *denarii* if you can find the poisoner, double if you can find firm proof of guilt and bring him to my court.' He shot me a keen glance. 'I mean it, citizen. Use any means you wish. No public mention of the letters, though – I assume that's sensible?'

I shook my head, a bit reluctantly. A hundred denarii would keep my family comfortably for several moons. 'I fear I can't accept your offer, councillor. I have a task to do for Marcus, and that must take precedence.' I saw that he was disappointed at my words and I added hastily, 'But if I do discover anything, I'll try to let you know. In the meantime, ask around the town. I'm sure that there are people who would jump at your reward. But now, excuse me, I must be on my way. I have other errands that I must do in town and I must be home by noon. I've already kept my servant waiting far too long.'

I bowed and kissed the garnet seal-ring on his hand, and hurried off towards the stable gate, where Minimus and Arlina were awaiting me. As I emerged, his slave-boys hurried in, and the last I saw of Porteus was him staring after me, biting his knuckle in evident dismay while his pretty young attendants fluttered round on either side.

ELEVEN

I did indeed have several errands in the town – Gwellia had asked me to bring back some supplies for the journey from the forum marketplace – and while I was there I used the opportunity to stop at the basilica, and speak to a passing member of the curia I knew. I could scarcely spare the time, but I wanted the news of Julia's departure to be known, though of course I didn't specify where she planned to go. Happily I'd found a councillor I hoped would spread the word, but he was more concerned to pass on the news to me that Varius and his brother had died the day before.

But I had done what I could. I hurried back and packed the cheese, spelt-flour bread and salted beef onto Arlina's back, and – leaving Minimus in the street to mind the purchases and mule – I risked the time to call in at the workshop, too.

'Father!' Junio was sorting coloured stones when I arrived for the large new commission that we were working on. 'I am glad to see you, but what brings you here? Worried that I wouldn't find the tanner's wife? I've already spoken to her – I saw her in the street – so the story of Julia's flight to Corinium will be all over town by noon. In fact I let the woman think that you're going there as well – or rather she seized on that conclusion and I did not contradict.'

I grinned at him. 'Well done. That's the tradesmen and the street-folk answered for. And I've been doing the same among the curial class. Though they're not much interested in what I plan to do. People are too shocked about the death of Varius. Porteus is even offering a very large reward for tracking down the poisoner – so if you learn anything, be sure to make a claim! As well as sending word to me at the same time, of course.'

'Porteus? Great gods!' My adopted son looked shocked. 'I'm surprised he has the money to make such promises. And why would he . . .?' He trailed off and his face cleared suddenly.

'Don't tell me Porteus got a threat as well? That's what you came to tell me?'

'Not entirely,' I replied. 'I do have another reason for interrupting you. I wanted to pick up a weapon to carry on the road – I've got a knife, concealed about me even now. But there are laws against these things and it's already been spotted by a sentry once, so I'll have to keep that firmly out of sight. I need something that looks innocent that I can keep to hand. One of our stone-breaking mallets would do the trick, I thought.'

'This one?' He dusted off his hands and handed it to me.

I weighed it in my palm. 'And perhaps you should carry the smaller one yourself. I wish you'd brought your house-slave with you into town. He's not much help with cutting stone, perhaps, but I don't like you walking through the woods alone, the way things are.'

'You are Marcus's confidante, not me. I should be safe enough. Anyway Brianus was required at home today to help with preparations for the trip. Which reminds me, while you're here, you can take the warmer cloaks with you as well. I've just fetched them from the fullers, and you will be glad of thicker plaid.' He handed me the bundle and I slipped the mallet among the pile of woollen cloth. 'You worry about me, but do take care yourself. Even the main road south won't be as safe as it has been of late. If the legions are marching eastward towards Londinium, you can't rely on the usual random route-marches to keep the peace.'

I shook my head although I knew that he was right. 'I don't think I'm under any special threat, myself,' I said. 'I'm part of Marcus's extended household, I suppose, but with Julia conspicuously leaving town the letter-writer won't be watching me.'

'Let's hope not, but that doesn't mean you're safe. Mother is right to fret. When the law breaks down, then any road is dangerous – you said as much yourself. There are always bandits, not to mention wolves and bears and without the legions . . .' He spread his hands. 'I mean it, Father. Take especial care and send me word as soon as you've arrived where you are going. May all the gods be with you. Please Jove, I see you soon.'

I squeezed his hands, and nodded wordlessly. There was really nothing useful I could add and, besides, there seemed to be something prickling my eyes. So I simply took the cloaks and left him to his work, while I hurried back towards the gate where Minimus was still waiting patiently.

With this extra bundle and the purchases there was no room for my bulk on the mule, but I perched my young slave up her back somehow and we were soon hurrying back towards my roundhouse once again. I hardly needed Junio's warning about the forest track – it was an anxious journey, and I kept careful watch. The presence of the mallet was absurdly comforting, but I still jumped each time a creature rustled in the woods. My eyes ached with the constant swivelling and I began to wish that I had used the longer, more frequented road or ridden in the ox-cart when I had the chance.

I did not have long for such regrets, because we caught it up. I was amazed to find it on this route at all. The old track is steep and muddy, precipitous in parts, and generally too difficult for carts of any size, as the driver had clearly discovered for himself. It was a smaller, lighter vehicle than I'd expected it to be – not so much a plaustrum as common *carruca*, and a smallish one at that – but it was clearly the wagon that I'd contracted for: the famous wicker super-structure had snagged against a tree.

The driver had climbed down, as I arrived, and was trying to prevent the massive ox from simply plodding on and tearing off the flimsy upper-works, but without his guiding hand the wagon had slewed round, so that it was now neatly wedged across a boggy bend, right at the bottom of a steep and sticky hill.

This route is unfrequented, in a general way, but this obstruction had so blocked the way that several travellers were backed up the other side: a fellow with a donkey-load of cabbages, an ancient woman with a basketful of gathered herbs, and a red-faced farm-boy in a heavy russet cloak, whose frisky goats were threatening to escape among the trees. None of them was doing anything to help, though the man with the donkey was loudly cursing ox-carts with every oath he knew (including some inventive ones I'd never heard before).

I gestured to Minimus to slide down from the mule and gave him the leading-rope, while I went forward to see what I could do. The driver of the ox-cart, a huge, lugubrious-looking fellow in a grimy yellow tunic, was tugging on the ox's horns without effect. He looked up as I approached and called across to me.

'It's no good you cursing at me, citizen, I'm doing what I can. That fool Jummilius assured me that the cart could come this way – but it has been a nightmare from the start. I should have gone the long way round on the military road, but some citizen has contracted to have this cart by noon, and if I don't deliver it I suppose I won't be paid.' He glanced towards the sky. 'Though Jove knows how I'm supposed to guess when it's midday in any case – there's too much cloud about to see the sun, even if we weren't surrounded by so many trees.'

'You unyoke the ox,' I answered, 'and I'll climb up the tree and see if I can free the branches from above, then perhaps we can push the wagon around the bend.'

He made a doubtful face. 'It won't be easy to get past,' he hollered back.

He had a point. He was an enormous man and the cart was wedged between dense bushes either side – brambles and hawthorn, in particular, seemed to grow particularly thick and prickly in this spot, no doubt encouraged by the prevailing damp. It was clear why the other travellers had not tried to pass by striking off the track.

'Well, if you pull, I'll push it from the back!' This whole strange conversation was conducted at a yell. 'You've got one of those fancy pivots on the front, I see.' I gestured to a massive metal spike on which the axle sat.

He nodded. 'It lets the front wheels turn more easily on bends, I will say that for it, otherwise I would not have got as far as this with it. But apart from that, the hirer's welcome to the thing. It's the most confounded cart I ever handled in my life – it sways about with that wretched frame on top and though it's supposed to have a pole-spring underneath, those solid wooden wheels are horrible, for all their iron rims. It almost shakes your teeth out when you hit a root or stone. I don't know why a sane man would want to hire it, but it seems that someone does. Well, I wish him joy of it, and of this ox as well. It might be sturdy but it's a stubborn, wayward brute.'

These words – delivered so loudly that the gate-guards back at Glevum might have heard – were hardly comforting, since I was planning to drive this very cart for many miles – and several days. However, he was unyoking the creature as he spoke and, despite the unflattering description, the ox did nothing more alarming than give an irritated snort and wander off to munch some muddy herbiage beside the track.

'I've freed him from the yoke. Now see what you can do at your end,' the driver called to me. 'And try to save that wickerwork as much as possible. There will be Dis to pay if we have damaged it.'

I nodded, though I hardly needed his advice. That flimsy homemade cover was all the shield that my party would have against the rain and I wanted it intact, if possible. At least it was no longer in danger of being torn off by the ox – though I knew that there were other overhanging branches further on ahead. I made a private vow that if I got it clear, I would drive this cart only on main military roads, which are wide and have cleared areas on either side.

I glanced up at the tree now. There was a branch that I could climb on, if it would take my weight, and from there, perhaps . . . I sighed. If I fell off, I would tumble into thorns. I am too old for such adventures, but the ox-driver was stranded on the wrong side of the cart, and in any case was even heavier than me. I grumbled inwardly and hitched my tunic up into my belt. I was just about to try to find a handhold overhead when my thoughts were interrupted.

'Let me do it, master.' It was little Minimus. 'I've tied Arlina safely to a tree. I'm younger than you are, and much lighter, too.'

Gwellia would have chided him for his impertinence but I said gratefully, 'You think you can climb it? It's a long way if you fall.'

'I'm certain that I can – especially if you give me a hand up to that big branch over there.'

I interlocked my hands to make a step for him, and he grasped the bough, swung himself up and swarmed along it

like a cat. He disappeared a moment among the foliage and
then his face appeared again and he grinned down at me.

'The branch has gone right through it – caught it like a fork
– but it hasn't done much damage. If I use my weight to pull
the forked bit back the way it came, I think it will come free.'

'You want a knife?' I still had one slung around my neck,
underneath my outer tunic. 'It might be easiest to cut it clear.'

He shook his head. 'I'll try my method first.' He disappeared
again. The leaves above me churned, there was a lot of rustling;
then a sudden sharp crack overhead, an oath, a shower of falling
leaves and twigs, and a moment later Minimus was tumbling
after them, snatching vainly at the passing twiglets and the air.
Instinctively I tried to catch him as he fell and – before I knew
it – both of us were sitting, winded, on the ground.

The slave-boy jumped up and grinned at me, unhurt. 'Thank
you, master. I got the forked branch out. It's made a nasty
tear at the spot where it went through, but a bit of woven osier
will fix it in a trice. It's done no damage to the frame itself,
that I can see, or the leather straps that hold it on. And I am
not hurt either, I just fell through lots of twigs.'

'Well done, Minimus,' I managed, though his descent had
knocked the breath from me. 'It's a wonder that you did not
fall into the cart!'

He helped me to my feet. 'There was no fear of that. The
branch sprang back and knocked me off my perch, but when
the cart was freed it swayed the other way.' He dusted down
my garments as he spoke. 'Now let's see if we can move it,
with the driver's help.'

In fact it needed the donkey-man as well, before we got the
cart lined up again and edged around the corner, where there
was more room on either side. Once we had done so the
donkey sidled past, disdainfully lifting its neat hooves to clear
the mud, followed by the ancient woman with the basketful
of forest herbs. The boy, though, was trying to round up his
rebellious goats, which had roamed off in all directions while
he helped to push the cart – and suddenly I glimpsed a flash
of blue underneath the cloak. My heart skipped several beats.
Could this be the watcher who had spied on us before?

'Citizen?' The driver had turned his attention to the ox. Glad of his burly presence, suddenly, I went and tried to help as he tugged the horns of the reluctant animal. The creature clearly preferred to stay and eat the grass but in the end the pair of us prevailed and it was installed between the shafts again.

The fellow climbed into the driving seat and turned to me. 'Stranger, I must thank you for your aid. I have no coin to give, but if you follow me, I'm sure that the citizen who hired this cart will give you a reward. I'll gladly tell him how you helped to get it free.'

I grinned at him. 'That will not be necessary. I am the man himself.'

He stared at me a moment. 'Is this some kind of jest?'

'I am Libertus the pavement-maker,' I explained. 'Was that not the name?'

He jumped down from the cart. 'Then why in Dis did you not tell me that before? You let me go on struggling with this stupid vehicle and all the time, I'd done what I was paid to do.'

My turn to stare. 'What do you mean by that? This plaustrum – if it deserves the name – was to be delivered to my roundhouse, at the crossroads with the major road.'

'Not as far as I know, citizen. My instructions were simply to deliver it to you. And I have done so. I wish you joy of it.' And with that he forced his way back past the cart again and set off tramping back towards the town.

'Hey!' I called. But there was no reply – and the driver was too big for me to argue with. There was nothing for it, I would have to drive the cart and leave Minimus to follow with the mule.

TWELVE

The driver was quite right about the ox – it was a stubborn brute – but after a little I got the hang of it. When I put away the lash and let it have its head and simply plod along the path at its own chosen pace, it tolerated my attempts to guide it with the goad. By imitating the cries and whistles that I've heard ox-men make I even managed to urge him to one side at one of the rare clearings and let the mule go by, so that Minimus could ride ahead and clear the way for us by holding back the branches that might have snagged the wickerwork. All this made for slow progress, though, and I began to fear that I would not manage to get home by noon.

On the other hand, I felt a good deal safer on the cart. In fact, I was so intent on driving and getting back in time that I almost forgot to worry about possible attack – though I did retrieve the hammer from its hiding place and keep it where I could reach it, just in case. I could not entirely dismiss the memory of that flash of blue. Was there someone out there spying on me still?

So I was delighted when we reached the outskirts of the wood and the crossroads where my roundhouse came into sight. But, I was not so delighted when I saw a cloud of dust out on the larger road and realized that a carriage was approaching from the main track on the right – almost certainly the raeda already on its way. The ox was impervious to my attempts to speed him on – I was almost tempted to use the whip again – but in the end I simply gave it up, called Minimus back to come and lead the cart and ran as fast as my old legs would carry me. I reached the enclosure just in time before the carriage did.

The raeda swept around the corner and drew up at the gate, with two armed horsemen riding either side. They fell back as the driver peered down from his perch. 'Are you the owner here?'

I nodded.

'Then you are honoured, citizen. The lady Julia is leaving for Corinium today. I am instructed that she wants to call and say goodbye to you and your good lady. Be so good as go inside to ask her to come here.'

I bowed. 'My wife, I fear, is aged and not able to venture out today,' I said, hoping that the ancient gods would excuse this version of the truth, 'or she would be the first to come and greet my patron's wife. But if the lady Julia would care to come inside, she is most welcome to our humble dwelling.'

I could see that he was doubtful, but Julia already had the carriage-shutter down and stuck her head out now to answer me herself. 'Of course I will. Nourissa! Help me to alight.' By this time the maid was already on the ground and had come around to the nearer door to let her mistress out. Julia, in a crimson travelling cloak and veil, climbed from the conveyance, pulled her hood up modestly and leant upon my arm.

'I am sorry to hear that Gwellia is indisposed,' she said, making sure that everyone escorting her could hear. 'She will grieve to miss the children. She is so fond of them – and they of her, of course. Nourissa, bring them in and let her say goodbye. The gods alone know when we shall return this way again.'

'You're quite sure, mistress? There might be spotted fever in the house. Or some other illness that might affect the children and yourself.' If I'd rehearsed Nourissa, I could not have improved her choice of words. 'Is there a miasma? No infectious smell?'

I shook my head. 'Gwellia is suffering from frailty and age,' I answered, hoping that my wife was not listening to this unflattering account. 'I do not think there's any risk of her transmitting that.'

Julia laughed softly. 'My servant is careful of our health, that's all. But, Nourissa, if Libertus says it's safe, I'm sure there is no risk. He is as anxious for our welfare as you are yourself. In any case I have that amulet you gave me, against danger and ill-health, and all the children are wearing theirs as well. So bring the babes, Nourissa.' She turned to me. 'We'll have to carry them. Marcus gave them poppy juice to help them sleep and pass the journey without too much distress.

Marcellinus will be sorry not be awake, but my husband thought it best to give it to them both.'

I nodded sagely. 'I can see the sense of that.' I should do, since I'd recommended it! But I said nothing more, just took the sleeping infant in my free arm while the nurse-slave scooped the toddler up and brought him after us.

As we entered the enclosure Julia turned and called, 'We shan't be an instant. Turn the carriage round, so we're ready to depart, and let that ox-cart past!'

I glanced along the road and there was Minimus, leading the ox-cart as though he had been born to it, with Arlina tied behind the vehicle and following along. In all the excitement, I had almost forgotten my cumbersome ox-wagon and my slave. 'Take it round the corner,' I called out to the boy. 'My patron's wife is here, so I can't stop to load it now. Turn towards the villa, but don't go very far. I'll come and fetch you when the raeda has gone.'

Minimus cast me an exasperated look but prepared to do as he was told and I led Julia and the children right into the house.

The next few moments were frenetic ones. Gwellia came hurrying from the shadows at the back, so anxious to greet us that I had to shoo her back and close the door, before anybody saw that she was fit and well.

'What kept you, husband? I was so relieved to see you at the gate. We feared something had happened and you wouldn't come in time! Cilla and her family are here and everything's prepared. We've given the children each a sleeping-draught.' She already had taken Julia's slumbering baby girl from me, taken off its outer wrap and was swaddling my small grandson up in it, instead. My household slaves and Cilla's Brianus were watching open-mouthed.

'Greetings, Julia! May life go well with you!' Cilla had jumped up from beside the stool beside the fire, and began to help Julia to remove her outer clothes. 'You think the raeda driver will be convinced?' She was pulling on the pale pink *stola* as she spoke. It was comically tight on her far more ample form, and she was slightly taller than her former mistress too, so the hem of her under-tunic and her ankles were on view, but once the flowing crimson cloak was on these defects were disguised. With the veil and hood to hide her face and hair, she would pass muster at a casual glance.

I nodded. 'People will see what they expect to see. Now if Nourissa puts Marcellinus down and you give her your elder boy instead, we can—'

'Me!' The nurse-slave startled me. She clutched the sleeping Marcellinus closer to her breast. 'But I'm going with my mistress. I'm sorry, citizen. She whispered to me that there was a plan to swap, but I naturally assumed that I was to stay with her and someone else was going to take my place.'

'But the raeda-driver's seen you. You don't have a veil. That's the whole point, don't you see? The whole scheme hinges on him seeing you again. It lures him into thinking that things are as they were. If someone else appears he'll know at once that something's wrong. Didn't your mistress tell you?' I glanced at Julia.

She was climbing into a plaid robe of Gwellia's, assisted by my slaves. Her face, I noticed, was a careful blank. She was trying to disguise her natural distaste at the home-woven fabric, I was sure (which must feel coarse against her fine patrician skin, accustomed to silks and finest wool) and the ministrations of well-meaning boys, instead of her usual skilful handmaidens. All the same she forced a smile and shook her head at me. 'I haven't really explained things to Nourissa, I'm afraid. I haven't had a chance. I could not find a moment when we were alone – and I could not be sure that in the villa there were not spies around. I could only whisper to her as we got into the coach, that we were in peril and there was a plan to swap.'

The nurse-slave shook her head. 'Well, I'm sorry, citizen. I agreed to help to keep my mistress safe and of course I will – with my own life, if that is what it takes. But if she's in danger – as it seems she is – then I must be with her. Besides, the baby girl's not weaned. She will take a little semi-liquid cereal, or watered wine and honey from a spoon, but she still needs the breast.'

'But surely, Julia . . .?' These were matters I knew nothing of.

The wet-nurse shook her head. 'She won't have milk by

now. I can't just abandon my mistress and the babe. You can't ask that of me.' She looked as if she were about to burst into floods of tears.

For a moment it seemed that my whole scheme was going to fall apart. The nurse's role was vital to the plan. Of course, at Julia's command she would do as she was told, but one word out of place – any sign of untoward reluctance or distress – and the plan would fail. She no doubt could be persuaded, given time, to act her part, but we had no time to spare. This visit had already begun to take too long.

It was Julia who found the way to manage things. She had pulled the plaid robe on by now and tied it round her waist, and loosed her long hair from its customary coiled Roman plaits, so it hung loose round her shoulders. 'Look at me, Nourissa, and listen carefully. My life and the children's safety may be in your hands. We'll find another wet-nurse, if we have to, on the road, but I'm sure the child will manage goat's milk from now on. When I was young, that's what they gave to me and I've survived. If you stay with us, the whole family is at risk. If you want to help me – and I'm sure you do – you will walk out to the raeda and help Cilla and her children into it, as though nothing untoward had happened here at all. Treat her exactly as you would have treated me. No tears, no drama, nothing to cause remark. I am depending on your loyalty, so that I can safely get the children far away from here.'

The nurse-slave stiffened. 'You can rely on me. Give me the other infant, then, since that's what you require.'

'And don't forget to call him Marcellinus,' Julia said with a smile. She looked wholly different, though still extremely beautiful. It was going to be difficult to take her anywhere without her being noticed, even in this guise. But that might work to our advantage in the end. 'If we all survive this, I will see you're well rewarded.'

'If you survive this, mistress, that is my reward.' The nurse had handed Marcellinus to my wife and taken Cilla's own sleeping toddler in her arms.

'Come, Nourissa!' Cilla was already at the door. Her imitation of Julia was so accurate that the nurse looked startled for a moment, but then she followed her and I went with them out into the lane. Cilla did remember not to climb straight into the coach, but stood back and waited as I'd told her to.

'Coachman, drive on! We have tarried far too long.' It was almost too imperious, but the raeda-driver did not hesitate. He leapt down from his seat to assist her up the step, helped Nourissa to hand the children in, then closed the door and hurried back to take the reins again. The escort fell into position front and rear and, as I stood and waved a last goodbye, the carriage rattled round the corner and disappeared from view. I watched the cloud of dust that followed it until it, too, had gone and then I turned and went back to the house.

Julia came to meet me. 'Thank you, pavement-maker,' she said earnestly. 'Now the worst is over. That went without a hitch.'

I shook my head. 'Lady, that was the easy part. The hard time is to come. For you, more than for the rest of us, I think. But we must make a start. I'll go and find Minimus and bring back the cart – it's primitive but it's the best that I could do. We'll load it quickly and then make a start ourselves.' I saw that she looked doubtful and I added hastily, 'Oxen are strong but much slower than a horse. If we don't set off within the hour we won't get far by dark and we need to reach a place where – speaking frankly, lady – no one has ever seen or heard of us. You in particular.'

THIRTEEN

The hard part was indeed to come, especially for the lady Julia, I knew. The next few days were bound to be a dreadful shock to her, accustomed as she was to wealth and luxury – in fact, only pressing danger would ever have induced me to subject her to this trip. Fortunately, she had no concept of what lay in store. If she had realized what hardships she'd be called on to endure, she might have resisted the project from the start – and certainly Marcus would have vetoed it.

To do her credit, she did her very best – did not even grumble when we packed her in the cart, although the seating was a simple wooden plank and only the flimsy wickerwork protected her from rain and wind and dust. In fact she seemed less concerned about her own discomfort than seeing that her children were settled under the cover in the back, and wrapped in home-spun blankets to keep out the cold – though she had to bite her lip when she saw the straw and reeds that I'd put down to make a bed for them.

'It's clean straw,' Gwellia assured her, briskly. 'We bought it specially. And Tenuis cut the reeds up at the spring this very day.'

Julia nodded though her eyes were shocked. She was obviously doubtful about this makeshift palliasse, though her children seemed entirely content. They simply stirred when they were laid down on it, opened their eyes a moment and went serenely back to sleep. I sent up a grateful prayer to the ancestral gods for that; when Marcellinus eventually woke there might be tears and shouts, and he had sufficient language to put at us all at risk. But I would worry about that problem when the moment came. For now it was enough to be safely on the road.

We closed up the roundhouses and left them to the slaves – Brianus to tend Junio when he got home again and Kurso, our little kitchen slave, to guard our home for us, feed the chickens, tend the crops and keep our fire alight. (He was proud as an emperor to be told that he could sleep in the big roundhouse while we were away, instead of in the slave-hut at the door, so he could feed and fan the embers and make sure they did not die.) Tenuis and Minimus we crammed in the cart with us – though with Gwellia, Julia, the children and myself, there was not a lot of room – while Arlina, laden with our goods, was tethered to the rear.

And so, before the raeda had been gone a half-an-hour (judging by the angle of the sun above the trees) we were on our way ourselves. I was very tense, at first – and not only because of possible attacks. I'd made it no secret that I was leaving with the cart, but my family and I are well known locally so the sooner we were out of territory where we might be recognized, the happier I'd be. Julia was wearing one of our Celtic travelling-capes by now, which both disguised her form and covered up her hair, and we'd washed off her Roman make-up with water from the jug so she looked a little less spectacular, though of course she wore no veil and she clearly wasn't Cilla if anyone looked twice.

We were lucky, I had timed our departure with some care – the road was not so busy at this time of day – and the only neighbour we encountered merely raised a hand, and trotted past us on his donkey without a second glance. I looked across at Julia, and realized with a start that I would not have recognized her in this guise myself – without the red ochre with which she tinged her lips and cheeks, or the kohl with which she emphasized her eyes – and her white, fair skin was already travel-streaked. I began to breath again. From now on we looked like any peasant family on the move, escaping some fire or failure of their crops – at least, I hoped we did.

'We shall have to find a Celtic name for you,' I said to her, as at last we turned onto the major road and I urged the lumbering ox away from Glevum and towards our destination in the south. 'I can hardly call you "lady" while we are travelling, you are supposed to be a member of my family.'

Julia was sitting squashed up by Gwellia, clinging grimly to the bench as the ox-cart rattled and lurched along the road.

Here on the military road the wheel-ruts were deep, and the homemade plaustrum did not fit exactly into them, so she had to clench her teeth and her words came out in little bursts with every jolt. 'But why not simply . . . call me Julia? Lots of Celtic people use . . . Roman names these days . . . indeed, you do yourself . . . Oooh!' She broke off as we bounced across a specially violent bump. The year had been a wet one and even the Roman military roads were suffering.

'Because someone might have heard the name of Marcus's wife,' I pointed out. 'He's a very famous man. They'll have heard of him in Aquae Sulis, I am sure, and possibly of you. I don't want people making awkward connections.'

'I see . . .' A little silence. Then: 'But . . . why not Cilla then?'

'Calling you Cilla would confuse your sons,' I replied with a smile. 'Besides, it's almost certain that one of us would get it wrong; it's much more difficult to misapply a name than learn a different one. A Celtic one is best. We'll call you Kennis – that means "beautiful". You heard that boys?' I called back to the slaves. 'The lady Julia is Kennis from now on. Though you can call her "mistress" as you always did. It's Gwellia and I who have to watch our tongues.'

'A good choice, husband,' Gwellia agreed. 'Kennis is as much a description as a name and easy to recall. As long as Julia remembers to respond to it!'

The new-named Kennis nodded, taking the compliment as no more than her due. 'I'll do my very best. And we'll tell Marcellinus . . . it's polite for us to use . . . that designation while we are travelling . . . He'll understand . . . he's used to his father . . . being called by different titles . . . in different company. And of course he won't have to . . . call me that himself . . . I am simply "mater" as far as he's concerned. It won't . . . matter that we speak no Celtic . . . you don't think?'

'Lots of Celts speak Latin for preference nowadays,' I said, wishing that I really felt as confident as that. 'Take Junio, my adopted son, for instance. He is half-Celt, of course, you can see it in his face – probably his mother was a household slave – but he never spoke anything but Latin in his life.'

'So if anyone asks, you used to be a slave.' Gwellia had

adopted an instructive tone, exactly as if she were the mother-in-law she was supposed to be. 'It makes good sense – you have the manners of a Roman house, but if you'd served a great lady as special handmaiden, it's just what you'd expect.'

'Rather like Cilla?' the new Kennis enquired.

If there was irony in this (Cilla had been maidservant to Julia at one time but had not acquired many Roman airs at all) Gwellia did not acknowledge it. 'Exactly like Cilla – though, of course, you're more refined. And you're supposed to have married our adopted son, so you should call me "mother",' Gwellia went on.

'And Libertus "father". I suppose?' My newfound daughter leaned forward on her bench and looked coyly up at me from underneath her pretty eyelashes. 'Forgive me, *Father* . . . I'm sure I shall forget.'

It was almost flirtatious and I saw Gwellia frown. Julia had always had the ability to charm – it was how she asserted influence over people close to her – and it was not unpleasant to be in receipt of it, but if this expedition was to succeed, I had to stop it now.

'Then do not call me anything at all.' I made sure I sounded brusque. 'In fact, speak as little as possible when anyone's around. Your Latin is so perfect that it might cause remark and your accent is an educated one. Just remember to treat us with apparent deference. The safety of your children may depend on it.'

Kennis – as I must learn to call her now – looked humble and rebuked. 'I'm being foolish . . .' she muttered contritely. 'Of course I'll play my part . . . as best I can. Though you might sometimes have . . . to remind me what to do . . . But it won't be hard for me to show respect to you . . .' She turned her warmest smile on Gwellia. 'You've both earned it. If this enterprise succeeds . . . our whole family will owe our lives to you.'

'It's no more than our duty,' Gwellia said with a sniff, but she sat back, satisfied. I own I was relieved. My wife is genuinely fond of Julia, who has shown us many signal kindnesses, but she is not entirely immune to jealousy. I didn't want to prejudice this journey from the start.

Soon though, I had other things to think about. The road, which had been largely empty until now, was filled ahead with a line of heavy wagons either side. There is room on a Roman road for two carts to pass, with care, but there seemed to be some sort of obstruction now in front of us, and as we drew nearer I realized what it was.

The first of the approaching vehicles was filled with timber baulks – great trunks of forest trees which overhung the back and side – some of which had worked against the ropes, escaped their lashings and fallen off onto the road, where they now lay in a haphazard heap, completely blocking it. The driver had unhitched his animal and was trying to use it to move the trees aside, while other wagons had banked up behind; some of their drivers were trying to assist, others stood cursing and railing at the gods. Meanwhile those travelling on our side of the route were forced to leave the track and, one by one, take to the muddy verge beside the ditch to pass the obstacle.

If it had been a legion marching past, of course we would have had to leave the road and do the same, so it did not especially bother anyone, although of course it slowed us down. After a considerable wait – and a little assistance from Minimus, who got out and led the ox – we took our turn and edged around the blockage, at the price of violent bouncing which make Julia squeal aloud. One of the lounging wagon-drivers opposite looked up at her at this, and gave an appreciative whistle through his teeth.

'If you want to marry off your daughter, carter, let me know,' he hollered, his broad smile showing a set of broken yellow teeth. 'I am looking for a wife. I lost the last one in an accident – and she'd do very well. Young and strong and pleasant on the eyes.'

I tossed my head at him. 'You'd better ask her husband,' I called back to him. 'He'll want a hefty dowry, because he's very fond of her.'

Several of the other drivers laughed aloud at this. The fellow, finding himself the object of a joke, turned away and spat into the ditch, while I urged the ox and the plaustrum back on to the road and we joined the queue of wagons that had formed and were now lumbering south.

I was pleased with my prowess with the ox and said aloud, 'Well, that seemed to be no problem, although it slowed us down, of course!'

'No problem!' I saw that Julia's dust-stained face was white with rage. 'How can you say that? It is preposterous! That man insulted me, though I held my tongue as you required me to!'

'I'm sorry, Kennis,' I said, gently. 'Cart-drivers talk like that. There's nothing meant by it. He intends it as a compliment to you, if anything.'

'Compliment!' She sounded horrified. 'He was impertinent. He impugned my dignity. Marcus would have had him taken off and flogged! And why did you not make people move aside and let us through?' She was genuinely outraged. 'They can see this is a carriage – even though it's primitive – and there are people in it, not just logs and turnips and smelly fowl in crates.' She gestured to the line of wagons still in front of us.

Of course! She was used to outriders having to clear a way for her! I was about to point out tactfully that such priority is a privilege of rank, when Gwellia spared me the necessity.

'You're not travelling in a fancy carriage now,' she said. 'You're supposed to be a Celt. And that is what the wagon-driver took you for. People don't cede precedence to common folk like us – or think that we have any special honour to impugn.'

Under the dust I saw Julia blanche. 'I'm sorry, Mother.' She sounded penitent. 'You mean that every time you travel . . . you are liable . . . to be spoken to like that? And caused all this delay?'

'Most people are,' I told her. 'It's not unusual. And if we met the army, we'd have to wait for them – though I expect that, knowing Marcus, he would produce a seal or an imperial warrant and be given precedence?'

Julia nodded. The whole experience had clearly sobered her. She sank into silence and nothing more of consequence was said until the sun was dropping in the west and we reached the outskirts of a little hamlet – scarcely more than a scattering of buildings at a crossing in the road – but where a bush suspended on a pole outside a door announced the presence of a public tavern on the premises and a range of window-spaces on the upper floor suggested the possibility of accommodation for the night.

FOURTEEN

Kennis was horrified when I pulled up outside the tavern and made it clear I was ready to get down. 'Are we not going on to find a mansio?' she said, in distress. 'We've already been travelling for hours. There must be a proper place not very far away.'

'A military inn?' I shook my head. 'Not in an ox-cart, Kennis, I'm afraid. The next mansio will be twenty-five- or thirty-thousand paces from the Glevum one. We'd scarcely cover that, if we'd been on the road all day. In any case, they'd want a warrant, saying who we are, before they'd let us in.'

'We're carrying a letter under Marcus's seal,' she said. 'I'm sure that would suffice. Anyone of consequence would recognize his name. Apart from the officers in charge who run the inn, important people always use these places when they're on the move. There's certain to be someone who has heard of him.'

'Exactly why it's vital that we stay somewhere else. You might encounter someone who's met you at some time – been entertained to dinner at your villa, even, or seen you at the games. And what would happen to your safety, if you are recognized?'

Julia's face was eloquent but she said nothing more, and I was about to get down and make enquiries for a room when all at once there was a whimper from the back.

'Dear Juno!' she exclaimed. 'The babes are waking up! They've been rocked by the motion of the cart all afternoon, and now it's stopped, they're stirring. I hoped that they would stay asleep till we were somewhere safe.' She tried to stand up and climb across the seat to get to them, but the remorseless miles and unyielding wooden bench had left their mark on her. She sat down with a groan and clutched her back. Meantime the protests from the rear were rising all the time.

'Juli . . . Kennis . . .' Gwellia murmured urgently. 'The

baby doesn't matter, however loud she wails, but we must make sure that Marcellinus is kept calm. I'll comfort him, if you're too stiff and sore – or get the slaves to do it – but something must be done. If he starts shouting for his toys, or for his nursery-slave, he'll sound so clearly a patrician's son that he'll give us all away.'

Julia stood up stiffly. 'You're right. I'll see to him myself.' She climbed – with difficulty – back towards the rear and lifted her still sleepy son into her arms. Her face, when she smelt him, made me realize that it was not something that she'd often been required to do – normally the child would have been washed and dressed before he was presented to his parents for the day. Gwellia meanwhile had scooped up the baby girl and was pacifying her by gently bouncing her against her knees.

'Mater!' Marcellinus's piping voice was slurred with poppy juice. 'Where are we? Where's Nourissa? Why are we in a cart? Where's the servant with my breakfast? I don't like it here.'

I stiffened, thinking we'd have a noisy tantrum on our hands, but his mother murmured soothing noises in his ear and he slowly quieted.

'He's hungry,' she informed us. 'And frankly, so am I.' She sighed, resignedly. 'Is it likely we can get some food in this dubious place? And something for the baby, if it is only milk and wine?'

'Time for action, slaves!' I called and they scrambled from the back. Tenuis helped me to the ground – slowly, since I was travel-sore myself – while Minimus went round to check the mule.

'Arlina's fine – though very tired and thirsty, I am sure.' He popped back to report. 'I've been watching through the wicker-work to keep an eye on her and she hasn't started flagging until the last few miles. But now she needs some water. I'm giving her some straw!' He showed me a handful that he'd taken from the mattress in the cart and hurried off to offer it to Arlina.

He was proving good with animals so I left him nuzzling her neck and standing guard over the ox and cart while I took the smaller slave and went inside the taverna.

As these places go, it was acceptable – no sign of prostitutes
or thieves or drunken tramps, for which such inns are famous
in the larger towns – only a one-eyed fellow and a scruffy
youth who looked up from a plate of nuts and cheese and stared
as I came in. They both wore sweat-stained tunics and – apart
from the blank eye-socket – were so alike that they could only
be father and his son. Their dusty cloaks lay close beside them
on the bench, together with a tray of ribbons, trinkets and small
goods. The three eyes watched me as I crossed the room.

There was a moment's awkward silence and then the old
man spoke. 'If you want the owner, he has gone outside to
oversee the stabling of our horse.' He had been speaking Latin
but suddenly he switched. 'You looking to stay here?' he asked,
in Celtic.

'If it's clean enough,' I answered, using the same tongue.
His dialect was slightly different from my own, but we could
understand each other reasonably well.

A smile. I had obviously passed some kind of test. The fellow
nodded. 'Clean enough,' he said. 'They change the bedding
straw at least three times a moon so you won't find bedbugs
– though there are sometimes fleas. Depends on who you're
sharing with and who was there before.'

'You come here often?'

'Always, if we're travelling this way. I'm a merchant and
I'm always up and down to Glevum with my goods – and
this the best inn for miles either way. There's even a wash-
pot provided in the yard and a latrine right opposite the
sleeping-cubicles.'

By 'merchant' he meant 'peddler', that was obvious – the
tray of trinkets was evidence of that. But I wasn't quibbling.
I was glad of his advice.

'Separate rooms for women?' I enquired. 'I've got my wife
and family with me – including a toddler and a babe in arms.'

He grunted. 'I wouldn't bring my own here, if I had a
choice. But I dare say you will cope. There's not a separate
room. They'll get an area which is curtained off, that's all.
So leave your slave on guard. And if the women have any
gold and jewels at all, make sure they lie on them. You never
know who might be passing through.' He'd reverted to Latin

for this last remark, but I did not realize at once what he was hinting at.

'Perhaps I'll let the women have the bed,' I said, falling into the same tongue automatically. 'And I'll sleep in the stables with the infants in the cart . . .'

'Traveller, you will do nothing of the kind. I've just come past the ox-cart and I saw your family there.' I whirled around to see who had come in behind me, unobserved – as the peddler had been trying to warn me earlier. This was clearly the woman of the house: a dumpy little person, as wide as she was tall, dressed in a stained green tunic – obviously home-spun – with a leather apron draped around her waist and with a pair of wooden clog-shoes on her feet. Her wispy hair was straggling from its plaited coils and her fat face was lined and worn, but wreathed in knowing smiles.

'That little boy's a charmer. Your grandson, I suppose? I can see the likeness. He's got your nose.' This was so preposterous I could not answer her, but there was little need. The woman was burbling, in bad Latin, like a leaking tub. 'I'm very fond of children – I never had my own – so I stopped to speak to them. The little fellow bowed and greeted me – it almost made me laugh. Like a little emperor, he was – the gods forgive me if that's blasphemy. Father a high-born Roman, I suppose?'

The peddlers were both goggling by now and again I was considering how best to answer this, and account for the boy's manner – but I need not have worried, the woman had not paused.

'Free your daughter, did he, and let her keep the child? Well, that was good of him! Most masters would have had him killed at birth and kept the mother to use another time. And now she's got another babe, I see.' She shook her tangled greying locks at me. 'Find a husband for her, did he, once he let her go? I presume she wasn't caught consorting with another of the slaves or her master would have had them whipped to death, not simply thrown her out.'

'They are both his children. He is very fond of them. He has relinquished Kennis back into my care,' I said, with more truth than she could possibly have guessed. Her imaginary version of Julia's past was safer than the truth.

'Ah! I wondered why the husband wasn't travelling with you! But now I understand. Her owner must have been very fond of her indeed. I suppose that he is married? Otherwise he would have freed this one and married her?'

'He is. And you are right, in part. She does have her freedom – and both her children too – and so, in fact, do we. My wife and I were both in bondage once, but I was made a free citizen of Rome and all my family share my status now.' If she was so interested in Marcellinus, she might well have noticed that he wore a child's toga *praetexta* underneath his cloak – but this would explain it, perfectly. Tomorrow, however, I vowed we'd take it off and leave him just his tunic, like a proper peasant child.

The woman's face had lit up with delight. 'Three proper citizens? With rich connections too. Dear Jupiter! This is an honour, sir. Well, don't you worry, citizen. I'll take good care of them. I'll tell my worthless husband he can have a cubicle for once, and the women and children can share our room with me.' She cocked her head at me. 'Supposing you've got money to pay for it, of course.'

'That entirely depends on how much it will cost. And whether you can offer something suitable to eat.'

She named a modest sum. 'And I'm sure we'll find you something. There is always bread and cheese – or a duck's egg for the little boy if he would fancy that. Or there's some vegetable broth that I could heat for you.'

'Stick to the nuts and cheeses, citizen.' Behind me the peddler was rising to his feet. 'I wouldn't trust the stew. I swear she only boils the same thing up each day and adds fresh scraps to it. But the cheese is fresh and the bread is not too bad.' He gathered up his cloak and tray and left the room followed by his sullen-looking son. I saw them climbing up the staircase in the yard towards the upper floor.

The woman frowned. 'I don't know what he means. Our broth is excellent – at least we've never had serious complaints. And it's a great deal better than what you'd get at a hot-soup stall in town. But if you don't want the soup I can do some duck eggs for you all – I've even got a bit of celery I can boil into a sauce. And nobody can say the eggs aren't fresh, I

picked them up from our own ducks today. I'll throw in a bit
of bread and cheese, goat's milk for the children and a jug of
watered wine. Let's say a half-denarius for you all – what do
you say to that?'

I was about to agree that it would be excellent – in fact I
was surprised that she had not asked a higher price – when
we were interrupted by a strident voice.

'What are you saying, woman? Do you want to ruin us all?'
The speaker was a tall, spare, shaggy man, who now shambled
through the door, making no secret of the fact that he'd been
listening in. He was a surly-looking fellow with suspicious eyes,
and his flowing hair and beard and side-whiskers were unkempt
and none too clean, like his grubby brown tunic and his country
'boots' (pieces of rawhide tied around his feet). With his tawny
mane and thin distrustful face he reminded me of a mangy lion
that I saw in the town arena once – and he looked about as
friendly. Clearly the proprietor of this establishment.

I muttered a greeting.

He jerked a chin at me. 'And who's this, anyway? The owner
of that wretched ox and cart outside? How does that entitle
him to special rates?'

The woman put her hands upon his chest and pushed him
to a corner of the room, where she hissed at him, as though
I might be deaf. 'He's a Roman citizen, and one with wealthy
friends. You mind your business, Aonghus, seeing to the cart
– and let me see to mine. And, while you're at it, move your
things into a cubicle. The last one on the right is free and the
bedding's fairly fresh. I'm going to let his family share my
room tonight.'

'Have you taken leave of all your senses, wife?' He folded
his enormous arms and looked askance at me. 'This is no way
to run a public inn.'

'Aonghus, be quiet. I know what I'm about. We give him a
good deal and see his family is well fed – in fact, his womenfolk and children can have the bed and I'll sleep on the floor
– and he'll tell his acquaintances how well we treated him.
He'll make our reputation – or he would have done if you
hadn't come in here insulting him and spoiling everything.'

'I'll be happy to recommend you,' I said, in a loud voice,

making it quite clear that I was listening to all this. 'If our accommodation is satisfactory.'

'You see!' She barely reached his shoulder but she shooed him to the door as though he were no bigger than a goose. 'You go and bring the ox and cart inside. And see the guard-slave has clean straw to sleep on, too. Who knows what trade might come our way from this? I've always said we need a better class of people staying here – that's where the money is.'

The lion gave me a resentful look and shambled off to do as he was bidden. The woman turned to me. 'So, citizen, you go and fetch your daughter and that lambkin in – the poor mite will be tired after travelling all day – and I'll get the eggs prepared and show them where to sleep.' She bustled off towards the courtyard, where I suppose the kitchen was.

She had been charmed by Marcellinus, that was very clear, and in some ways that was very fortunate. But the boy was far too young to understand our plight, and – if he and his mother shared a bed with our hostess – I feared that he might start to talk too much. But there was nothing for it: at least we would be warm and safe and fed, and at a reasonable price. Most travellers on the road would have to settle for much less.

So accompanied by Tenuis (who had been standing by) I went out to tell the women the good news.

FIFTEEN

Julia (or Kennis, as I should call her now) was predictably appalled. 'Share my bed with strangers? What were you thinking of . . .?' she protested, but Gwellia put a finger to her lips.

'Remember you're a peasant and we have to sleep somewhere. You are being treated very well. Not many people find the landlord giving up his bed. Now here's the man himself coming out to take the cart, so it's time to go inside. Remember to be pleasant, and look grateful if you can.'

Kennis nodded, though her cheeks were fiery red. She even submitted to the man's rough grasp as he reached up to help her down, but she did not relinquish Marcellinus to the outstretched hands. 'I'll take him, or he'll fret. He is tired and hungry and not used to strangers. I'll look after him. Look after Gwelli . . . Mother, please, instead. She has the baby and may want some help with her.'

But Gwellia was already on the ground, with the infant snuggled expertly inside her cloak, so when Kennis and her son had struggled down themselves, I left Minimus to oversee the cart and led my little group inside.

At once the woman came bustling out and when she saw Marcellinus she bent down and tried to chuck him underneath the chin. 'I've got a duck's egg boiling for you. Won't that be nice, young man?' She had put on a special voice she seemed to think was suitable for dealing with the young.

Mercifully, he was still so sleepy he was disinclined to speak and simply buried his head against his mother's skirts, otherwise, who knows what affronted outburst he'd have made.

'Dear little fellow. Gone all shy, have we? Tired out with all the travelling I expect. And no doubt the babe is, too.' She turned to Kennis. 'Perhaps you'd like to take the children straight upstairs – you'll find some river water in the pitcher by the door so you can wash and change the infant straight away, and then I'll bring a tray and you can eat up there.'

It was a better arrangement than I could have hoped – less chance of anyone betraying who we were – and I agreed at once. I'm not sure that Kennis was particularly keen – I doubt she had ever changed an infant in her life – but Gwellia had brought a bag of rags with her in preparation for this very task. My wife looked meaningfully at me, then murmured graciously, 'That's thoughtful, tavern-keeper. We all are very tired. If you'd like to lead the way?'

The woman lit a smoky taper from the fire and pushed open a small door, through which a narrow inner staircase could be seen, clearly leading into the private quarter of the house. 'This way then, lady citizens! Come on, little man. You're going to have the best room in the house.'

Marcellinus did not look impressed but the little party went straggling upstairs.

I could do nothing but let them go and trust the Fates. It was up to Gwellia to manage matters now. I could only hope the children would go back to sleep again (their father's potion had been very strong, so there was every chance of that) and that Kennis would not say something that betrayed her rank in life. Meanwhile I would be forced to find a bed in one of the public cubicles elsewhere.

However, there was first the matter of the meal. I'd hardly had the time to sit down on the bench (the same one that the peddlers had been using earlier) before a grubby slave-boy came sidling in with it – a plate of nuts and bread and soft, strong-smelling cheese. He thrust it on the board in front of me.

'The master says that if you change your mind, there's plenty of hot stew.' The words were delivered in a lifeless monotone, and I wondered whether he just resented customers, or whether his master had beaten all interest out of him.

'I was warned against it, I'm afraid – to my slave's regret, I'm sure,' I replied, aware that Tenuis was wriggling with delight at the prospect of something warm to eat. 'But we can't risk upset stomachs while we're on the road.'

The inn-slave shrugged. 'Well, you'd better tell my master,

then, before he sends your servants some. He's a stickler for seeing that nothing goes to waste, and if the guests don't eat what they are served, he gives it to the slaves. There's been at least one plate of stew sent back today.'

'Is this just the servants of your customers? Or you as well?' I asked. He was as skinny as a bird and his Latin was so halting that I spoke in Celtic now, guessing that he was more fluent in that tongue.

I was obviously right. He shot me a doubtful glance. He clearly wasn't used to clients being interested in him. Then he decided I was harmless. 'Mustn't eat the profits. That's what he always says.'

'Then my slave would sympathize. When he was younger, and belonged to someone else, he often did not have enough to eat.'

The inn-slave looked at Tenuis, then at me, and clearly concluded that it was safe to speak. 'Mouldy bread and curdled milk sometimes – people are always complaining of the stew, but leftovers make a treat for us. He feeds his geese and chickens better – they give him eggs, he says – where me and the stable-boy are replaceable, and cheap.' He turned away and dipped a jug into a vat beside the fire and brought it over, dripping, together with a wooden drinking-cup, considerably stained, which he attempted to polish on his sleeve. (Neither item was improved by this.) 'And here's the watered wine. I'll dip a fire-brand in it, and warm it, if you like.'

This was not an appealing prospect – wood-ash was unlikely to improve indifferent wine – but the offer was clearly an attempt at friendliness so I gave the lad a smile. 'Thank you. I'll commend you to your master for your courtesy.'

A frightened look. 'Oh, please don't do that, sir – I mean citizen – I hear that's what you are. He'll only think that I have overstepped my duties and give me another beating.' He thrust the burning stick into the cup of wine and handed it to me, steaming and full of little fragments of charred wood.

'Your master isn't kind?'

He glanced round nervously. 'I was often hungry where I was before, but I wish that I was back there and that's the truth of it. Or that someone else had been in Aquae Sulis on that day, and come to the market looking for cheap slaves.'

'You haven't been with your present master long?' My mind was racing now. He'd mentioned Aquae Sulis. 'Where were you before? Not a servant of Eliana, I suppose?' I spoke without much hope. I knew that she'd disposed of all her slaves quite recently, but that would be too much of a coincidence.

It was. The slave-boy shook his head. 'This master is my first. I wasn't born in servitude. My father is a trapper, and there were seven children in the house, but we had a dreadful winter and not enough to eat. I was the eldest so he sold me on to feed the rest of them. I don't know if it worked. The slaver didn't give him very much for me – too small to be of any proper use, he said. And he was right. I was the last one left before the market closed, but then the tavern-owner bought me for a trivial price and here I am.' He stopped and frowned at me. 'Who is Eliana, anyway?'

'Just an old woman with a rundown farm who had to sell her slaves,' I said, carefully picking the black fragments from my wine. 'She lived near Aquae Sulis, I believe. I simply wondered if you were one of them.'

'I'm sorry, citizen.' He flinched as though he might be slapped for being ignorant.

His fear was so pathetic that I was moved to say, 'It was only the remotest possibility. I understand the place is very large – the family was extremely wealthy at one time – so it is probably well-known in the vicinity. It was just possible that you had heard of it.'

He glanced sharply at me. 'You don't mean that place where there was once a fire?' He handed me a spoon to help me with my task. 'The woman living there was widowed recently?'

I stared at him. 'So you do know of her?'

'Only by repute. One of her land-slaves was on sale with me, and he was talking in the cell the night before they put us on the stall. Used to be a fine place, he was telling us, but gone to ruin in the last few years. Orchards, woods and grain fields – all neglected now – even a vineyard and a wine-cave once, although the wine was pretty poor. The slave-quarters had got so bad they couldn't sleep in them and had to live in the stables in the end – but they never saw their owners from one Kalends to the next. The master was an invalid and she scarcely left the house.' He was busying himself, with fetching nuts and cheeses from a barrel by the wall and arranging them on a wooden platter by this time.

This was clearly Eliana's farm. 'Do you know where I might find it?' I tried to sound as casual as I could. My plan had been to take my little party there – partly on the pretext of inspecting it on Marcus's behalf – and hide them there, for a little while at least. The estate was currently unoccupied, I knew, and Varius's heirs – whoever they might be – could take no steps until the will was read, giving me time to seek a different hiding place. But I had only the most vague idea of where to go and had been relying on asking people when I neared the site.

But the servant could not help me. 'No idea at all. Somewhere near the main road, that is all I know. Apparently you can still see the main house through the trees, though part of the roof is at risk of falling in. But there's no one who can help you when you get there, I'm afraid. The steward bought his freedom and all the slaves were sold.'

'And the place is unattended!' I was unprepared for this, though from my perspective it was splendid news. I'd been expecting at least a gatekeeper or two – relying on Marcus's sealed letter as my authority to move into the house, on the grounds that Varius and Claudius were dead. 'Not even a guard? Were the new prospective owners not afraid of theft?'

'I understand there was nothing left behind that would attract a thief. And the land-slave says the place has got a reputation for ill-luck – nothing but death and evil fate for years. Even local tramps and beggars will not sleep there, so he says.'

'Tell me about that land-slave?' I said eagerly. Finding someone who had worked on the estate would make my task easier, and a great deal more discreet. I'd planned to ask questions in the nearby town. 'What became of him?'

The skinny servant shook his head again. 'I don't know, citizen, he sold quite early on.' He looked up from his task, and gave me what I realized was a hopeful look. 'Are you looking for a servant-labourer of some kind yourself?'

I had to disabuse him. 'On the contrary. I can't afford new slaves. But I heard that the estate will shortly be for sale and I know a wealthy Roman who might be interested. In fact we're travelling down to look at it on his account.'

He made a face. 'Then I hope he's not afraid of curses and bad luck. Though I suppose a new owner would have it ritually cleansed.'

'Its evil reputation might reduce the price,' I said, heartily. 'So I'm pleased to hear of it – or anything else that you can tell me of the place.' I reached into my purse (the drawstring one that dangled from my waist, not the heavy leather bag full of my patron's gold, which was slung around my chest next to my skin) and pulled out a small coin.

'Of course I'd help you, citizen,' he said, regretfully. 'But I'm afraid that's all I know.'

'Then take this, anyway, for your help so far,' I said. 'More if you remember anything.'

I handed him the coin. Only a quadrans – any more would raise suspicions in the boy – and in his master, if it were ever found. From the eagerness with which it was taken from my hand, I knew it was enough.

'Thank you, citizen.' He slid it underneath his tunic. 'If there is ever anything . . .' He broke off as his owner came in through the doorway from the court, and reverted to broken Latin. 'Is that all, citizen?'

'What do you mean by loitering, you wretch? Don't keep the citizen waiting for his meal. Go out to the kitchen-block and fetch the man some bread. And mind it is the best bread, not the coarser stuff.' He turned to me with an ingratiating smile as the slave-boy scuttled off. 'I've made a bed up in the stable for your slave – so he can watch the ox. Do you want this one to go out with him, or accompany you?'

'He can stay with me,' I answered. 'And he'll eat with me, as well. And you can take a portion of my bread and cheese out to the other boy.'

'But I've put some broth out for them.' A frown accompanied this.

I shook my head. 'They both have nervous stomachs when

we are travelling, and I dare not risk hot food. Give it to your
own slaves – at my expense, of course.'

The frown cleared instantly. 'As you command, citizen, of
course. Ah, here's the bread and I see that you already have
your wine. Enjoy your meal, and your young servant, too. I'll
see your other slave is given something similar, and than
I'll come and show you to your cubicle.'

It was not luxurious, when we got to it. Simply a curtained
recess with a mattress of cut reeds and rushes on the floor, a
doubtful pillow stuffed with prickly straw and a pair of tattered
blankets. From behind the curtain there were already snores
– from the peddler, I suspected. But it would suffice. So after
a brief visit to the latrine in the yard and a rub-down with
some chilly water from the trough, I wrapped my cloak around
me and settled down to rest, with my lumpy purse beneath
my pillow and with Tenuis lying at my feet.

SIXTEEN

I t was not the most comfortable night I've ever spent – what with the fleas and smell and the constant snoring from next door – and I was glad when the dawn came creeping through the ill-shuttered window-space. When I encountered Minimus in the yard, however, I learned that the stable had been snug and warm, and when Gwellia appeared a moment afterwards – as Minimus hastened off to take water to the ox – she told me that her party had been comfortable too.

'Fairly primitive, but clean enough,' she said. 'Both Julia and Marcellinus slept, surprisingly, though the baby girl was fractious all night through.'

I murmured something about regretting that.

'Probably still hungry, I'm afraid,' my wife went on. 'I did everything I could, gave her sops of milky bread that she could suck, but she did not take much of that. Poor little infant, she hasn't even any teeth as yet. I hope this expedition won't be the death of her. A child of that age really needs to nurse.'

I shook my head, unhappily. 'That's my fault, I'm afraid. I'm not really used to infants, and when Julia said that she'd been weaned quite young, I simply supposed it could be done.'

'I know that, Husband, and so does Julia. The problem is that it should not be done so suddenly. But in the circumstances, you've done the best you could. Better that the child is here with us and has a chance, than stay to be discovered and be murdered in her crib,' Gwellia said. 'And Marcellinus and his mother had some proper rest, rather more than I expected – they are used to proper Roman beds, with stretched goatskins to support the mattresses, not straw-stuffed palliasses on the floor – not to speak of sharing bed-space with the woman from the inn. But Jul . . . Kennis . . . was tired out from trav-elling, and the boy was still half-drugged with poppy juice.'

'But you didn't give the baby any, so you could sleep

yourself? There is a little of Marcus's potion left, I think?' I could see that Gwellia's face was grey with wakefulness.

She shook her head. 'I did not dare. The child is far too young to keep drinking poppy juice. But I was lying on a mat beside the door, in any case, so I took her down with me and tried to keep her soothed by dipping my finger in the milk for her to suck – otherwise she would have kept everyone awake. Even so, she's very hungry now, and she needs a wash and change of swaddling. I came down for the water. I must get back to them. Juila has no idea of how to deal with such things.' She waved a jug at me and hurried back into the inn.

I watched her go, and as I turned to dip my face into the trough I heard footsteps on the stone stair from above, and then a voice behind me said, in Celtic, 'Good morrow, traveller. You rested well, I trust?'

It was my snoring neighbour from the night before – the one-eyed peddler – cloaked, dressed and apparently ready to depart and uglier than ever in the morning light. I returned his greeting. 'Not easy to sleep here,' I said, forbearing to mention that he'd prevented it. 'But at least the children and their mother rested well. Fortunately the inn-woman was so enchanted by the boy, she volunteered to let them share her room.'

'Is that what she told you?' He gave a knowing laugh. 'If you believe that, traveller, you are less intelligent than I supposed. No doubt she likes your toddler well enough, but that's clearly not the reason that she let them share her room.'

I was genuinely puzzled. 'I'm not sure I understand.'

'Surely even a Vestal Virgin could work it out! Your daughter's beautiful – and this way the woman could keep an eye on her, and be sure her husband did not visit in the night. Or anybody else, for that matter!'

Such a possibility had never crossed my mind – though if I'd really had a daughter perhaps it should have done. 'But my wife would have been with her!' I protested.

'Exactly, traveller. And she was obviously a beauty once, as well! It's clear you're not accustomed to public hostelries. Without a slave to watch the door, even my ugly grandmother might not be wholly safe!' He sketched a little bow. 'And now, if you'll excuse me, traveller, we must make an early start. My son is fetching our belongings from upstairs, and here's the slave-boy with our horse, I think.' He gestured to the open stable to one side, where our skinny servant of the night before was leading out a mangy animal. At the same time the sullen son came clattering down the stone steps from above, gave me the briefest of curt nods, and busied himself with strapping on the panniers and reloading trays.

'You don't intend to break your fast before you go?' the little slave asked, using the awkward Latin that I'd noticed earlier.

The peddler shook his head and answered, with a fluency that put the boy to shame, 'We have reserved some bread and cheese and we will eat that on the road. We must reach Glevum in time to sell our wares today or we won't eat at all tomorrow. I've already paid your master what we owed, so now the horse is loaded it is time that we were gone.' He nodded me a bow. 'Your servant, traveller. Go well – and take good care of your handsome wife and daughter, that is my advice.' He chuckled at the slave's bewildered look and, accompanied by his offspring and unlovely animal, he went out through the arch and I saw them plodding off towards the north.

I did not altogether envy them the trip. It was a long way to Glevum – especially on foot – and the first hint of drizzle was already in the air. Very soon it would begin to rain in earnest, I could see.

'Thank all the gods I have a covered cart,' I said aloud, to no one in particular. 'At least we won't get drenched. Though rain will obviously slow us down and we won't reach our destination before nightfall, as I'd planned. Mars knows where we'll find to stay tonight.' I shook my head, remembering the peddler's warning about the womenfolk. And this was the best *hospitium* for miles around, he'd said. But there was nothing I could do about it, in advance. I turned back to the slave, who had picked up a broom-bundle and begun to sweep the court. 'Tell me, young fellow, did you get your broth last night? I don't want to pay your owner and then find he'd cheated me!' I was using Celtic which was easier for him.

'So that was your doing, citizen? The master did not say

so, but we knew it had to be!' The lad leaned on his broom, looked earnestly at me. 'The stable-boy was very grateful too. He made sure your slave had extra straw and a nice warm blanket that the master uses for his horse. I'm only sorry that there's nothing I can do myself, to thank you for your kindness . . .' He broke off suddenly as the sound of the infant crying came loudly from within. 'That child is hungry,' he remarked. 'I know that cry of old.'

I nodded, with a sigh. 'Unhappily her mother has no milk for her.'

He brightened suddenly. 'Then perhaps I can assist you, after all.' He glanced around the yard. 'I could not help hearing what you said just now. You were speaking Celtic . . .'

'You were listening to my conversation with the peddler?' I know I sounded sharp.

'Not really, citizen. But I did hear you wondering where you might choose to stay tonight.' He looked at me enquiringly, but I did not reply. I was still a little irritated at his eavesdropping.

'Because you would not reach your destination, as you'd hoped?' he urged. 'Believe me, citizen, I only wish to help. I thought perhaps you might prefer to avoid a public inn. A lot of them are merely dens of pick-purses and whores – especially the taverns nearer to the towns. Even my master says so privately, though if you ask, he'll recommend one readily enough – and expect commission from the owner by and by.'

'You think you know of somewhere?' I said, more kindly now.

He gave a little shrug. 'I'm not sure if you would think it suitable. But I do have one idea. It's just a simple roundhouse – small and cramped and smelly – but it would be safe. And the household would be grateful for any money earned. But you would not be cheated, citizen. I can answer for the owner's honesty.'

'You are thinking of your own home?' I exclaimed.

He nodded, placing a warning finger to his lips. 'But be careful that the master does not hear me saying this. He'd flog me if he thought I was advising you against the tavern trade – as I say, he gets a tip for recommending people on. But I thought this might be better – for the children, specially.'

'A roundhouse would be crowded,' I demurred, though I was seriously considering the possibility.

'There's a storage roundhut outside the door where you could sleep, if you preferred, and there will be hot grain pottage, if there's nothing else. There might not be much comfort, but it would be cheap.' He had dropped his eager voice till he was almost whispering. 'And then there is the child. My mother has suckled other people's children once or twice before, and she has an infant so there will be milk – and some to spare. That might be a solution for the baby, do you think?'

I found that I was nodding, all at once. Perhaps my ancient gods had listened to my prayers. And for once I did not think that Julia would object. Many citizens farmed out their children to the poor until they were old enough to wean, to save the mothers inconvenience. Only the very rich – like Marcus – could afford to keep a wet-nurse in the house. So this arrangement was a common one. Julia would almost certainly agree, if only for the infant's sake. It was indeed an answer – from an unlikely source.

'We'd pay her handsomely,' I said. 'If you think she'd be prepared . . .'

He nodded. 'I think she'd be relieved. It was because the last one weaned and had to be sent home, that they were forced to sell me on to pay for food. But there is one problem, citizen. She does not speak Latin – no one does at home. Only my father has a word or two – just enough to help him sell the creatures that he traps.'

'Yet you speak well enough.'

The slave-boy made a face. 'He taught me what he knew before he offered me for sale, and the rest has been beaten into me since I've been working here. Another reason why they sold me cheap, of course. But you speak Celtic, so there'll be no problem there.'

'I do,' I answered, 'though not all the family does. The boy and his mother have lived in Roman households all their lives – as many slaves do nowadays – but I should be able to translate

for them.' In fact, that was a positive advantage of the scheme,
I realized. In a Celtic-speaking household there would be no
chance of Marcellinus – or his mother – accidentally saying
something which betrayed their lofty rank. 'A splendid notion,
serving-boy. I think you have repaid me for your plate of stew
– and more!' I fished into my purse and produced another
quadrans. 'How do I find this family of yours? And how can I
be certain that they'll agree to this?'

He glanced around again. 'Fifteen or twenty miles down
the road, you will come to a crossroads by a twisted elm,' he
whispered, seizing the coin and slipping it into his tunic hem.
'The house is a hundred paces up the trackway to the left.
You'll see my father's traps outside the door, and skins and
animals nailed up against the fence. His name is Esadur. Tell
him that Caeder sent you – that was my name at home. And
tell them too that I am safe and well and happy in my work.'

'And are you?' I was surprised at this.

'I want them to think I am,' he answered, ruefully. 'But
here's my owner coming, I must be about my chores.' He
seized the brush again and began to sweep the court as if his
life depended on its cleanliness. Perhaps it literally did!

I turned to greet the landlord – in Latin, naturally. 'Good
morning, innkeeper! Tell me what I owe – and add the price
of breakfast for my party too. It would be wise for us to eat
before we make a start.'

'I'll send some bread and watered wine in to your slaves,
if that will do? Though you'll be wanting cheese with it,
yourselves, I suppose? I don't have fruit and olives, or fancy
things like that. My wife's already taken goat's milk and sops
in for the child. That will be an extra . . . Let me see . . .' He
made a calculation on his fingers and then named a price – a
lower one than I'd expected. He flashed a crooked smile. 'And
think of us if you are ever coming back this way. Now, have
you made arrangements for tonight? Or would you wish me
to commend an inn or two?'

'I have a place in mind. So now, if you will see that we are
fed, I'll get my little party on the road again. I'll settle with you,
just before we leave.' I glanced at the slave, but he was busy
with his broom, so I followed the landlord back into the house.

The meagre breakfast did not take very long though the landlady still tried to make a special fuss of us, and Marcellinus in particular. I was anxious to move on before he said too much, so I paid the bill quickly – and within the hour we were on our way again, lurching towards Aquae Sulis on the cart.

SEVENTEEN

The day that followed was one I would be happy to forget: long nightmare hours of rain, mud, wind and cold. Everyone was wet and weary to the bone; the infant was hungry, and within an hour or two of starting – having eaten all our damp provisions – so were the rest of us. Marcellinus (who'd been protected from discomfort all his life) was awake and fretful now and added to our wretchedness by raging, weeping and whimpering by turns. The baby bawled. The women were exasperated and exhausted with it all. The slaves sat shivering in silent misery and even the ox and mule seemed unusually reluctant and intractable.

The road was relatively empty, for which small mercy I still thank the gods, because the verges were becoming more sticky by the hour, until they were near impassable in parts. When forced off the main track – as happened now and then when we met a group of soldiers or supply-carts on the move – we were quickly axle-deep in mud and several times I feared the cart would break. By noon or thereabouts (in the sullen light it was difficult to calculate the time!) I was tempted to abandon travel for the day, and would have sought shelter in the first habitation that we happened on, if a man on horseback had not ridden by.

I would have paid no particular attention to this other traveller, but he reined his horse and turned to squint at me. 'Greetings, citizen.'

'What news from Glevum?' I called out to him, recognizing him as a tax official to whom I'd paid my rates for the workshop once or twice – and cursing the fact that he'd identified me too. But best to sound as casual as I could.

'Libertus, the pavement-maker, isn't it? Bad tidings, I'm afraid,' he shouted back. 'There's been a spate of sudden deaths in the colonia. Some of them people that I'm sure you know.'

Varius and his family, I thought. I decided to feign ignorance.
'That is unfortunate. Something in the water, possibly?'
'Not this time, citizen. This looks deliberate. Only certain
people seem to be involved. The town is full of whispers – as
it always is – and it's difficult to know what to believe, but
there are rumours of some sort of crazy vengeance feud, aimed
at members of the curia and their families and friends. Three
patrician citizens are already dead – that is a certainty – and
there are stories of other victims, not discovered yet.'

I looked at the two women, and they looked at me. I knew
what they were thinking, although they didn't say a word.
'Three patricians dead?' Two I was prepared for, but who then
was the third? Had Eliana already managed to starve herself
to death? She was a patrician, certainly – but in such calcula-
tions of the dead, women were not usually included in the
count.

I must have sounded genuinely shocked. The tax-collector
smiled and nodded. 'Varius Quintus Flavius was the first to
die, I hear, and his brother Claudius did not survive him long.
Those two I can vouch for with some certainty. Their funeral
has already been publicly announced.'

'And the other?' I hardly dared to ask. 'It wasn't a woman
relative by any chance?'

The horseman shook his head. 'A senior member of the
curia, I heard. Another councillor discovered him at home,
apparently, stabbed, hanged or poisoned – it is not clear which.
There's some kind of mystery. The name and details have been
officially suppressed until the magistrates have met and decided
what to do – enquiries are already underway. But secrecy has
caused a greater stir, of course. People are beginning to talk
of leaving town.' He paused and frowned at me. 'Your name
was mentioned, come to think of it, as someone that the curia
wants to interview.'

'Me?' It shocked me to my veins. But I understood now
why the man had paused to talk. Was he hoping to report me
found, and ask for a reward?

'There's talk of an unsigned document in which your name
occurred, found in the dead man's hand – or that is what I
heard, though I don't know how reliable that is. Anyway,

there's obviously been some mistake. By yesterday you must have been already on the road.' He gestured to the cart. 'And perhaps you're fortunate to be elsewhere! I'm not sorry to have business in the south, myself – and I must be on the way or I won't get there tonight! Go well, fellow-townsman!' He raised a hand in brief farewell and galloped off – still travelling away from Glevum.

I breathed out heavily. There would be no report – at least till he returned to the colonia.

'What shall you do?' my wife, beside me, muttered urgently. 'Turn back and see the magistrates?'

I shook my head. 'If I'm summoned formally, of course I will appear, but for the moment, I am on my patron's business. This is only hearsay,' I replied. I did not tell her what was really in my mind – and anyway, I was in no mood for talk.

Because I was certain that I knew why the curia wanted me: it could only be that Marcus was the murdered councillor. When I first heard of the third death, I had thought of Porteus – he had received that second warning, after all – but the detail of the unsigned document convinced me otherwise. The document named me! I realized what that had to be, of course: the warrant naming me as guardian, which Marcus had drawn up, and wanted Varius and his half-brother to witness at his house. Which raised a sudden thought. No one but my patron would have need of such a thing (most certainly Porteus would not) or even known that it existed. So why had Marcus brought it out before he died? Was it to get it witnessed and countersigned, perhaps?

Fortunately, the womenfolk did not appear to be especially concerned. They would not know about the warrant, I realized suddenly, only the letter of authority which he had given me and which I was carrying underneath my robes. I still had that, of course, but it was merely a general letter under seal. It would not have the force of a legal contract if it came to court – especially if the owner of the seal was dead.

But I was not about to tell the women of my fears. For the moment they had sufficient woes to bear. But I was shaken to my sandal-straps. My mind was in a whirl. The letter-writer had clearly found a way to strike – Marcus's precautions had not been good enough and his courage in remaining at his post had been a tragic, terrible mistake. Or was this perhaps the handiwork of the new Emperor – a decree of indictment that had been issued recently, and acted on now that the legion was no longer in the town – exactly the thing that Marcus had originally feared? Either way, I thought, it hardly mattered now. The outcome was the same.

My patron – whom I'd loved, in spite of all his faults – was dead, and that increased the present danger for us all. My heart was cold with grief, but there was no time for tears. I was charged with keeping his little family safe. It was the last thing I could do for him.

'I know of a safe place to stop, I think,' I said aloud, thanking the gods for prompting me to pay for an unwanted plate of stew, and leading the skinny servant to try and help me in return. No one would think to find us in a humble trapper's house, especially one that wasn't even on the major road. If somebody did trace us to the inn we used last night, they would ask the landlord where we planned to stop – not the serving boy. And he would not volunteer it, for fear of being whipped – though I did not believe that he'd betray us anyway.

There was no thought of stopping, after that, and with one accord we huddled down against the wind and rain, wrapped our damp cloaks around us and ploughed on doggedly.

We found the roundhouse just as dusk began to fall. It stood in an enclosure not unlike my own, except for the skins of animals nailed up on huts to dry – clearly the place that we were looking for. It was as small and humble as the boy had said, but I have rarely been so pleased to see a building in my life. A thin plume of wood-smoke was rising from the central chimney-hole, and through the open doorway came the faint glow of a fire.

Even Marcellinus brightened. 'Are we stopping here?'

He looked so woebegone I melted instantly, forgiving him the tantrums of the afternoon. Poor little fellow, he did not know what tragedies had struck.

'I hope so!' I told him, cheerfully. 'It will be warm and dry at least. Wait here while I go and ask them if they have room for us.' The ox had already shambled to a stop, and I got down stiffly and walked over to the gate.

A figure detached itself from the shadows of a hut. 'Who there?' The Latin was atrocious, but the meaning was quite clear. 'What your business here?' The speaker came towards me, brandishing a wicked-looking skinning-knife, and in the fading light I got a better view. This must be Caeder's father, Esadur.

He was a tall, spare fellow, every inch a Celt, from the long moustaches to the traditional plaid trouser-leggings and the matching cloak. His face was gaunt with hunger but under the huge eyebrows his eyes were very bright. They glittered with suspicion and – I guessed – with fear.

'Have I the honour of addressing Esadur?' I asked, politely, in my native tongue.

The dark frown deepened, but the knife-hand dropped. 'How do you know my name?'

I pressed my advantage. 'You have a son called Caeder, I believe?'

'I used to have one, traveller, but he's no longer here. Why do you seek him? Is he in some trouble?'

'I could wish him happier,' I answered, with some truth. 'But I saw him just this morning and he is fit and well – owned by the landlord of the tavern where we stayed overnight. He sends his greetings and commended me to you. He suggested you might provide us food and shelter for tonight – we have small children with us, and would pay you well, of course.'

He looked at me a moment, then past me at the cart, where Kennis was sitting with the baby in her arms attempting – ineffectually – to rock it back to sleep. The trapper seemed to make his mind up, suddenly. He stuffed the knife into a holder at his belt and gave a piercing whistle through his teeth. A mangy dog came racing from the house with a small thin harassed woman hurrying after it, holding a lighted taper in her hand.

She paused at the doorway when she caught sight of me. 'What is it, Esa?'

'Someone Caeder sent. A Celtic family by the look of it. Offering money if we'll feed and shelter them.'

'How many of them are there?' At the promise of silver there was such relief, that I knew that we would find safety here – for overnight at least.

'Two women, two small children and myself,' I said. 'Together with a mule, and ox, and a pair of little slaves. I'll pay you what I would have paid an inn. Would that suffice?' I named a sum – twice what I'd given the landlord earlier.

It was more than handsome and she seized on it at once. 'Well, they'll have to take us as we are – there's nothing been prepared. But I think there's enough grain porridge in the pot – I'll throw some extra herbs and oats and eek it out a bit. It will be warm and filling, if it's nothing else, and we'll find a bed for all of you somehow, if it's only on that pile of reeds I cut to weave a mat. We can turn the ox and mule out on the grass around the back. Will that be adequate?'

'More than acceptable,' I said with gratitude.

'Then, Esa, you had better show them in.'

Esa grunted. He untied the gate and gestured me inside, while he went off to help the family from the cart.

I followed the woman into the house. It was made of daub and wattle, like my own, but much more crowded and less luxurious. It was warm and smoky and extremely dim, with only the fire and two small tapers giving light – a question of economy I guessed, because the woman quickly lit another candle at the hearth. By its extra glow I gradually perceived – from what seemed to be a pile of straw beside the wall – a dozen sleepy eyes regarding me. A row of children of assorted ages lay huddled underneath a blanket made of rough-sewn skins.

'You go to sleep,' their mother said – as though that were possible, with a crowd of strangers in the room. 'This man and his family have come to stay the night.' She turned to me. 'I only hope that there'll be room for you in here. I'll move the loom away.' She moved towards the stones that held the weft in place.

'And spoil the cloth that you were weaving? You'll lose the tension if you move the weights,' I said, preventing her. 'Caeder suggested we might use the storage hut. I'm sure we'd manage there.' It was not a pleasant prospect but at least it would be dry and we could rest, I thought.

She seized on the suggestion instantly. 'The hut – that is a good idea. But not for guests! I'll put my boys out there, this once, and you can have the fire. And children, don't complain! This is man is going to pay – tomorrow there'll be vegetable stew and eggs for all of us. Now take this taper and go out to the hut – you'll find those reeds out there to make a bed. Lasticus, you're in charge. Make sure they settle down. Your father and I will come and join you later on. And take your cover with you – it will be cold out there. The guests can use our blanket – we'll wrap up in cloaks.' She was already setting the stew-pot back onto the fire and throwing more grain and herb leaves into it.

The children went out, grumbling. I thought of protesting about disturbing them, but I restrained myself. I was so weary that I could have lain down on the earth floor where I stood, and slept so that only a thunderbolt from Jove could have awakened me, but there were others in the party and I must think of them. Besides, a handsome tip would be more welcome here than simply another night beside the fire.

No sooner had they gone than my own women and children from the cart arrived. Julia looked rather dubious at first, and stood uncertainly beside the door, but then the smell of porridge began to fill the air and she consented to come in. The baby, however, began to wail again.

'We're all of us tired and hungry,' I murmured to our hostess, as we took our wet cloaks off and hung them up to dry on nails around the wall. 'The infant specially. In fact we're rather hoping that you could help us there, as well. Caeder says you have a baby at the breast? But perhaps he's weaned by now?' I remembered the small toddler I'd seen trailing to the hut.

'My latest child was too feeble to survive,' Caeder's mother said, as though this misfortune were a matter of mere fact. 'But I still have milk, if that is what's required. Doesn't the mother have enough for it?' She enquiringly turned to Julia, who looked blankly back.

'Kennis speaks no Celtic,' I hastily explained. 'My wife and I were sold to slavery and did not bring her up. She was raised in Roman households all her life.' There was not a word of this that was not strictly true, though it gave a different picture from the reality.

However, it earned me a sympathetic nod, as I had hoped. The woman understood – if anybody did – that parents sometimes have to sell their children to be slaves. 'And the baby's father?'

'Head of the household that she lived in, a very wealthy man, and genuinely fond of her, I think. In fact, the little boy is his as well, but there was trouble in the house and it proved no longer possible for him to keep them there. Indeed we now have reason to think he since has died, but he's provided for her very handsomely.' I did not dare to look at Gwellia, who – as a native Celtic speaker – was listening to all this. It was the first indication that she'd had of my suspicions that Marcus might be dead. I heard the stifled gasp which showed she'd understood.

'You think it was Marcus, who was discovered dead?' she murmured, using Latin in an undertone.

I gave a little nod. 'It was the mention of the document which persuaded me. I'll tell you later on. And why else would the curia want to talk to me?'

There was a moment's silence and I feared that she was going to weep. But I underestimated how resourceful my quick-witted wife could be. She turned to Caeder's mother, as though nothing had occurred. 'He even provided a wet-nurse until recently,' she put in, joining the conversation in Celtic as before. 'But now the woman has been sent elsewhere. And the child's not thriving, sucking just from sops.' Any quaver in her voice appeared to be concern about the infant's health.

Caeder's mother clearly thought so. She made a clucking noise. 'Poor little creature. No wonder that he cries. Bring him here to me and I'll suckle him at once.' She was already loosening her bodice as she spoke.

Julia had not understood a word of our exchange, but the meaning of that gesture was unmistakeable. She brought the wailing infant, and handed her across. The woman cradled the baby in her shawl, gave the breast and as the child suckled greedily, she turned to Gwellia.

'What's the mother's name? I heard you mention it.'

'We call her Kennis,' my wife replied, with more composure now. 'And the baby is a girl.'

'Then please tell Kennis to stir the porridge pot for me, and you can serve the food. You'll have to use our bowls and spoons, I fear. You'll find them in a stack beside the fire.'

Gwellia was soon gathering them up, and showing Kennis how to stir the pot – not a task, I guessed, that she had ever done before. 'Keep it from the sides and bottom so it doesn't burn,' my wife said, forcing a cheerful tone. (Latin gave her the freedom to explain the obvious.) 'And as soon as it starts bubbling we can put it on the plates.'

'And here are your slave-boys,' a Celtic voice behind me said. 'They will be wanting gruel as well.'

I turned. Minimus and Tenuis were standing in the entrance way, looking so wet and woebegone that any heart would melt. Esadur, behind them, pushed them firmly in, closed the wooden door and used a hempen loop to fasten it. He gestured to the boys to hang their cloaks.

'Don't have a word of Celtic, either of them,' he muttered to his wife, 'but they are willing and – between us – we managed in the end.'

'Arlina and the ox are safe and fed?' I said, addressing Minimus. 'I didn't see a barn or stable anywhere.'

'I don't think there is one, master. But there's a field of apple trees around the back,' he answered, eagerly. 'We put the animals in there – there's grass and water and a gate so they'll be safe enough, and there's some natural shelter underneath the trees. The householder has pushed our cart in too, and put some leather hides across the roof – to help to keep the inside portion dry, I think. I tried to ask him, but he doesn't understand a syllable.'

I translated and expressed my satisfaction to our hosts, and we huddled round the fire, while Gwellia and Kennis served up the bowls of food. Grain gruel with herbs is not the tastiest of food, but it was hot and nourishing, and we ate it thankfully. Only Marcellinus baulked at such a meal – until I told him it was what brave soldiers ate, after which he downed his supper without more complaint. There was a home-brewed drink to follow, fermented apples mixed with meadowsweet.

It was strong and – even for myself – had to be diluted with water from the ewer by the door. I am not generally very fond of apple-beer, and never serve it to my slaves and womenfolk, but now – when heated to sizzling with a hot brand from the fire – it seemed like nectar and everybody drank.

There was no need of poppy juice tonight. The children's eyes were drooping with fatigue and – after brief ablutions – we set them down to sleep where Caeder's siblings had been lying earlier, with Julia beside them and the slave-boys at their feet. Esa brought some deerskins in to cover them. Gwellia and myself were given the bed-space of the owners of the house – with cleaner, warmer bedding than I'd had the night before. (A glance from me ensured there was no further talk of Marcus, while there were ears to hear.) We did no more than strip our outer clothes and footwear off, and – exhausted by the efforts, griefs and worries of the day – before our hosts had even raked the fire and tiptoed off, I was already in the arms of Morpheus.

I dreamed of my patron, lying on a bier, and a great dark cloud that seemed to rise from him and roar towards me down an empty road, stretching its nebulous fingers out to seize me as it came.

EIGHTEEN

I awoke the next morning to the acrid smell of burning bread. I raised myself on one elbow and stared stupidly around. For a moment I could not work out where I was – except that the room was empty and clearly not my own. There was the sound of children's laughter somewhere quite nearby. Too many children to be Junio's! Then, with a sinking heart, I remembered yesterday.

Of course, I was in Esa's roundhouse! In daylight it looked a very different place. The stools and straw were missing, the hanging smoke had gone, the door was wide open, and the sun was streaming in – clearly, the summer downpour of the day before had passed. The room looked swept and ordered – almost bare, in fact – apart from the cloth-loom and a few tools hanging round the walls.

But I had a faint impression of alarm – a memory of some stealthy movement very close to me. My purse? I felt beneath my pillow for it, but there was nothing there. Alarmed, I sat upright and looked around to find my clothes. I could not see them anywhere. There was no sign of Gwellia, either – or of anybody else. Meanwhile, a single flatbread loaf was scorching on the fire.

I scrambled to my knees and pulled it from the iron tray. It burned my fingers, and I dropped it instantly, cursing myself for bothering with such a trivial thing. My instinctive cry of pain, however, had been heard and a moment later Gwellia came in.

'Ah, you are awake then, finally?' she said, as if there had never been the least cause for alarm. She put down a plaited basket as she spoke and pulled my missing clothing out of it. 'Well, you are just in time. You can come and have some breakfast with the rest of us. I've aired your cloak and tunic in the sun, as you can see. They were still a little damp from yesterday and you were so exhausted that we let you sleep.'

I started to whisper the news about the purse.

She waved my words aside. 'Husband, I needed a few coins. I took it while you slept to give the woman the money that you'd promised her and she sent the elder children to a nearby farm to buy some food for us – and, naturally, for the family as well. They got back a little while ago, with homemade cheese and milk for everyone, but we've saved some for you, so when you are ready you can come and eat. Meanwhile, you'd better put this away again—' from the basket she produced the purse – 'and take more care of it another time. It may not be me who steals it.' But she said it with a smile.

I did not feel like smiling. The events of yesterday hung too heavily on me, but relief enabled me to give a sort of rueful grin. As I slung my money around my torso once again, and pulled my clothing over it, I gestured to the loaf. 'I did not wholly save it, I'm afraid. But it won't go far, in any case, between fifteen of us.'

'That one was keeping warm for you,' my wife explained. 'All we others have taken ours outside. We're eating in the orchard – though it's a little damp – there wasn't really room for everyone in here. Esa has taken stools out for the adult guests – including you, of course. So put on your cloak and come. You won't believe what Marcellinus has been doing while you slept.'

I wouldn't have believed it, if I hadn't witnessed it. He rushed towards me proudly as soon as I appeared. 'I caught a caloman,' he said, dangling a dead pigeon proudly by the legs and using the Celtic name for it. 'Esa showed me how.'

'The children have been with Esa, emptying the traps. Your little fellow went along, and did it very well.' Caedler's mother had not understood the words, but had deduced the sense. She had been suckling the baby again, and it was gurgling happily, but now she laid it down and did her bodice up, gesturing me towards the empty stool beside her. 'I'll teach him to pluck it, later, if you like. And my husband caught a hare. He's skinning it this moment, and with the coins you gave us I can get leeks and turnips too, so there'll be stew tonight. Are you going to stay another day with us?'

She looked so eager at the prospect that it was hard to shake

my head. 'We must be on the road. But it's possible that there
is something you could do for us. Though I'll have to discuss
it with my family.' I turned to Gwellia who had broken the
scorched spelt-bread into two and was now spreading it with
runny cheese for me, and said in Latin, 'We could leave the
baby here, and have it wet-nursed, do you think? Just for a
day or two. It's thriving so much better, I'm sure Kennis would
agree.'

'If we're going to do that, why not leave him here, as well?'
She glanced at Marcellinus, who had put his pigeon down and
was sitting on damp grass with the other boys, absorbed in
trying to whirl a buzz-bone on a string. They had not a word
in common – except for 'pigeon' now – but they seemed to
understand each other well enough. He made the pig-bone
whistle sing and they all laughed heartily. 'He doesn't speak
their language, but he would be safer here – for all kinds of
reasons.'

'Kennis would not bear it,' I said, biting my breakfast, which
– surprisingly – tasted not unpleasant, apart from the charred
crust.

Gwellia glanced at the so-called Kennis anxiously, but she
was paying no attention to our conversation: she was sitting
on a rough, three-legged stool beneath a tree, tired and dishevelled, but watching her young son indulgently.

'I suspect she'd be persuaded,' my wife said, thoughtfully.
'She'd agree to any hardship to keep the boy from harm.
And if we are in greater danger than we were – as seems to
be the case – better to split the party. If anybody comes
seeking us, it will be the cart they follow, and they won't
come looking here. She'd see the sense in that. Though she
does not know the truth about her husband yet. When are
you going to break the news to her?'

'Time enough for that when we get official word,' I
answered. 'I fear the authorities will find me soon enough,
and then she'll have to know. I'll try to negotiate on her behalf
– it should be clear that Marcus had intended that I should,
even if the document was never signed.' She was looking
puzzled, so I explained about the formal appointment of myself
as guardian, and how Varius and his brother had never

witnessed it. 'But I have that other letter under seal, of course, which gives me some authority.'

'So you will be needed to act for Julia?'

I nodded. 'Even if Marcus has been subject to an imperial interdict – in which case everything he had will be forfeit to the Emperor – she should at least be entitled to the Corinium estate. I'm not certain of the details of the law, but I'm sure that Marcus said that if a husband dies anything his widow brought as dowry reverts to her at once, and is no longer counted as part of his estate. If I can prove that he was dead before the interdict was served, the Corinium house would not be forfeited.'

But Gwellia was not listening. Her eyes widened, suddenly. 'An imperial interdict? You think that someone killed him to oblige the Emperor?'

'If Marcus was subject to an *infamia* decree, he would no longer have the protection of the law – anyone could kill him, with impunity, and even expect the Emperor Didius to be pleased and suitably grateful. And that seems probable. He's had several of Pertinax's friends disposed of elsewhere, I believe.'

'But in that case, why the need for secrecy? The murderer would surely want to make it known, in the hope of winning a reward.'

I made a helpless gesture. 'That did occur to me. So it's more likely, don't you think (supposing that there was such an imperial decree), that Marcus took his own life, rather than be banished to some barren rocky isle, and have his family reduced to penury? The indict would not then apply to them at all – presuming that they were not named in it themselves.'

'But if the Emperor issued an edict of banishment it would be served by the authorities and put in force at once. More so, if infamia was declared. How would your patron know in time to kill himself?'

'Suppose that someone warned him that a decree was on its way? He had his friends among the councillors, and it would be like my patron to have seen the threat, and sacrificed himself for Julia's sake. It would account for why the curia want to talk to me. And it would explain the secrecy as well – Marcus was much-respected among the Glevum populace. The authorities might fear there would be riots if the people knew that he'd been driven to an honourable suicide – though they could not safely protest against the Emperor's edict, of itself.'

My wife was shaking her head unhappily. 'It won't be easy to persuade the courts of Julia's claim, if you have the Emperor as an enemy.' She sighed. 'It's worse than I supposed. I simply thought that Marcus been been killed by whoever wrote that note – like Varius and his brother.'

'I know,' I said. 'And it's still a possible explanation, I suppose. He did receive that threatening letter, after all. The idea of an edict is speculation, nothing more – though it does seem likely, given all the facts. But either way, it's clear that Glevum is a dangerous place just now, especially for my patron's family. That's why I propose to carry on as planned, and hide Julia and the children as I promised Marcus that I would.'

'At Eliana's vacant property, I assume? You haven't changed the plan?' She handed me a pitcher of cold water as she spoke.

I nodded doubtfully, and – since no cup was offered – tipped back my head and poured some down my throat. 'That is still my intention,' I agreed, wiping the droplets from my beard. 'Though, if they're seeking me to answer to the curia, it may not be safe for long. But it will give us a few days, at least. I had been proposing to send Marcus word from there, through Junio, perhaps – but now I am not certain what to do. If no one comes to find us, perhaps we'll stay awhile – at least until there's certainty from Rome.'

'You still think that Didius will fall?'

I glanced around, but no one seemed concerned at this protracted conversation in a foreign tongue. Caeder's mother even smiled at me, and I returned the grin, nodding appreciatively at the water jug. Then I turned to Gwellia again. 'I'm certain that he will, if what Marcus told me turns out to be true. So when – and if – a new emperor is proclaimed, we may be able to appeal to him on Julia's behalf. Especially if Septimius Severus succeeds – he was a one-time friend of Pertinax, and is likely to be sympathetic to my patron's widow's cause . . .' I broke off as Marcellinus came proudly up to us, to demonstrate his new-found skill of whistling the bone. I hoped he hadn't heard me mention widowhood.

At his approach his mother brought her stool across and came to join us too. Gwellia raised an expectant brow at me. 'Libertus has something he wants to say to you. About the children, as I understand.'

Kennis looked enquiringly and I was forced to speak. 'The boy seems very happy,' I muttered awkwardly. 'The company of other children, possibly?' It sounded pointed, but she did not take offence.

She nodded. 'He's never had a playmate other than a slave. And I think he's had more fun with that old piece of bone than most of the elaborate toys his father's bought for him.' She sounded almost rueful, and I seized my chance.

'Then there is a proposition I would like to make to you. It will not be easy, but I think it would be best.' I offered the suggestion which we'd outlined earlier. 'I know it would be hard to leave the children here, but it might be better for us all. The fee would help this struggling family as well. I'm certain they would take good care of him, and the infant's health could well depend on it. And it would not be for long. Once we are safely settled we can think again.'

She bit her lip and drooped her head into her hands 'I think their father would be horrified,' she said. 'But there may be a certain sense in what you say. For the infant in particular.'

I was so anxious to convince her that I hardly heard. 'After all, it's not unusual,' I urged. 'Lots of rich parents farm their children out – at least until they're weaned. And look at Marcellinus. Have you seen him happier? Do you think he would be better on the road with us, subject to discomfort and the risk of who-knows-what? To say nothing of betraying who we are, by some childish chatter, and bringing danger down on all of us. Even his father would have understood.'

If I'd used the wrong tense, she did not notice it. 'Then I will trust your judgement, my old friend – I know my husband does. He has placed me in your hands.' She glanced at Caeder's mother who was watching us, still cradling the gurgling infant in her arms. 'You think the woman will consent?'

'I think she'll be relieved,' my wife put in. 'I own I am, myself. I was anxious for the baby. Libertus, speak to her.'

I shook my head. I know how things are managed in a Celtic house. I went and spoke to Esa, who was busy with his hare. He pretended to be doubtful, but I could read his eyes and I knew he was delighted at the prospect of the silver coins which I produced out of my purse. 'Four at once, and in advance, to cover all expense – and the same again when we return, if we find both the children clean and fed, in good health and – most of all – content.'

He pondered for a moment, then put down his skinning knife and wiped his bloodied hands on the damp grass. 'I'll have to talk it over with my wife!' He went across to her.

I heard them murmuring. I could see that she was nodding eagerly, though he shook his head at her. He came back slowly, 'Well, traveller, we would have a contract – it appears – if we had any notion of how long this will last. When do you expect to be this way again? And what kind of surety can you offer us that you will not simply leave the babes and disappear?'

'You have my word as a Celtic nobleman,' I said. 'Which happens to be that of a Roman citizen, as well. And look at the children's mother, if you have any doubt. Do you suppose that she would just abandon them? Her one concern is for their health and happiness.'

He took up the knife again, and set to work. 'Then make a proper oath!'

'I make a solemn promise before the ancient gods, that I'll be back again, at the latest, within a half a moon. It may be – if we are satisfied with what we find – that we'll renew the contract then. Either that, or we will pay you what we owe and take the children back.'

He nodded grudgingly. 'Agreed.' He spat on his palm and I did the same, then we clasped our dampened hands, in token of a contract. 'Though this arrangement may not be for long, you say?' There was disappointment in his tone – despite his reservations of a moment earlier.

'That depends on what awaits us when we get where we are going.'

He looked at me suspiciously. 'And where is that, exactly, citizen?'

'I wish I knew,' I told him truthfully. 'Somewhere on the road to Aquae Sulis – I believe. I'm hoping that I'll recognize the house – or failing that, that I'll find someone who can tell me where it is. It used to be a profitable farm and orchard, once, but then there was a fire and it has grown ruined since. The story must be well-known in the neighbourhood. The owner was crippled in the blaze and died quite recently.'

'And what is your interest in the place? Do you inherit it?' He stopped to stare at me.

I shook my head. 'Unfortunately not. The presumptive legatee is dead. It is not clear who'll have it now. Possibly the widow, or perhaps the Emperor. Or the courts may have to sell the whole estate, to settle debts. My patron is – or rather, was – an important magistrate, with a professional interest in the case.'

'So the search for the treasure never came to anything?' He eased the knife into the space above the head and pulled the skin off in a single piece.

'Treasure?' It was my turn now to stare. And then I realized the implications of what the trapper had just said. 'You know the place?' I could hardly believe it. 'I don't think Caeder did?'

He shook his head. 'I don't suppose he would. I only heard the rumour after he was sold – when I'd passed him to the trader and was on my way back here. I fell into conversation with a man I met, who'd also sold a slave to the same dealer at the same address. Apparently that was the very last of the staff of that estate. His owner had instructed him the day before, to sell on all the servants and shut up the place – only this old manservant was going to stay with her.'

'You can't mean Hebestus!' I was thunderstruck. 'A tall, thin, bald fellow in an ochre uniform?'

'Was that his name? I don't remember it. But he did tell me this. She had conceived a sudden notion that there might be something hidden in the fields – something that her husband tried to say before he died – and she was going to make this fellow go out with a spade and see if she was right. I did not envy him. He was of advancing years and never a land-slave by the look of him. Besides he was quite sure that there was nothing there – the steward would have had it years ago, he said.'

He put the skin down on the tree-stump he'd been using as a bench, and picked the hare up by its two hind legs. 'This is the real treasure of the fields,' he said, triumphantly. 'There will be stew and plenty for us all tonight.'

Perhaps Eliana's steward had found some hidden gold, I thought – that would explain how he had bought freedom for himself. But then I changed my mind. If the steward had found money, he would not have stayed at all – unless the sum concerned was very small. And clearly Eliana had not discovered it – she would never have come to Varius if she had money in her purse. Perhaps I'd look myself! I turned to Esa. 'Can you tell me how to get to the estate? Did he describe the place? On the road to Aquae Sulis, I believe?'

'We travelled back together – we were both on foot. Like me, he did not have the coin to pay anyone a fare, though of course he was not going as far as this. He stopped to make an offering at his owner's tomb, a handsome family vault on the road outside the town – apparently his mistress was concerned that she'd no longer be able to perform the rituals. I waited while he poured some oil into the sacrificial urn – it did not take him long and frankly, I was glad of company. We hadn't much to steal, but when you are foot-traffic and you're travelling for hours, there's always the possibility of someone robbing you, even if you're walking on a major road. When we reached the farm estate, he took his leave of me and I came on alone. But he did point out the house, which you could just see through the trees. I can't describe exactly where it was – but I could show you the turning where he joined the lane into the farm.'

NINETEEN

I was so astonished at this unexpected news, that I called out to Gwellia in delight. 'The Fates have spun a lucky thread for us. Esa can guide us to the property. He knows where to find it.'

I had spoken in Celtic, and the man's wife heard me too. 'You'll take him on the ox-cart?' she said, delightedly. 'He can go on to Aquae Sulis and buy supplies for us – that would be wonderful. Things like flour are so much cheaper in the town. And perhaps he could bring back a pair of live hens, too? We used to have some until quite recently, but we were forced to eat them when times got very bad – and ever since we've sorely missed the eggs.'

'And how would you have me bring them back again?' Esa was clearly unimpressed with this idea. 'Bad enough to manage what we bought with Caeder's sale – cooking pots and turnips – but live poultry and a sack of flour? On my back for twenty miles, like some beast of burden, I suppose? Or give half the money to some farmer on the road, for the privilege of riding in his cart?'

'It might be worth the outlay, given such a chance,' she said, stoutly. 'When will you next get free transport halfway to the town? And you'll have to make your annual visit sometime, anyway. Make a day of it, and get everything we need.'

'And where do you suggest I spend the night? The slave-trader gave me floor-space, last time, but only because I had a boy to sell. There's a room at the temple, where travellers can go, but that's reserved for pilgrims to the shrine and one would be expected to provide an offering. I always could sleep beside a hedge, of course, I've done so many times, but you don't want your provisions spoiling in the dew – or worse still, in the rain.' He shook his head. 'Better for me to simply guide our visitors and then come straight back here, while you bargain at the crossroads as you always do. I'll go to Aquae

Sulis when we've been paid the rest for fostering the children for a half a moon. Then, perhaps, we can afford these little luxuries.'

His wife was disappointed and she shook her head. Kennis saw the gesture, and came hurrying across. 'They won't agree to have the children?' she enquired. I had forgotten that she would not have understood a word.

'Not at all,' I reassured her. 'That is now agreed.' I explained the source of the discussion and she made a face at me.

'Couldn't Esa use the mule to take his purchases? Minimus could go with him and bring it back to us.' She glanced towards our hosts. 'I suppose it's always possible that something unfortunate will happen to the beast – or even to the slave – but it seems a tiny price to pay to have a guide. Otherwise we will be forced to ask someone locally, possibly revealing who we are. Besides—' she gave me her most charming smile – 'it's not only Esa's family who will benefit if Esa gets to town. Marcellinus will flourish better on rye flour and fresh eggs.'

Put like that, I could hardly disagree, though I was reluctant to part with Arlina, even for the necessary day or two. I had been planning to use her to ride into town myself, mostly to make enquiries about Eliana's husband and her farm, but also partly out of curiosity. I had never been to Aquae Sulis in my life, though I knew its reputation, naturally. It is famous as a place of religious pilgrimage, with a temple and bath complex at the heart of it – and an associated market settlement has become a busy town, straggling towards the fortified river-crossing further north.

But it was not the thriving market which attracted me. I'd been hoping to visit the fabled spring myself and see if it was true that Minerva Sulis really sent hot water bubbling directly from the earth. If so, no wonder people come from miles around to offer sacrifice and pray at the shrine for justice or good luck; such a marvel would be proof of supernatural hands at work. It's probably just rumour, but I would like to know for sure. I'm not a follower of Roman goddesses, but I'd be tempted to purchase a curse-tablet of my own, directed at whoever had caused my patron's death, once I was certain that a deity was there!

Such plans, however, would clearly have to wait. My most important task was to get my party safely to the farm and this was too good an opportunity to miss. Kennis was looking expectantly at me, so I turned to Esa and his wife. 'It has been suggested that Esa might travel down with us, and then use the mule to go to town and bring back purchases. We do have panniers for her, as you see – and once we're at the farm, we can unload, of course. Would that be satisfactory? We can collect the animal when we return – provided that you feed and water her meanwhile. It would be a great deal easier than your journeying on foot.' I did not suggest involving Minimus. There were too many hazards on the road – and once we'd found the farm we'd need our slaves in any case.

For a moment I thought the trapper was ready to refuse – or perhaps to haggle, in the hope that I would pay him extra for his time – but his wife was already nodding eagerly. 'So you get transport both ways, husband, and they get you as a guide. What could be better? Now, joint that hare for me and I will put it in the pot, and the stew will be ready by the time that you return. If you set off quickly you will be back by dark, now that you have an animal to ride.' She turned to me. 'And tell your Kennis that I'll go down to the stream and cut some fresh new rushes for her children's beds and Esa will find some skins to cover them – they'll be as comfortable as little emperors.'

I doubted that, in fact. Marcellinus was accustomed to a frame-bed, with a pillow and cover stuffed with down from ducks – though he'd slept well enough last night on nothing more than straw. But looking at him now, chasing the little wooden image of a pig which one of the other boys had tied onto a string and, when it was jerked away from him, toddling laughing after it with his unsteady run, I could see that he would be healthily tired long before tonight. So I nodded and translated, not quite word for word.

Gwellia had been listening to all this, of course, and she sprang to her feet. 'Then if that is decided, let us call the slaves and depart as soon as possible. The earlier Esa reaches town, the more chance he can get home before it's dark. The first part will be slowest, I'm afraid. The ox will not be hurried – so the sooner that we get him yoked onto the cart, the better for us all.'

Esa nodded and whistled to his sons. Our slave-boys came running too – they'd been at the spring, watering our animals – and a whirlwind of activity ensued. Everybody helped and by some miracle – perhaps Minerva Sulis was active here as well – within a half an hour we were ready to depart. Caeder's mother stood beside the cart, cradling the infant in her arms, and Gwellia handed her the roll of rags and the single change of clothing that we'd contrived to bring – much needed by both children by this time, of course. They were received with so much pleasure that you would have thought that we'd provided new garments for the whole household here.

'I had wondered how I'd manage to keep them dry and clean,' the woman said. 'But I'll rinse their old clothes in the stream this very day. And Esa, see if you can bring me a bronze needle from the town, so I can mend the boy's tunic where he tore it earlier. The bone one that you fashioned me has broken at the eye.'

Esa, who had hauled himself up beside me in the cart, muttered that he would, but he hoped that there was nothing else she wanted in the town, otherwise four silver pieces would not stretch to everything.

'Then take some skins with you,' she said. 'There will be lots of room, now that the children are no longer on the cart. You might find someone who wants to buy direct – I'm sure the trader that you deal with now only gives you half of what he gets for them.'

'If the citizen is willing?' he murmured doubtfully. But she had already unhooked the pelts of an otter and a squirrel that were nailed to the wall, and passed them up to him.

Gwellia and Kennis were in their place by now – no longer sitting on the wooden form but stretched out in more comfort on the straw mattress (or what remained of it), under the protection of the wicker frame. I signalled to my slaves. Minimus tethered Arlina to the cart again, then he and Tenuis squeezed in as before – though, as the woman had predicted, there was far more room for all.

So we were ready and would have gone at once, had not

Marcellinus caused a short delay. He seemed to realize that we were going to leave him there. He dropped the buzz-bone he'd been playing with and came rushing to the cart and – when he wasn't lifted into it – burst into furious raging tears, stamping his feet and bellowing inconsolably. For a moment I feared that we would have to stop and take him after all, but then the oldest boy came out and took him by the hand and led him off to show him how to bait a trap. Thankfully, the crying stopped at once and as we shambled off Marcellinus did not even glance at us again.

Esa shook his head. 'Dependent on his mother! And he must be two or three! I sometimes think the ancient Celtic system was the best, when children were farmed out to relatives, so that their parents didn't bring them up at all, and they learned independence from an early age. But that's all disappeared – like many of the fine traditions of our ancestors. The most you hear of these days is what we're doing now, wetnursing an infant who is no kin at all for money, and only for a year or two at most. The Roman way, I suppose. But it will do your grandson good to be more self-reliant – and a little less indulged.'

I did not translate for Kennis. I had seen her face when her son began to cry and thought that she was going to start to weep herself – though when he was so easily consoled, she was still more upset because he'd forgotten her so fast. It would not be tactful to share Esa's views, so I changed the subject. 'How far is this estate that we are looking for, trapper?' I enquired.

He squinted at the sky   still blue and cloudless after yesterday. 'Eight or ten thousand paces, possibly. With luck we might be there by noon,' he said.

We did a little better than that, in the event – partly because there wasn't a great deal on the road. We did encounter an ox-cart here and there, and once a fancy travelling gig with outriders which forced us to the verge, but aside from an errant herd of cows which seemed to have escaped and a couple of imperial couriers who galloped past at speed, we saw almost no one else except pedestrians.

We had been travelling for perhaps four hours or so – no

constant stopping for the children's needs today – and had fallen into a sort of silent reverie, each lost in our own thoughts, when Esa startled me by shouting suddenly, 'That's it! That's the place, I'm almost sure of it. I recognize that hillock and that fallen oak. And there's the house, look, you can see it through the trees.'

I looked where he was pointing and whistled in surprise. Whatever picture I had formed of Eliana's home, it wasn't this.

It was a proper Roman villa, though on a modest scale: a handsome pillared central doorway and a range of rooms each side, with small upper storey (almost certainly for storage and a sleeping-space for slaves), all fronted by a little courtyard with a gated entrance arch and what had clearly once been a shelter for a gatekeeper, though – like the wall which ran around the house – it was in ruins now. There was even a broken statue and a fountain in the court. Hebestus had been right. This had clearly been a very prosperous household at one time.

I glanced around at the surrounding land. There was evidence of what had been a sort of orchard once, and traces of straggling crop-rows in the fields either side, though these were now either barren or wholly overgrown. Here and there gaunt blackened trunks remained, towering over the surrounding undergrowth – silent evidence of that ancient fire, which no one had taken the trouble to remove. No one had pollarded the trees or mended walls for years and the track that led towards the gate had turned to mire. Even the paved courtyard had become a wilderness of weeds.

'You'd better let me down then, if you mean to go inside!' Esa startled me a second time. 'Though you may require assistance to broach that gate, perhaps.'

I followed the direction of his glance. The wooden gateway was probably not barred – that would have had to be done from the inner side – but it was secured by a hefty length of iron chain, passed through a hole in either gate and fastened with a sturdy lock-bolt. It was intended to deter intruders – and it certainly presented quite an obstacle.

I signalled to Minimus, who slid down to the ground, then

came and took the ox-ropes from me while I got down myself. I picked my way along the muddy track and was examining the heavy hinges of the gate, wondering if they could be somehow lifted free.

Gwellia came to join me and I explained my thoughts. She made a doubtful face. 'That looks impossible. Eliana clearly did not mean that people should get in. But over there the boundary wall is falling down – why don't we get the slaves to move a few more stones and make a gap that's big enough to get the ox-cart through?'

She was quite right, of course – it was the easy way, and I should have seen it for myself. I tried to look judicious. 'A sensible suggestion. Of course there is no track on either side that way, but given the condition of the lane that hardly makes a difference, I suppose.'

She looked so pleased and proud to be of help, that I regretted being churlish with my praise. I raised my voice. 'My clever wife has had a good idea. We'll move the stones from that collapsing wall and get in through the hole. We may need to push the cart – Esa, if you'd be good enough to stay a little while?' I tailed into silence. He hadn't understood. I repeated it in Celtic and he broke into a smile.

It was the first time that he had done so, and it transformed his face. 'A splendid notion, but you'll need stronger arms than yours.' He all but elbowed me aside and strode up to the wall. 'Or perhaps we'll use the ox. If we can move this section . . .' He laid hold of a stone, then all of a sudden gave a barking laugh. 'On second thoughts, you don't need strength at all. Even your little slaves could manage this, I think.' He put his shoulder to the wall and heaved and another great section of the stone collapsed. He stood up, dusting off his hands. 'It's so decayed that only custom is holding it in place! One more shove like that and we will be inside.'

It proved nothing like as simple or as quick as that, of course, though everybody helped – except for Julia, who looked so shocked at the idea of moving stones that I gave her the task of 'staying with the cart' – thus freeing Minimus, who was a lot more use. Even when the lumps of wall had been pushed down – and some of them proved most reluctant to come loose – they all had to be moved to clear a route for us. That was no easy task. They were heavy, awkward, dirty and recalcitrant. Some clung in big clusters – with sharp edges too – threatening our toes and fingers constantly, others crumbled into piles of dust and fragments at our touch making humps and hollows which needed stamping flat.

But just as I was wishing that I'd tried to move the gates instead, the last enormous wall-stone in the gap yielded to my shoulder, and fell down with a thud that made the ground vibrate. When the dust had settled and I'd regained my breath, Esa and the slave-boys dragged the rock away (rocking it on one corner) and the way was clear.

A cheer from the main road behind us greeted this, and I turned round, surprised. A small knot of passers-by had gathered at the entrance of the lane and had evidently been observing our antics for some time – though nobody had offered to assist in any way. So much for our attempts to get here unobserved! I cursed the Fates, but to ignore the watchers now was to excite more interest, so I smiled and waved. 'Forgot the key,' I shouted cheerfully.

There was a mocking jeer and they waved back to me, then – presumably convinced that there was nothing more to see – they drifted on.

I heaved a sigh of some relief and while the slaves helped Esa empty the panniers on the mule, load in his pelts and climb up on her himself, I took the ox from Kennis and got up onto the cart.

I turned my head. Arlina was already trotting down the road in the direction of Aquae Sulis and the market-stalls. So, leaving my passengers to walk, I edged the wagon through the gap that we had made – and found myself in Eliana's old estate at last.

TWENTY

O f course, there were problems still awaiting us – though entering the house itself did not prove one of them. The front door yielded very easily, and I found myself inside a large and gloomy area, which must have been the main reception room. It was damp and empty-smelling, and devoid of furniture, though a well-worn mosaic still adorned the floor and a broken oil lamp in a niche showed where the statue of the household gods had stood. There was a small stone altar against the wall below, still stained with the signs of a parting sacrifice – Eliana had obviously had the final leaving rituals performed.

That was fortunate, because when Julia came in she looked around the empty atrium apprehensively. 'A fine house once. I hope there are no ghosts,' she whispered, shuddering. 'There is an awful empty feeling to it now, and didn't the owner die here only recently?'

I gestured to the shrine. 'It's clear that proper cleansing procedures were carried out. There are signs of bones and feathers on the altar still – and stains from wine and oil.'

'And there's the remnant of a recent funeral pyre out in the field as well.' Gwellia had just entered and overheard us. 'I noticed it when we were walking past. A large one, by the look of it – and burnt right to the ground. Eliana's husband had a decent funeral. So there is no fear of restless spirits.' She gave me a little grimace of relief that Julia did not see. 'Well, we are safe and dry – Minimus is finding a secure place to leave the ox, and Tenuis is gathering the makings of a fire.'

'There is a wood-pile somewhere?'

'Not that I could see. But there were a few logs stacked at the cremation site, and there's no lack of sticks to use as kindling. Though where we shall put it, is a mystery. There's no fireplace in here and we don't have braziers – though there might be a hypocaust somewhere, I suppose. That might move the chill, though it won't be possible to keep the furnaces alight. Shall we see what else the house can offer us?'

There was not as much as I had hoped, in fact. Hebestus had been thorough in his clearing of the place. There was a three-sided wooden box-bed in one *cubiculum* – obviously an object too difficult to move, and equally obviously the place where Eliana had spent her final night, since there was a half-burned taper on a spike, and a discarded mattress still lying in the frame.

Julia had been exploring with us – largely because she did not want to be left alone in the cold and echoing atrium, I think – and when she saw the bed-frame she gave a little cry. 'A proper bed to sleep on!' She flung herself down upon it like a child – and then seemed to recollect that this might not be polite. 'May I have this tonight?' She gave me that coy, winning smile again. 'There's sure to be others elsewhere in the house. And perhaps – at least while we are in the villa, where I feel at home – I can relax and be Julia again, and forget that I am supposed to answer to another name? It wasn't easy to remember to be Kennis, anyway.'

'All the same,' I told her, 'we should keep the fiction up, at least when others are about, until we're sure we're safe. That trouble in Glevum that we heard about may be much more serious than you realize – and it may be wise for "Julia" to have disappeared. Though have the bed by all means – we are used to reeds and straw, and as you say, there may be other beds elsewhere.'

We left her to enjoy her little luxury and went on with the search. I was expecting little, and I was right to doubt. Apart from one lopsided table with a broken leg, we found no other furniture whatever in the main part of the house.

We tried the attic next, up a narrow wooden staircase which creaked alarmingly at every step. The area was much as I'd imagined it to be: one large empty sleeping-room, divided into two – one side for maidservants, no doubt, and the other for the men – with a steward's cubicle between: a row of marks showed where the rows of narrow mattresses had been, but only a few wisps of stuffing straw remained. A dark storage room next-door was little better stocked, producing only two dusty wooden serving-bowls, and a box of faded ochre tunics – in a variety of shapes – no doubt discarded uniforms for long-forgotten staff. There was evidence of rodents elsewhere in the room: we found half-eaten tapers in a pile, but the box was wooden and the tunics were unharmed.

Gwellia, ever practical, took the box from me and piled the other items into it. 'We can use those clothes as blankets for a day or two, if we smoke out the moth, and a few of these tapers are still useable,' she said, decisively. 'You've got a knife, so we can cut some reeds for bedding – or straw, if there is any to be had. Though we had better choose a sleeping-space down on the floor below – the roof is leaky in some places here. We could even use the outside kitchen; it would be warmer there – I suppose the villa had one! It won't be very big but at least there will be provision for a fire. And meanwhile we'll see if there is anything available to eat.'

I looked at her, surprised. 'We finished our supplies?'

She nodded. 'We ate the last crumbs yesterday, I fear. And I dared not ask that little family to sell us anything – they have so little, they would deprive themselves. But the woman did give me a handful of apples from her store. Last year's, of course, so they're small and wizened now, but at least we will not starve. Tomorrow, I will venture out and try to find a roadside stall. There is sure to be something, on such a major road. But that can wait until we've settled in. For today, let's go and see what's here.'

I assented. 'Though don't expect too much. I know that Eliana took her own supplies with her.'

In fact, an exploration of the kitchen area revealed a small amphora which still contained some oil, and a large container set into the ground outside which held a few parched peas. These (with the discovery of an ancient cooking pot, much-patched) offered some promise of a warming meal – if we could only contrive to make a fire.

I said as much to Gwellia, but she simply grinned. 'I told you I'd sent Tenuis out to find some fuel. Come and see what I've got in my luggage roll.'

When she unrolled it I saw what made her smile. 'A box of half-charred linen and a flint and striking stone!'

'I packed them while you were in Glevum for the cart,' she said, 'I thought they would be useful. And I've brought a spoon or two, a twist of salt and a bit of barley grain I stuffed into a pouch.' She produced these treasures with triumph as she spoke. 'There were other things I thought of, but I had no room for more.'

'Well managed, wife!' I could have hugged her for her thoughtfulness, but Gwellia does not care for such displays. Instead I tried a jest. 'I'm glad you brought the spoons. Julia would not like to use her hands to dine.' I grinned and squeezed her arm. 'So there's a chance of pottage?'

'Even tastier, we could have broth, perhaps. The kitchen patch is wholly overgrown but there may be something edible still there beneath the weeds, and I can't believe that all these fields are quite devoid of crops. I'll show you what I mean.' She led the way into the rear walled garden as she spoke and plunged her hands among the foliage. 'Look, I told you – there's a skinny leek.' She gave a tug and held up the bedraggled thing triumphantly. 'And that looks like borage!' She waved a hand at it. 'And I'm sure I saw some turnip-tops out on the field. Even if the roots are rotted we can eat the leaves.' She sat back on her heels. 'I'll send the boys out on a search, and I'll go on hunting here – between us we shall manage something nourishing, I think.'

This was so encouraging I tried another joke. 'All we need now is Marcellinus and his pigeon trap!' I said and made her grin. 'I'll see if I can find the means to set one for myself. There may be something in the sheds that I could use. Though here comes Minimus – he's been dealing with the ox – perhaps he's looked inside the outbuildings.'

But when I asked, the slave-boy shook his head. 'There is almost nothing left in any of the barns – just some wisps of hay and a few frayed lengths of rope. All the sheds and stores are empty, except for where I've put the ox, of course. There is one small enclosure – it might have been for geese – with a trough that's full of rainwater, so I've tied him there where he can reach a drink. It's overgrown with grass and weeds, so he can graze on those. Tomorrow we can mend the wall and put him out into the field. Though we'll have to find some water.'

'Isn't there a well?'

'I couldn't find one, so there must be a river or a spring somewhere – if we can find a container anywhere. There's nothing in the land-slave quarters, because I've looked in there. This was the only useful thing that I found anywhere—' he held out the broken pail which he'd been carrying – 'and there's a sort of barrel set into the ground, with a spindle in the middle and a heavy tree-trunk made into a press. I don't know what it's for. Crushing something, by the look of it – there's a runnel at the bottom, so liquid can run out.'

I glanced at Gwellia, who was collecting turnip-greens. I recognized a wine press when I heard one described. Marcus had once talked of having one installed. And Hebestus had mentioned that there'd been a vineyard here – though I hadn't imagined anything so grand as to require a mechanical device. (Most vine-growers just use their slaves to tread the grape-juice out and leave it in a clay-pit for a fortnight to ferment – unless they aim to sell it, instead of drinking it. It's an efficient system for a small estate, because the skins left over can be fed to animals – or, in same cases, even to the slaves!)

'It's for crushing grapes,' I told the slave, and he answered with a grin.

'Well, master, if you're hoping that you'll find a few amphorae that the owner left behind, you will be disappointed. That machine's not been used for years – the pit is full of rotting leaves and spiders' webs and the pulley ropes have failed.'

I laughed. 'Most private wines will only last a month or two before they sour,' I said. 'One of the reasons I prefer my mead. So if there is a wine-store on the property the contents would be scarcely drinkable by now.' I frowned. 'Though there was talk of a wine-cave, somewhere, I recall. That might be cool enough to keep the vintage fresh, at least a little longer. After we've eaten and rested, I'll go and look for it – it must be within the bounds of the estate. Perhaps in that hillock that we noticed from the road – and that's also where any spring is likely to be found.' I broke off as Tenuis came into the garden seeking us. His arms were full of assorted lumps of wood.

'Look what I've found, mistress,' he said, importantly – not waiting to be spoken to, as a well-trained servant should. He let go of his load, which clattered to the ground, on the broken paving of what had once been a path.

Gwellia did not chide him for impertinence. 'Well done! Now we can make a cooking-fire and eat! You take Minimus and go back into the field and bring back anything that's edible.'

I was already busy with the tinder and the flint, and using a handful of the straw-heap from the cart, I soon had a little fire burning in the kitchen cooking-hearth. It would be some time, of course, before the meal would be prepared, so I shook out the tunics and held them in the smoke – though fewer moths fell out than I had feared – then hung them on the broken wall to dissipate the smell. Then I joined the hunt for herbs while Gwellia warmed the pot – and was delighted to add a clump of wood-sorrel to our increasing store.

The boys' return brought turnip-roots as well as leaves – though many had been partly eaten by other creatures, first – and a few slug-ridden cabbages. But cleaned and chopped and thrust into the pot, with the peas and grain and a little water from the ox's trough, it soon began to smell invitingly like soup.

Julia clearly thought so, because she came out to us – full of apologies for sleeping while we worked, though it was hard to know what use she might have been. Now though, she was keen to help, so she supervised the boys as they cleaned the wooden bowls that we had found. Then she and Gwellia ladled out the broth, dividing it unequally between the two – one for the adults and the other for the slaves. There were no stools or benches, so we squatted on the floor and ate from our communal serving dish – in comparative comfort, thanks to Gwellia's spoons.

When we had finished, Julia turned to me. 'That was more delicious than I thought possible. I don't know how your wife contrived it, with such ingredients. When I get home, she'll have to show my cook-slave what to do.'

I could not answer. The poor lady had no idea at all of how her life was going to change – though, given her good looks and background it was possible that some other patrician husband could be found for her, especially if I could persuade the new authorities that the Corinium house was rightfully her own.

'You're thoughtful, husband!' Gwellia remarked. She looked anxiously at me. She knew what I was thinking, but I shook my head at her. The time had not yet come to tell Julia what we knew. My wife, as ever, found a way to disguise what might have been an awkward interchange. 'If you are worrying about the morning, husband, there is no need to fear. There's still a little broth remaining in the pot – unusual, perhaps, so early in the day, but perfectly sustaining, and after that I'll go and find a farm, or a roadside market that will sell us something more.'

I shook my head again. 'I was thinking that I ought to go and try to find a spring while there's still light enough to see. It must be almost the eleventh hour by now, and it will soon be dusk. Now that we have a pail, I could bring fresh water back – better than using what is in the trough after the ox has been drinking out of that.' I clambered to my feet. 'I'll take Minimus with me.'

'And try to find that cave, if you have time,' my wife suggested. 'One never knows – there might still be some wine!'

Julia's eyes brightened. 'A wine-cave?'

I nodded ruefully, remembering the fine imported Rhenish she was accustomed to, and what Hebestus had told me about the bitter stuff that Eliana had brought from this estate. 'Perhaps,' I said, 'but don't expect too much.' I repeated what I'd said to Gwellia earlier. 'Wine from this province does not keep in storage very well, and I hear that the last vintage wasn't good in any case!'

Julia looked disappointed and ready to protest, but by this time Minimus was waiting with the pail, and I made a swift escape.

TWENTY-ONE

There was a spring – though it was sluggish at this time of year – which trickled through a reedy pond to form a pebbly stream. The water, though, was sparkling and we filled the pail. (It had no handle and was difficult to hold, but we contrived between us.)

When we had finished I set it on a flat part of the bank and said to Minimus, 'We'll leave this for a moment and try to find that cave. If it's a natural cavern it must be somewhere on this hill. There's a rocky outcrop over there, which might conceal an opening, and another darker shadow over by those trees.'

The dark patch yielded nothing but a fox-earth, but at the outcrop there was a sort of cleft between the rocks – wide enough to walk through, when one got close enough to see – and evidence that there had once been a well-worn track to it. The entrance was largely overgrown with weeds and brambles now, of course, but some of it was trampled down, as though some animal had been this way quite recently, using the rock-space as a lair, perhaps?

That made me thoughtful. There are still wild beasts about in forest areas, and although this did not exactly qualify, there were thick trees nearby, where the orchard had degenerated into a tangled wood.

'Aren't we going in there, master?' Minimus was clearly eager, rather to my shame. 'You'll want to tell the mistress that we have found the cave, if it is the right one, and we won't know till we look.'

His enthusiasm – and this latter argument – persuaded me to take a careful peek. When I poked my head into the space beyond (very, very cautiously and half-prepared to flee!) I could see that there was indeed a cave and something lying up against the wall.

The place however did not smell of animals – and dens are

very aromatic, as everybody knows. Instead there seemed to
be a faint sweetish rotting smell, if anything. I withdrew my
head, perplexed. This called for light – and though we had
scarcely any tapers in the house, I was willing to sacrifice one
or two for this.

I explained my thoughts to Minimus and we struggled back,
carrying the water – to Julia's delight, though she was disappointed when she realized that it was not to wash her dusty
feet. Instead we poured it out into the larger of the now-clean
bowls, and when everyone had taken a refreshing drink from
it, I turned to Gwellia and told her what we had found.

She was more pleased than I'd expected, and bustled round
at once. 'If you need lights, let's see what we can find. Here's
that little oil lamp that was standing in the niche; the spout is
broken, but I've still got a little oil and we'll find something
that will make a wick. A piece of this old tunic will do very
well.' She tore a strip of linen from the hem and fashioned it
into a tight twist even as she spoke. 'There! Now we can light
it at the kitchen fire, and here's a piece of taper you can take
as well – it's the longest one we have. Save that till you need
it and then light it from the lamp.'

I was tempted to demur. 'I was only proposing to have a
glance inside. Tapers may be more necessary back here at the
house.'

She withered that suggestion with a look. 'If it's indeed a
wine-cave there may be racks in it, or an old barrel in the
Gallic style – something that will burn more slowly than those
small logs we found, and keep the kitchen embers glowing
overnight. If the cave is dry it might even be a warmer place
to sleep. Shall I come with you, and have a look myself?'

'It won't be warmer, it is noticeably cool – ideal for storing
wine, no doubt, though I didn't see any,' I said. 'Nor any of
the racks or barrels that you're hoping for. But come with me
by all means – there is no danger now, I'm sure. There have
been animals at some stage, judging by the tracks, but it's
clearly been some time since anything was there.'

Gwellia gave me an impatient frown and handed me my
knife, which she had used to chop the stew ingredients. 'All
the same, you can carry this with you. And I'll take that

stone-mallet that you brought on the cart! We haven't come so far to have you set upon by some drunken vagrant who is lying there asleep – or bitten by a nest of snakes that you've disturbed.'

I hadn't considered the possibility of snakes, though perhaps I should have done. 'I don't think that we'll find vagrants,' I protested mildly. 'From what Hebestus said, the villa has a local reputation for ill luck. But we'll take our makeshift weapons to make doubly sure and we'll go and see what we can find.'

She nodded and then turned to Tenuis, who was hovering nearby. 'You can spread some bedding-reeds for us while we are gone – somewhere in the villa where it's relatively warm – and make a bed for you two slave-boys at our feet. Then bank up the fire, and help Julia select which of the tunics she would like as bedcovers. We'll share the rest between us. Then help her to her couch – poor lady, she has enjoyed few luxuries of late. We'll go to bed as soon as we get back, to save on candles – just in case there's any problem in the morning getting more. We don't know how far it's going to be to find a marketplace.'

The little slave-boy scurried off to start his tasks, and with Minimus proudly holding up the lamp, my wife and I and set off together for the cave. I was encumbered by the mallet and the extra taper-reed, which I thought superfluous, but I did not complain: I was anxious to complete our mission before it got too dark.

In the event I was glad that Gwellia was there – and that I had taken her advice. Not that there was anything of value in the cave, as we realized when our eyes became accustomed to the gloom. Our shadows loomed enormous on the rock walls round about, but by the flickering oil lamp it was clear that everything portable and useful had been moved out long ago. There were indeed some wine-racks: but one was carved in stone beside the entrance way, so that amphorae could be safely stored upright – (though the floor was stained in patches, suggesting some had smashed) – while a smaller free-standing wooden version at the back – which might have been of use to feed the fire – had been reduced to fragments by a fall of rock, which had half-buried it.

A fairly recent rockfall, I realized with alarm. I put down what I was carrying and took the oil-light from the little slave. Lifting it overhead revealed the fresh scar where the huge hunk of stone had fallen from above, bringing a tumble of rubble as it came, judging by the hundreds of pebbles and small stones which now lay in a ragged slope against the wall.

The thought that more of the roof might suddenly descend was not a happy one, but otherwise the cave seemed quite a pleasant place. No bats, no snakes, no uneven lumps to trip one underfoot; one could see why it was chosen as a storage space. Even the pale shape that I had noticed from the entrance earlier proved to be nothing more sinister than a heap of foliage. The source of that vague, unpleasant smell, perhaps? I kicked it over, but nothing scuttled out, other than a startled spider.

I thought I knew what it was doing there. 'I was wrong about the vagrants,' I called out cheerfully. 'Obviously they come here, sometimes, after all – whatever the reputation of the place. Probably they think the curse does not include the cave – though you'd think that falling rock might persuade them otherwise. All the same, some beggar has made a bed here, by the look of it – perhaps they were simply desperate for a place to sleep. But at least we can guess who trampled down the plants beside the door.' I turned away to leave. 'Let's follow his example and go back to our beds. There's nothing here of any consequence and we don't want to be caught up in another fall of stones.'

'Just a moment, husband!' Gwellia had brushed past me and was stooping by the pile of leaves that I'd disturbed. 'Let me have that lamp!' I did as she instructed and she moved the dried plants with her foot to get a better look. 'I thought as much. When you disturbed the heap I recognized the smell. Hyssop, myrtle, parsley . . . rosemary! This is no casual beggar's mattress, husband. These are funeral herbs, and some expensive ones, at that.' She straightened up and looked anxiously at me, her face shadowed in the flickering light. 'You don't suppose that Eliana laid her husband here, rather than in that family tomb we heard about?'

I looked around the empty cave and shook my head. 'I can't

imagine so. We know there was a pyre beside the house, not here, and Esa said that Hebestus had made an offering at the vault, on the road near Aquae Sulis. No one would do that if the ashes were not there, for fear of offending the spirit of the dead – and Hebestus would know where the cremation urn was put; he must have been at his master's funeral. He probably arranged the details, in fact, since Varius certainly did not and I don't think Eliana would have managed it alone – she seems to have relied on her slave for everything.'

Gwellia's silence acknowledged the truth of what I'd said, but finally she spoke. 'Then I don't understand the presence of these herbs. No one of any honour would bring their husband here to cleanse the body and prepare it for the pyre – the dead man's ghost would haunt the place for years, if he'd been denied the dignity of lying in the house, and even there he'd want his feet towards the entrance so his soul could find its way – not to be lying in a darkened cave. Unless he died here?'

'He could hardly have done that. I believe that he was crippled and confined to bed for years. Anyway, whatever herbs were used for ritual would have been put into the fire and cremated with the corpse.'

She shook her head. 'This is more like the offerings that the Romans used to put onto a grave. I remember when I was a slave, and my owner's grandmother was very old and died, they buried her in the ancient way, and they had herbs like this. There's even parsley mourning wreath among these leaves, I think!'

I lit the other taper and knelt to look, myself. 'You're right,' I said, bewildered. 'And there's another of wild roses – all dried and withered now. Part of Eliana's leaving rituals, do you think? Some kind of ceremony when she said farewell? It seems unlikely, but I suppose it's possible. She is a forceful lady, and if she chose to have a private sacrifice . . .?' I did not believe this theory myself, so I abandoned it, and looked around for something to help me to my feet.

My first thought was to lean on the piece of fallen stone, which was lying at an angle just within my reach, but when I put my hand on it, it rocked alarmingly. I let go quickly and looked round for something else, holding my taper up to illuminate my search. There was a jagged crack which ran down the back wall of the cave and – rather gingerly, in case there might be something lurking there – I put my fingers into it, and pulled myself upright. And discovered something that was rather a surprise.

'Dear Mercury!' I cried. 'There is a draught through here. I can feel it on my hand. It is coming through the crack.'

'There are too many shadows and you are tired tonight!' Gwellia sounded indulgent and amused. 'Your imagination is playing tricks on you! Of course there's nothing of the kind. How can there be a draught from the inside of a cave?'

'There is!' I persisted. 'Feel it for yourself.' I looked a little closer. 'That's not just a crack, it's a space between the rocks. And look, it widens there – behind that fall of stones. You can just see where it starts to broaden out. I think there might be a proper aperture – one you could crawl through, probably, if that heap of pebbles wasn't in the way!' I held my taper up enough for Gwellia to see the gap I meant.

She bent to look, then put her hand where mine had been. 'Dear gods!' she said. 'You're right. I wonder if there's anything inside. There was talk of treasure somewhere, wasn't there?' She began to scrabble at the stones, and I worked with her, using the mallet head to sweep the rubble clear. As we cleared them it grew evident that there was indeed a hole, which seemed to lead to another space beyond. The cool air that I'd noticed was more perceptible, and that sickly smell was growing stronger too.

After a few minutes of this activity I paused in my labours and sat back on my heels. I looked down at the pebble I was holding in my hand. Something about its shape and smoothness struck me, suddenly. 'Of course!' I muttered. 'How could I be such an idiot? This is a pebble – rounded by a stream. It's not a fallen stone. So what's it doing here? Someone must have brought it here, deliberately!'

Gwellia took the stone from me and fingered it. 'I think you're right again. Most of these stones are jagged – just as you'd expect – but some of them are not. They are not even the same kind of rock as what is in the cave.' She stared at me, her face troubled in the flickering light.

My brain was working properly by now. 'And look at where

the stones are lying – in one single heap. If they had come down with that hunk of rock they would be scattered everywhere. I even noted that the surface of the floor was smooth – but I did not realize the significance!'

'Someone brought the stones here to block the entranceway?' She shook her head. 'It can't be that. The way that hunk of stone has fallen, it's blocked it anyway. There's no room to crawl through the opening, with that lying there. And that's a natural rockfall, that is evident. No one could have moved it there deliberately, it's such a massive piece of stone.'

It was indeed enormous – taller than a man and almost twice as wide – and though it was not very thick, it was heavy enough to have completely splintered the old amphora rack. A wooden rack which had once stood against the wall!

I looked at Gwellia and she looked at me. 'Are you thinking what I am thinking?' she enquired. 'It was the rack that used to hide the hole – and when the rock fell down, it half-revealed the space, and someone brought in extra stones to block it up again?'

I nodded. 'It seems the likeliest explanation, doesn't it? And with the smell I think that I can guess what's in that space. Perhaps Eliana's husband was never on that pyre. I wish that I could move that stone and crawl in there and see. Though perhaps that's possible. It's only balancing. When I leaned against it, I made it rock before.'

I placed more weight experimentally against the stone. It moved a little more – just enough this time for me to glimpse the space behind. That was enough. I handed the lighted taper to my wife – this needed two hands – and I pushed with all my might.

'Be careful, husband!' Gwellia cried out in alarm.

But the warning was too late. Minimus had added his efforts to my own and the stone had lost its equilibrium and was falling as she spoke. It tumbled with a crash that made the ground vibrate, raising choking clouds of dust and sending deafening echoes eddying round the rocks. If I hadn't stepped back smartly and snatched Minimus away it would have fallen where we stood, and crushed us as surely as a wine press smashes grapes. As it was, it barely missed my toes.

I was so shaken I could hardly speak, but I tried to hide my fright behind a feeble jest. 'We almost had another use for all those funeral herbs!' I said.

Minimus managed a sickly grin at this but Gwellia did not smile. She had seized the guttering lamp from where the slave had put it down – the falling stone had blown my taper out – and was staring past me with her mouth agape and a look of horror dawning on her face.

'I think we're right in our suspicions about the funeral,' she said. 'Look what's behind you!' She gestured with her hand. 'Is that Eliana's husband, do you think? And if so, whose ashes are in the family grave? That is a human body, or it used to be – and one that has never been cremated on a pyre. And don't tell me it's a vagrant mendicant who crawled in here to die – beggars don't wear neatly hobnailed sandals like that!'

I turned, and saw what she was pointing at. There was still a pile of rubble in the way, but now discernible through the gap between the rocks was something that was clearly a human leg and foot.

TWENTY-TWO

glanced across at Gwellia, who was looking anxious in the flickering light. I was loath to abandon this mystery unsolved, but it was already late and soon it would be dark. 'Shall we come back tomorrow?'

But she shook her head. 'None of us will sleep if we just leave this now! Minimus, come and help your master to move the rest of the rubble which is in the way. I'll hold the lamp for you. It may be that we'll want you to crawl in through the hole when it is clear – you are the smallest, so it's easiest for you.'

That suggestion clearly terrified the slave, though he set to work as he'd been ordered, naturally. I felt for him – even an adult might be nervous of uneasy spirits here. I was not entirely without concerns, myself. However, I was the paterfamilias, and responsibility in this household was ultimately mine.

So I cleared my throat and said, as casually as I could, 'I think it's best if I'm the first to go. Once we've moved this remaining pile of stones there's obviously room to let a grown man through, provided that he bends down low enough.' I was rewarded by a grateful glance from Minimus, who worked to clear the blockage with a much greater will.

A few more minutes of combined effort proved that I was right. The aperture was low, but it was wide enough for a stooping man to pass with care. Furthermore, the area beyond was now partially revealed. It was clearly another, rougher, colder and much smaller, cave – little bigger than a plunge pool at Marcus' private baths – and what seemed to be a human body took up most of it.

It was not entirely unexpected, but it still made us gasp. It seemed that our speculations about the corpse had been correct. The body was largely swaddled in a stained and faded cloak, and partly obscured by large outcrops of the rock – the floor was as uneven as the outer one was smooth – but it was possible to see that the owner of the sandalled foot had been a full-grown man. (Presumably the origin of that vague pervading smell, which seemed more pungent now the opening was cleared.)

I picked up the fallen taper and relit it at the lamp, then – feeling for some reason compelled to draw my knife – I stooped and walked into the little cubicle of death. To this day I don't know exactly what I hoped to find – except perhaps some proof that the dead man on the floor was indeed the former owner of the farm.

What I did find made me exclaim aloud. 'This isn't Eliana's husband!' My shout of surprise made the whole cavern ring.

Gwellia's anxious face peered through the aperture, illuminated by the lamp which she was carrying. 'How can you be certain?'

'For one thing the body has been dead for far too long!' I said, moving the taper to get a better look. 'Eliana's husband died quite recently. This body has been lying in this cave for years. The leg is reduced to scarcely more than bone.'

I did not add that it was more than usually macabre. All trace of flesh had vanished, leaving just the leathery skin to stretch across the tibia, under the tattered remnants of what had been the clothes.

If I had not seen a similar phenomenon before – a two-headed cat which had been preserved this way (brought to Glevum for a public festival and exhibited, for a quadrans, in a show with other freaks) – I think I would have dropped the light and fled, fearing the presence of some supernatural hands. But I managed, with an effort, to fight my panic down and force myself to take a rational view. Conditions in the cave had clearly kept the body very dry, I told myself, and it was ventilated by that cooling draught which seemed to come from a fissure overhead – so instead of rotting as you might expect, the leg had desiccated like a piece of salted fish. Exactly the process which the owner of the exhibition had described to me. But even as I convinced myself that this was possible, I was still shuddering. There was something unnerving about the way this body lay – under the covering cloak it seemed eerily misshapen and unnaturally wide.

I used my knife-blade to move the brittle rags of cloth aside – and had my second shock. 'And furthermore this is not one man, but two!' I called to Gwellia. 'There is another body half-underneath the first.'

The other cadaver was a slightly smaller one, lying on its side with both its knees drawn up (which is why it had been concealed by the cape) but it had clearly also been a male, and desiccation was equally advanced. Both sets of ribs were visible, standing out like those of skeletons, and – though something unpleasant had happened to the guts – under and around the stained and fragile clothes discoloured skin survived, looking like dark parchment – and about as thin. There were even a few remaining clumps of matted hair clinging to the two grotesquely grinning skulls. The effect was horrible.

I moved to rise and accidentally moved a fleshless arm, which flopped down gruesomely – revealing the grisly fact that it was incomplete. I let out an involuntary cry.

'Dear Mercury! Husband, what has happened? Have you fallen? Are you hurt?' There was a scrabbling sound and before I'd recovered my wits enough to speak, Gwellia had joined me in the tomb. I mentally applauded her bravery, of course, but I wished she hadn't come. I tried to protect her from the ghastly spectacle by standing to shield it with my arms outstretched. 'I am not hurt. Go back! Don't look! It's far too terrible!'

But she was already staring past me at the horror on the floor. 'Witchcraft!' she whispered in a shaking voice, clapping her free hand across her mouth. 'No wonder you cried out. This place is genuinely cursed. Skeletons should not have skin and hair on them!' She dropped the oil lamp suddenly and flung herself at me, and I could feel her sobbing as she clung around my neck.

Very gently, I disengaged myself and sat her on a rock while I picked up the knife that she had clattered from my grasp and managed to rescue the extinguished lamp just in time before the oil had all seeped out. I relit it from my taper – though darkness was arguably kinder in that awful place.

'No sorcery,' I soothed. 'This is something that can happen naturally – though it is very rare. Sometimes it's done on purpose.' I explained about the cat. 'The man who owned it told me that in the North African Province of the Empire, where he came from, it is not unusual – his tribal ancestors found dead bodies dried out in desert caves and perfected the technique to preserve their ancient kings. Making a *mumia*, he called it. Except that I don't think it was deliberate this time. No one meant to dry these bodies, it is just an accident.'

'Master!' An urgent bleat from Minimus came through the aperture. 'Grant me permission to come and join you soon. Forgive me, master, I know I shouldn't ask – it's a servant's job to wait where he is told, but you have both the lights and it is dark out here. In fact, it's getting dusk outside the cave as well . . .' He sounded terrified.

I looked at Gwellia and shook my head at her before she summoned him. 'Stay where you are, Minimus,' I called back to the slave. 'We are coming back to you in any case. We have seen everything we came to see, and more – and there's nothing further that we can do tonight.'

Gwellia clutched my arm. 'But we can't just leave the bodies lying where they are!' she murmured, urgently.

'Why not?' I too had dropped my voice so Minimus could not hear. 'They have been lying here for years and nothing we can do is going to help them now.'

'But their spirits . . .! They must walk abroad. There's been no funeral. No wonder that the villa is rumoured to be cursed!' The murmured words were quivering with dread.

I nodded. 'Tomorrow we will offer oil and wine for them – though you need not fear a haunting in the meantime, I don't think. Those herbs suggest that something has already been done to appease the spirits. However I want to go to Aquae Sulis anyway – so I'll find a priest to perform the proper cleansing rituals.' I ushered her back through the aperture ahead of me, then took one final look around the space before I followed her. When I had come through into the outer cave myself (and given Minimus the taper, to his visible relief) I voiced the other thought that had occurred to me. 'I don't think that a funeral pyre would be appropriate – but we could perhaps arrange to put them in the family sepulchre. Eliana would have wanted that, I think.'

'The family tomb?' Gwellia's tone was sharp with puzzlement, but now that she was no longer confronted by the dreadful sight, she began to sound her usual self again. 'You think these men were relatives of hers?' She had begun to move towards the entrance-opening, ready to light our way out of the cave, but now she turned and held the lamp aloft to frown at me. Then her face cleared. 'I see!' she said suddenly, in an altered tone. 'You think that these are Eliana's sons? I know you told me that their bodies were not found. So you suspect that they have been there ever since the fire?'

'Don't you? And I think Eliana found them only recently – after the fall of rock smashed down the wooden rack and revealed the entranceway. Possibly when she was preparing to vacate the farm. We know that she was hunting for that rumoured treasure, just before she left. And it would make perfect sense. Somebody left those funerary herbs outside the aperture.'

'But the opening was blocked by rubble. No one could see the bodies lying there.'

'Exactly so! The opening was blocked. But – as we agreed before – that was not by natural means. Someone piled those stones against it afterwards – even bringing extra pebbles from the stream to make sure it was sealed. I'm convinced that it was their mother.'

'And she didn't move the bodies?'

'She could not have moved that stone that blocked the way, alone, and by that time she would have sold her slaves.'

'Except for Hebestus, though he would be no help, from what I hear of him.'

'I don't think she ever told him what she found,' I said. 'He would have mentioned such a heartbreak when he spoke to me. Perhaps it was the day that Esa met him on the road, when she was here without a slave at all – it doesn't often happen for a matron of her rank. It would make sense, then, that she would try to bear the tragedy alone – she is not a woman to confide her griefs to slaves. Her pride would not permit it. And what could he have done? The cave itself had made a kind of sepulchre which held her sons. I'd like to think that she tried to do her best for them.'

'I hope you're right – that way at least their souls would

be appeased.' Gwellia spat on her finger and rubbed behind her ear. 'So the mystery is solved. They came here to escape the fire but perished in the smoke.' She shuddered. 'Poor young fellows! What a dreadful death. And poor Eliana – what a shock for her! Though I'm surprised that, having found them, she agreed to leave the farm.'

There were several aspects of this summary I did not quite accept, but this was not the time to stop and argue with my wife. I put my hand upon her shoulder. 'Assuming that all these speculations are correct,' I said. 'There are lots of questions that we don't have answers to. But that is for tomorrow – for now I think we ought to get back to the house. If we don't go soon, we will be trapped ourselves – out in unfamiliar fields in the dark! That lamp's already guttering and the taper's nearly gone!'

Gwellia nodded, and gestured to Minimus to pinch the taper out. 'Relight that when I tell you. In the meantime we'll just use the lamp, and try to catch the moment before the oil expires!' And she led the way outside into the gathering dark.

After the dimness of the cave, even the dusk seemed fairly bright at first and we walked quite quickly for a little while, though a brisk little evening breeze was springing up and when we had to light our taper it did not serve us well. Even our attempts to shield it with our hands did not protect it and it very soon blew out, leaving us to stumble blindly in the dark. Only the faintest of brief glimmers in the sky – sparks from the fire in the kitchen-block perhaps – glowed now and then above the trees to guide us back. If it had not been for an intermittent moon, occasionally peeping through the clouds, it might have been difficult to find our way at all.

As it was, it took us a long time to reach the house – more than once we wandered off the path and lost our footing in the dark – and when at last we stumbled up the steps and through the door, it was to find one single taper burning on the spike, and an anxious Tenuis awaiting us.

'Ah there you are, master and mistress!' he cried, as we appeared. 'You have been away so long, I began to fear that you were lost, or had encountered wolves. But I see that you are safe. I've made your bed for you – in the *triclinium*. I thought it would be warmer in there than the larger rooms. The other mistress has already gone to bed. I gave her a small taper because she does not like the dark, but she has been sleeping almost ever since you left.'

TWENTY-THREE

My wife inspected the sleeping arrangements that the slave had made for us, and nodded her approval. 'Very well, Tenuis! You may go and rest, yourself. I assume you banked the fire?'

'As well as I was able, mistress, with the few small logs we had. Though I was hoping . . .?'

Gwellia glanced at me. 'Unfortunately we found nothing that was suitable.'

'We found a corpse, though!' Minimus put in, excitedly. 'Two of them, in fact. The master thinks they were the sons of the estate.'

'The children of that bird-woman that spoke to you in town?' Tenuis paused in the doorway and shot me a puzzled look. 'I thought she said that they'd been dead for years.'

'They died during the awful fire at the estate. But the bodies weren't discovered. They were in an inner cave.' Gwellia gave a little shudder at the memory. 'The young men must have gone in there to shelter from the blaze, but found that they were trapped inside – and either starved to death or suffocated by breathing in the smoke. Perhaps that's what helped preserve them, in the end, so they were bizarrely smoked like cheese or fish.' She glanced at me. 'Do you not think so, husband? You are looking unconvinced.'

I shook a warning head. Tenuis was visibly pale, shaken and aghast. He had not seen the horrors in the cave, but his imagination was clearly painting pictures in his mind.

'Certainly the bodies were macabre – and I'm sure they date back to the fire,' I said, pacifically, sitting on the pile of bedding reeds to unlace my sandal-straps, while Minimus knelt at Gwellia's feet and undid hers for her. 'Though the circumstances might not be exactly as you think. But – enough of this for now. There is quite enough to give us nightmares, as it is! Tenuis, retire – and be ready to attend to Julia when she wakes. Minimus, help your mistress take her cloak and tunic off, then blow out the candle and go to sleep yourself. Thanks to my clever wife, we can kindle fire again tomorrow, if the kitchen fire goes out.'

Gwellia permitted herself to be undressed, then sank down on the bed-reeds at my side and spread the tunics so they covered us, but I could feel that she was sleepless and rigid, even in the dark. After a long time, she dug me in the ribs.

'Husband, there is something that you're not telling me' she pleaded, whispering. 'I understand you did not want to terrify the slaves, but if you don't share your doubts with me I shall not sleep, myself. What do you mean, "the circumstances may not be what I think"? You said yourself the bodies were preserved by chance.'

I thumped the reeds to shape a better pillow for my head. 'Indeed,' I muttered, sleepily, 'but they could hardly have been trapped inside the cave by accident. I'm surprised you did not see that for yourself, but I'll explain it in the morning. Try to sleep for now.'

I felt her whirl around beside me and sit upright in the dark. 'I shan't sleep for an instant if you don't explain it now. Of course it was an accident – what else could it have been . . .?' She tailed off. 'Oh dear gods – you can't think that someone came and walled them in alive? Not on purpose! That would be even worse than being trapped by some mischance.'

She couldn't see me, but I shook my head. 'It did not happen while they were alive, perhaps. The bodies didn't look as though they'd struggled to get out, so I presume they were already dead. But I'm absolutely certain that someone walled them in.'

There was a moment's silence while my wife digested this. 'Because of the stones and rubble piled up outside to hide the opening? But I thought we had concluded that Eliana did that, fairly recently.'

'I'm talking about the time when they were first hidden there. I don't believe that wine-rack moved itself,' I said. 'And it had clearly been in front of the entrance to the inner cave, until the fallen rock demolished it. Maybe it always stood there to disguise the opening – probably it did, and the young men came and moved it to get in. But absolutely certainly they did not move it back.'

Gwellia said nothing, as she thought this through. Then she murmured, 'I suppose you're right. So you suggest that someone came when they were dead, and closed the cave to hide them for some reason of his own?'

'Such as trying to disguise the fact that he had murdered them?' I said. 'I think that's very probable.'

'Murder?' Gwellia's gasp of horror made me instantly regret that I'd succumbed to the temptation of expressing it that way. 'I thought they simply had gone into the cave – perhaps looking for that family treasure that we've heard about, to save it from the fire – and been overwhelmed by smoke. Is that not probable? As sons of the estate they would have known the hiding place was there.' She had quite forgotten to speak quietly, and I heard the slave-boy stir. Now that he was listening there was no point in whispering – or in trying any longer to protect them from the truth. Imagination would be worse than facts.

'Dead men don't chop off their own hands,' I said. 'Nor move them afterwards. And the right arms of both corpses had been hacked off at the wrists – though there is no sign of the parts that were removed. Did you not notice when we were in the cave?'

I felt Gwellia shudder. 'I was trying not to look!'

A rustling at the bottom of the bed told me that Minimus had joined his sleeping pile to ours – obviously too terrified to sleep alone. 'But why chop the hands off?' His voice was wavering. 'That's just inviting ghosts. Now the spirits will have to walk the earth to look for them.'

I sat upright in bed 'This is ridiculous. If we are going to talk about these things, we will do it in the light. I was going to wait till morning, but I see that we shall have to do it now, or none of us will have a moment's rest. Minimus, there should be a piece of taper in the room where Julia is – if the Fates are smiling, it will be still alight. Go and fetch it, quickly, and bring it back in here.'

There was a bumping as the boy went stumbling about, then a creak as he succeeded in opening our door – an act rewarded by a faint glow from across the atrium suggesting that there was indeed a candle still burning in the room beyond. Minimus bent over and fumbled underneath his bedding-reeds. 'I've got the taper-end that I put out,' he said, triumphantly. 'I'll light it at the flame and bring that back to you.' And his dim shape disappeared in the direction of the glow.

In the semi-darkness, Gwellia caught my hand. 'And is there an answer to his question? Why cut off the hands? Simple cruelty? Some kind of evil sacrifice? Revenge? Or is this the curse that people tried to warn us of?'

'I think the killer had a use for them,' I said. 'I think he cut them off and plunged them in the fire, so that the rings could be identified. Remember I told you what Hebestus said about the sons – only a few fragments of charred bone were ever found? But how could anyone be certain whose bones they had been?'

'Seal-rings!' Gwellia breathed. 'Of course! Eliana would have recognized them as her sons'! But presumably the rings would come off easily enough. In that case why not simply just produce the seals?'

'That would not suffice to prove the boys were dead, or – more importantly – imply how they had died. There had to be some circumstantial bone as well – something to suggest that they'd perished in the fire. Those corpses were missing only one hand each – I noticed that at once. There had to be a reason, but it wasn't till I thought of seal-rings that the answer came to me. And that confirmed my theory about whose the bodies were . . .' I broke off as Minimus came back into the room, carrying the re-lighted taper-end.

Even a small flame gives off surprising light, and as the illumination drove the shadows back, my spirits lifted too. (I am not generally given to fear of the unknown, but tonight even I had been half-ready for unwanted visitations from the Afterworld.) Gwellia and Minimus simply looked relieved.

'Your master has a theory,' Gwellia began – and outlined to Minimus what I'd said about the hands. I did not interrupt her – though some of her account did not exactly tally with the conclusions that I'd drawn. I knew that, in explaining to the slave, she was calming her own anxieties, so I let her talk – it gave me the opportunity to clarify my thoughts.

My wife had clearly been thinking hard herself. She finished her recital and then she turned to me. 'But you still think that they were murdered, husband? They didn't simply die – even if someone did remove the hands? We know there was a fire. Perhaps they did not burn to death as everybody first thought, but could they not have suffocated as I had supposed? Or was there evidence of some other cause of death I did not see?'

'I think that someone stabbed them underneath the ribs, and virtually disembowelled them,' I replied. 'Did you not notice . . .'

She closed her eyes against the memory. 'I thought they had exploded, or something horrible . . . Part of whatever process preserved them in the cave.'

'I was inclined to think so, too, at first. Perhaps it even helped the bodies to remain – since the stomach contents were no longer there to rot – but the lower clothing was in tatters, as though it had been slashed, and stiff and stained with something dark that looked like blood to me. But there were no such stains around the wrists, which suggests that the removal of the hands was a kind of afterthought – done when the victims had been dead some time. A closer inspection would no doubt tell us more.'

'But shouldn't they be lying in a pool of blood, if that was how they died? And there was no sign of that! Of course this would have happened many years ago, but the floor of the cave was simply scattered stones – no discoloured patches on the rocks.'

'Exactly. I'm inclined to think the victims were murdered somewhere else – the outer cave perhaps, since there are dark stains by the stone amphora-rack which I supposed were wine – and dragged there afterwards. Though since the killer's dead, I suppose we'll never know.'

'Dead? Why do you think that he is dead?' my wife exclaimed. 'I thought the lazy steward must have murdered them, but isn't he alive?'

'The only person we know about who's dead, is Eliana's husband. Or do you think their father killed them?' Minimus was shocked enough to speak without requesting our permission first.

I did not rebuke him. 'On the contrary. I think that Varius did,' I said, and had the satisfaction of seeing my companions look surprised. 'And I'm just as certain that Eliana came to that conclusion too. She told me he was visiting the villa "just about the time that awful fire took place" – she even told me that he helped to fight the fire. In fact, I think, she realized that he was probably to blame for starting it. But she also said, "my sons were still alive" – those were her very words. Looking back, I see that she connected him with that event. So he cost her everything – her sons, her husband's health and finally the farm.'

'But she still accepted his hospitalit . . .' Gwellia trailed off. Her eyes grew very wide. 'She was the one who poisoned him? That's why she agreed to come to Glevum, so she could get revenge? Is that what you believe?'

'If I'm right about the moment when she worked out the truth, I think she had already consented to the move. But when she found the bodies, she did not change her mind. Quite the contrary, she abandoned her half-hearted search for treasure in the grounds – Hebestus had been fearing that he'd have to dig, but we've seen no sign that such a thing took place. Coming to Glevum gave her a proper purpose, now – the opportunity to avenge her family.'

'I wonder she did not seek redress through the courts. A mother may appeal for vengeance for a murdered son, in person if she has no one to speak for her – it's almost the only reason a woman may bring a case at all.'

'But Eliana did have somebody to speak for her,' I said. 'Varius himself had potestas. So there was no hope of justice from the magistrates. And what other recourse did she have? Even her wish to sue her steward was refused – probably because he was secretly in Varius's employ. He may have been the one who actually set the fields alight – someone was clearly paying him small sums for several years, though freedom was probably the promised recompense. But he could not get that until his former owner died and Varius was formally declared the residuary heir. It would be interesting to find that steward and hear what he has to say, now that Varius is no longer here to threaten him.'

Gwellia shook her head. 'And that's not very likely. He will have disappeared. And the same thing's true of every point you've made. You may be right in much of what you say, but how could it be proved? We have no evidence beyond the bodies in the cave – and the fact that someone left the herbs and closed the entrance up. You don't even know for certain that Eliana was responsible for that.'

'I think she would confirm it, if we asked!' I said. 'Now that Varius is dead, she has nothing more to lose. She might even welcome the fact that his treachery was known.'

'Though she has become a murderer herself? And not merely Varius, but Claudius too – and many of the household slaves as well! Would she not fear exile of the harshest kind, at least?'

'Even an unskilled advocate would plead she was provoked, and acted to avenge her family. The court might be persuaded to be merciful. Besides, Varius himself was guilty of a capital offence. Arson and the murder of two Roman citizens! I don't applaud her actions – she has killed a lot of people who did her no harm at all – but I can understand her motives. And as for punishment, I do not think she'd care. She's given up the will to live. She'd done what she intended and "outlived her usefulness", so she has given up food and may have starved herself to death by now. But I should have liked to speak to her and see if my conclusions were correct. It's only a pity Marcus is no longer here to help, or I'd –'

I was interrupted by a figure at the door. 'What is happening here?' Julia was standing with her candle in her hand, and little Tenuis attending her, behind. I had been so intent on speaking that I'd not seen them come. 'I thought that the agreement was that we should go to bed early and eke the tapers out. But obviously that's no longer true. First a slave came to my room and wakened me. Then I heard voices here and saw the light – and when I followed them I heard my husband's name. Is there some problem? Has something happened that I don't know about?'

There was a silence. Gwellia looked at me. 'We made a discovery in the wine-cave,' I explained. 'A fairly grisly one – but it does suggest that Varius's death was a revenge, within the family. In the normal way, I would have sent to Marcus, to tell him my suspicions and asking him to question the surviving members of the house. But—'

'So Varius was not a victim of those threats!' Julia interrupted. 'Or do you think the killer sent the other letters too, to disguise his real intention and divert suspicion from himself?'

The letters! After the discovery of the bodies in the cave, I'd almost forgotten the question of the threats. But if I was right about the death of Varius, it raised a whole new aspect of the affair.

'I don't believe that Varius got one after all,' I said. 'But I do have the beginning of an idea about those notes. I want to think it through before I tell you more, to make sure there's nothing that I've overlooked, but I think that I can promise you that there's no danger here. This estate will fall into the public purse, I think, and I'm carrying an authority to occupy the house – sealed by a magistrate – so we can stay until Didius' decrees are nullified, and it's safe to return to Glevum – or perhaps Corinium.'

'You think that Marcus has been subject to an imperial interdict? You don't mean he's been banished?'

I did not, in fact, of course. I was convinced that Marcus had evaded it. But I was saved from the necessity of saying so by the sudden expiration of the taper that she held.

'Dear gods!' she said. 'The candle has gone out. How will I find my way back to my room again?'

'Minimus will guide you,' I said, thankfully. 'Though that taper will not last much longer, either. It has almost gone. Go back to rest, and we will do the same. And don't concern yourself unnecessarily. There are problems in Glevum, I will not deny, but I don't believe that Marcus is in any immediate danger now.'

Julia needed no more encouragement than that, and in the sudden dark my wife reached for my hand.

'I'm very glad you told me what you thought. I feel less troubled now. And you managed an awkward moment very cleverly. Though sometime we'll have to tell Julia the truth.'

I settled down beside her on our bed of reeds. 'I'll do that when I'm certain that my fears are true. In the morning, I intend to go into the town. I'll take the ox-cart and bring back supplies – there is no danger now if we are recognized – and I'll try to find someone to take a note to Junio. I'll get him to tell the authorities what we've found here, as well. Then if the curia want to summon me, they can. I don't think there was ever serious danger from those threats.'

Gwellia answered with a sleepy, 'Mmm.'

'Esa says there is a guardhouse on the river crossing-point – the army may have left for Londinium by now, but if it's still manned they will have access to imperial couriers. Marcus's seal should be enough to get a message sent.' I was not altogether confident of that – news travels quickly in the military world, and if Marcus was disgraced there would be no hope of help. But I'd face that tomorrow.

I nuzzled up to Gwellia. 'What shall I bring back from the market?' But there was no reply. So I followed the example of my softly-breathing wife and went instantly to sleep.

TWENTY-FOUR

Next morning I was up before the sun, and so were Gwellia and the slaves. Although the hours of night are short at this time of the year, all of us had rested relatively well after the rigours of the day before, and in the misty half-light before dawn we ate our meagre breakfast and then lit the fire again. Cold broth is not the finest meal at that early hour, but it was sustaining, and there was at least the promise of better food to come.

Maximus and I went off to fetch the ox and entice him back between the shafts again, while Gwellia and Tenuis collected wood to feed the cooking-fire. Then, retracing our unorthodox route of yesterday, with Minimus tugging at the horns and my own judicious application of the goad, we urged the animal back into the lane and got the cart onto the major road again. Gwellia came with us for a mile or two, (leaving Tenuis to tend to Julia when she woke) but got down at the next farm-stead that we passed and set off – armed with some money from my purse – to see what she could buy from the tubby farmer's wife, who was feeding a flock of flapping chickens from a pail. The last I saw of Gwellia she was collecting eggs – which promised well for future purchases. She saw me looking, and gave a cheery wave, then we were past the summit of the hill and we lost sight of her.

The road was busy, even at this hour – surprising after the emptiness of yesterday – and there seemed to be a joyful mood about. Several drivers even waved their whips at us or called out cheerful greetings as they lumbered past. A mental calculation told me that today was not a public festival, which might have meant the usual market-stalls were closed, so perhaps the brilliant sunshine (which had now broken through) accounted for this outbreak of geniality.

We lurched on companionably for perhaps an hour or so, and very soon the river-crossing came in sight. There was a fine bridge, wide enough for carts to pass, with care, and guarded by the small military fort I'd heard about. And there was no doubt about the presence of the soldiery. A hefty fellow in full legionary kit, with bulging biceps and enormous legs was leaning on a spear and idly watching the traffic as it passed, only stopping one wagon out of ten or more.

Perhaps we were unlucky. He seemed to be concentrating on ox-carts in particular. He pushed his helmet back as we approached and uncoiled himself, revealing that he was immensely tall. He sauntered to the cart, but barely had to raise his head to talk to me. 'I've not seen you before. Your business in Aquae Sulis, traveller?'

'Visiting the market – and the temple, too, I hope.' I decided to gamble on this opportunity. 'But first I would be glad to talk to the commander here.' The man looked startled, unsurprisingly, so I played my winning throw. 'I carry a letter of authority from the senior magistrate in Glevum, written under seal and permitting me to act on his behalf,' I said, producing it from underneath my cloak. 'I may be on an ox-cart, and of no account, but it is in his name that I am making this request. There is an urgent message which I wish to send and I am in need of a swift and trusted courier – or even a rider from the imperial post. If this message reaches Glevum fort it can be forwarded.' At least, I thought privately, I sincerely hoped it could, now that the commander there had delegated power. But it was my best hope of reaching Junio.

The soldier was examining the seal with interest. 'Your patron's name?' he barked.

Ah! This might be where my task grew difficult! Was Marcus's disgrace already widely known? I said, with a swagger that I did not feel, 'His Excellence Marcus Aurelius Septimus. He has connections with the Imperial House.'

The huge brow wrinkled in a frown. 'I think I've heard of him.' He handed back the letter. 'You shall have your wish. I'll have you escorted to the commander's deputy, who is in temporary charge. But the boy and the ox-cart will have to move along.'

Minimus looked apprehensively at me, but I had come to trust him with the awkward animal. 'Get down and lead him,'

I instructed. 'Use the goad and walk. Go across the bridge and wait the other side – there'll be somewhere near the market where you can tie him up. Then you can sit up on the cart until I come. I shan't be very long.'

But in that I was mistaken. It would be many hours before I saw the boy again, but I did not know that as I walked into the cool gloom of the fort, following the sulky subaltern who'd been assigned to me as guide.

'In here, citizen!' he said, opening a heavy door and ushering me into a tiny cubicle. At other times it must have acted as a kind of holding-cell, the only window space was a small slit high up in the wall, and the only furniture a battered wooden bench. The walls and floor were made of solid stone, as I noted when my escort left me there and shut the door. I was gratified to notice that he did not turn the key.

I sat down on the wooden bench to wait, mentally running over the events of yesterday and composing the message I would send to Junio. There was nothing else to do and nothing here to see, though there were sounds of movement elsewhere in the fort. After what seemed an age my guide appeared again, accompanied by the soldier I'd encountered at the gate and a small, squat self-important officer – a centurion, judging from the sideways plume on the helmet which he carried underneath his arm.

'You are the citizen Libertus?' he rapped out, as the trio formed up in a standing row in front of me.

I was about to answer meekly, but I changed my mind. 'How do you know that? I don't believe I mentioned it,' I said.

That earned a sneering smile. 'We have our informants,' the centurion said. 'And you are staying at an estate a little north of here, that was inherited by a certain Varius Quintus Flavius?'

My heart was sinking to my sandal-soles. Of course, I'd been warned that the curia in Glevum were seeking me, but I'd not expected them to trace me yet. The traveller on the horse, presumably! It was foolish to have come here – effectively handing myself over to the authorities – but it was too late now. It was likely that I would be taken back for questioning – probably today – with no way of telling anybody where I was, not even Minimus, who would be fruitlessly waiting with the ox-cart until dusk.

'It seems you know already,' I said, bitterly. 'Though I can't imagine how. Few people knew the details. I take it there has been some sort of search for me?'

The centurion looked almost jovial at this. 'There's been a man from Glevum here this very day, enquiring about you, and asking us to put a watch upon the gate. Driving an ox-cart, that is what he said – and here indeed you are. My men will be delighted. He's offering a reward. I've sent a slave to fetch him, he'll be here very soon – and then we can decide what we're going to do with you.'

'But I am a Roman citizen,' I protested, unconvincingly. 'I came here in good faith to ask the commandant to get a message urgently to the colonia.'

The soldier from the gate gave me a nasty smile. 'Indeed. The letter with the seal. Supposedly from Marcus Aurelius Septimus himself. We had been warned that you would carry one – that is how we could be certain who you were. And don't worry about your message, citizen. It seems you may be able to deliver it yourself. I believe the intention is to send you back as soon as possible.'

'So this does concern my patron?' I said, unhappily. 'I was afraid of that. Some decree from Didius Julianus, denouncing him, I suppose?'

The massive shoulders hunched into a shrug. 'Don't ask me, citizen, I don't know myself. We are soldiers, not philosophers. We don't ask questions. We just do as we're told. Though I doubt that this concerns a decree from Didius, that would have been formally nullified by now.'

'Nullified!' I was so startled I leapt up from my bench. 'What's happened?'

This time it was the subaltern who spoke. 'Citizen, where have you been the last few days? Have you not heard the news? The Upstart was executed on the Kalends of this moon and the Emperor Septimius Severus wears the purple now. I thought that all Britannia would have known by now – yesterday was declared a public holiday to celebrate, by order of the Provincial Governor no less.'

'But I thought Albinus was a candidate himself?' I was still trying to take in the unexpected news. Ironic that it should have come too late to save my patron's life, but – since Septimius had been a friend of Pertinax – it might be possible to redeem his honour and estate and save his family, yet. I resolved that I would try – let them drag me back to Glevum, I would plead my rank and appeal direct to the imperial court in Rome!

I was so busy with these thoughts I only half-heeded the subaltern's reply. 'Oh, Governor Albinus has withdrawn his claim. He made a pact with the new Emperor, and promised him support, in return for being offered the Empire later on. Septimius has formally adopted him and even named him Caesar, to prove that he's the heir – that was the chief reason for the public holiday. Decimus Clodius Septimius Albinus Caesar, that's now his formal name – but, you know what such promises will turn out to be worth—'

'Silence, soldier!' The centurion's sudden bellow made me jump. 'You are showing disrespect to the Emperor of Rome. I should have you flogged, but I am short of men, so I shall simply put you on fatigues. Latrines for you tomorrow. In the meantime, stay here and guard this man. And no more gossiping, or it will be far worse for you!'

I looked at the subaltern, who had snapped to attention and was frowning horribly. It was clear I would get no further help from him. So I turned to the centurion, though without much hope. 'I consent to your arrangements – it seems I have no choice. But I do have one request. Can I at least send a message to my wife and slaves – specifically the one who is waiting with the cart. And I'd like to send him a *sestertius* or two – I promised I would take some food back when I went. There is nothing on the farm.'

The centurion appeared to find this very comical. He actually laughed. 'Well, you'll have to ask the citizen who set the watch for you. He asked us to detain you and he is paying us, so it is his decision what becomes of you. He has been staying at the temple complex overnight – they have facilities for visitors of rank – and he told us where to find him. He should not be very long. The temple is only a few minutes walk from here, along the riverbank. In the meantime, you can sit and think of any reason why he should accede to your request.'

They all three left together, and they locked the door this time – though presumably the subaltern was still on guard outside. I settled back on my uncomfortable bench, trying not to think about what lay ahead of me. However, my solitude was not to last for long.

The door flew open and the centurion peered in. 'Ah, there you are!' he said, as if I might have disappeared. 'You've got a visitor. The slave I sent has just come back – and he's brought the citizen himself. Ask him about contacting your family. You may be fortunate. A generous gentleman.' He gave me a smug smile. 'Though I would not count on it. And you'd better have that letter that you showed to me, and let him see the seal. He was asking me if you still had it and I said you did. Strangely, he has something similar himself. So now we'll see who really has authority.' He turned back towards the passage, all obsequiousness now. 'This way, citizen. Here is the wretch you asked to detain and he has admitted everything that you accuse him of!'

And he stood back to let the citizen come in.

TWENTY-FIVE

'Junio!' I could not believe my eyes. 'What are you doing here?' I jumped up from my uncomfortable seat and he came towards me with his hands outstretched.

The centurion was looking more astonished than I felt – if possible. 'You know this person in some social context, citizen?' The question was addressed to Junio, and the tone suggested total disbelief, though the enquiry hardly needed to be made. Far from merely mutually grasping elbows in the normal way, I found myself engulfed in a warm filial embrace – a most unbecoming exhibition for two citizens of Rome.

Junio, however, did not seem to care. 'This is my adoptive father,' he explained.

The soldier looked bewilderedly between the two of us. I, in a tattered tunic, stained with travel now – and Junio in formal Roman dress. I confess my son looked splendidly the part – barbered and fullered to perfection, in his well-draped tunic and expensive cloak – while I was grey and shaggy, and not especially clean. 'But surely, sir, you are a Roman citizen . . . How . . .?'

'And so is he – as I am sure he will have claimed. Indeed, I owe my status entirely to his. Before he freed me and took me as his son, I was in fact his slave.'

The centurion swallowed heavily, as if digesting this. Then he turned to me. 'Citizen,' he said, in an altered tone of voice, 'apologies for any disrespect I might have shown. I did not realize that you really were a citizen – I thought a false claim to the rank was part of the offence that you were wanted for.' He turned to Junio. 'And I suppose that seal is genuine as well?' His voice betrayed his terror at what he might have done.

'Just like the one that I am carrying!' Junio produced a bark-roll letter as he spoke. 'They are both authentic, as you'll see if you examine them.' He proffered it to the centurion, who backed away as if the scroll might poison him. 'But, no one is about to issue a complaint. I asked you to find the person I described, and you have certainly obliged.' He gave the man a magisterial smile. 'So, we'll say no more of it. Now if you would care to leave us, we have business to discuss. I've not forgotten that I promised a reward – I'll settle with you later, just before I leave. In the meantime, it is possible you could arrange some wine, and a few refreshments? My father is not young, and he has had a nasty shock.'

The centurion backed out, bowing and we heard him in the hall, bellowing instructions to his underlings. Junio grinned at me. 'I'm very glad to see you, and know that you are safe – though I'm very sorry that they locked you up in here. I was not expecting that. I did ask them to stop you, if you passed this way – gave them your name, told them what you looked like, and said that you'd be on an ox-cart or more probably a mule and would be carrying an authorizing letter under seal. I should have realized they'd assume that you'd committed some offence.'

'Lucky that I happened to come to Aquae Sulis then!' I felt I was entitled to be a little wry.

He made a face at me. 'If you hadn't come this morning, I was going to search for you – relying on some local to direct me to the farm. I have a gig at my disposal, and we looked out for the house, but somehow we must have driven past it on our way here yesterday. Not surprising, as it was getting dark. I knew that you had gone to Eliana's old estate, but nobody in Glevum could tell me where it was – and I could hardly interrupt the funeral to ask her where to come.'

'The funeral?' I murmured stupidly. Surely my patron was not cremated yet?

'For Varius and Claudius,' he said, suggesting that I could have guessed that for myself. 'They were her nearest relatives, and when the days of mourning were complete, obviously she had a funeral for them. Very well-attended, too, from what I understand – though obviously I did not go myself. The curia were unanimous that I should come at once, and bring you back as soon as possible. Marcus has insisted that no official statement should be made until they'd had the chance to question you.'

'Marcus insisted?' I was sounding like the famous goddess in the cave – repeating everything. 'But I thought that he was dead!'

Junio was staring as though he thought the moon had turned my wits. 'What gave you that impression? He's very much alive – relieved that Didius has been deposed, of course, and very pleased with you. Though how you managed to work out who the letter-writer was, and force a written confession out of him, I still don't understand – especially since you weren't even in Glevum at the time.'

It was my turn now to goggle. 'But I haven't . . .' I began, and then realized that perhaps I did know the solution – and that I should have known it long ago. 'Porteus?' I murmured. 'He sent that letter – then wrote a confession in a document and mentioned me by name?'

Junio nodded. 'I won't ask how you know that he had mentioned you,' he said. 'But you are right, of course – there was a writing-tablet in his hand when they discovered him. Taken henbane, by the look of it – which he'd mixed with poppy juice – though to read what he had scratched onto the wax you'd suppose that he had heroically fallen on his sword! He could not face the ignominy, that is what he wrote. He realized that you knew that he had sent the threats, but he had never intended Marcus any actual harm – he'd only hoped to frighten him away, so that he could stand for office in his place.'

I nodded. 'He deputized for Marcus when he went to Rome,' I said. 'He told me so himself. He was clearly disappointed that Marcus hadn't stayed abroad, as he'd intended to. I suppose that Porteus would have been the obvious candidate – and gained the higher office that he always sought.'

'But he swears by all the gods that he did not kill Varius, although you think he did. That's why Marcus wants you to come back straight away, and explain your reasoning before the curia. Obviously, there is no further risk to Julia and the children now – so if Porteus was the poisoner and it can be proved, his goods will be forfeited to compensate the crime – to the state, if there is no proper heir to claim. Though that will be the sum of punishment, I suppose, he cannot be exiled when he's already dead and it's agreed his daughter will not be penalized – beyond the loss of all his wealth and goods.'

'But he didn't murder Varius,' I said. 'Unless I'm much mistaken, Eliana did.'

'Eliana?!' Junio was shocked. 'And I had no idea.' He gave me a reproachful look. 'I know that Didius was a potential threat, and no doubt you were wise to take Julia and the children away where they were safe – but if you had worked this out before you left, could you not have confided it to me, if no one else? Especially since my own family were involved. Was it because you felt you had no proper proof?'

I shook my head. 'I could not tell you, because I'd no idea myself. I only worked out the letter mystery today, when you reported that Marcus was alive and I realized then that Porteus must be the suicide. Then pieces of mosaic slotted into place.' I shook my head. 'I have been an idiot. I should have suspected Porteus from the start – the way that he accosted me outside the fort, thinking I'd reported that there'd been a threat. Why should he imagine anything like that? I foolishly assumed that he'd had a threat himself – in fact I actually suggested that to him . . .'

'And he leapt at the excuse.'

I nodded ruefully. 'He even revealed that he knew about the contents of the note – and he was carrying a sequel – which he never sent, but which he accidentally showed me at the time. He thought quite quickly, I must admit the fact – claimed that it had been delivered to his apartment earlier. And I never questioned it – even though the writing-block was of similar design.' I could hardly believe my own stupidity.

Junio nodded. 'Probably the one that he wrote his death-confession on. Marcus noticed that the decoration was the same, and took that as further evidence of guilt. But you had already seen it at the fort?'

'He was waiting to approach me, as I realize now – wondering how Marcus had reacted to the threat. He was such a nervous fool that he could not keep away – which, bizarrely meant that I took for granted that he was innocent. It did not occur to me that a man who had written threats against a magistrate – and so committed a serious offence – would choose to draw immediate attention to himself. And right outside the garrison at that!'

'So he was waiting for you? But how would he know that you were likely to be there?'

'I think I know the answer to that question too. One of his servants had been near the villa keeping watch – no doubt the one who threw in the writing-block. I said to Marcus that was likely to occur. He obviously saw me leaving and reported back . . .' I broke off suddenly. 'Dear Mars – do you know, Porteus mentioned that delivery to me – the fact that it was thrown across the wall – and I did not question how he knew!' What is more, I thought wryly to myself, I'd noticed that Porteus dressed his servants in bright blue uniforms and did not connect it with my glimpses in the wood.

'You're right about the spy. One of the slaves has thrown himself upon the mercy of the curia – confessing to delivering the scroll, but pleading that he did not know what it contained and was only doing as his master said. But despite repeated questioning by the torturers, he cannot tell us any more at all – apart from the fact that he was watching you – further convincing Marcus that you'd solved the whole affair.'

Of course he had been watching me, I thought. He was the courier who ran past me on the forest track that first day – though since he was no longer attempting to disguise himself, I'd thought no more of it. Doubtless he was hurrying to his master then, to report that I was on my way – just as he informed him of my presence at the stables the next day.

'I realized that it was not mere chance that Porteus should happen by when I was hiring the raeda,' I said thoughtfully. 'He must have really hoped then that his threats had worked and Marcus was about to flee. He pretended to be interested in renting the villa, while my patron was away – which I did not believe – but I thought he was just frightened and looking for a pretext so he could run away himself.'

'But you did not suspect him of the letter? He was sure you did.'

'I've been wondering myself what gave him that idea,' I said, and then it came to me. 'Of course, I told him that Varius was dead, and asked if he knew if there had been a threatening note – but only because he'd happened to call on Varius on that day. But he assumed that I suspected him, I suppose. He panicked, naturally – kept insisting that he knew nothing about that and asked if I knew who'd sent the threats.'

'And you said . . .?'

'That I was working on it, and would find the guilty man, and – come to think of it – suggested he left town, saying that Marcus would understand why he had fled. I still thought he'd had a threat himself, of course, but he must have drawn his own conclusions from my words . . .' I broke off as the subaltern appeared, bearing a tray with the requested wine and dates. He put it on the bench – for there was nowhere else – while giving me a look that said I was the author of his woes.

'I'm instructed to ask if there is anything else that you require.' He could not have sounded less enthusiastic if he'd been asked to tread the wine himself.

I was about to say that there was nothing, when Junio chimed in. 'Perhaps it would be possible to send a messenger? Just to alert my father's slave to what is happening? You'll find him with the ox-cart at the marketplace.' He turned to me. 'We'll have to make arrangements about getting that back home. You and I can travel in the gig, and I have instructions to hire a travelling carriage for the children and the womenfolk. Marcus will pay the driver when they all get back.' He gave me a wicked grin. 'Hence my sealed letter of authority.'

I shook my head. 'I promised I would take provisions back to Gwellia. She managed wonders yesterday but there is nothing there to eat. And the children are not with us, we have left them with a wet-nurse we encountered on the way – the carriage will have to call there and collect them on the way. And Arlina, who is with the family too.'

Junio shook his head. 'No wonder it was difficult to trace where you had been. We made enquiries at several inns, but none had heard of you. One place sounded hopeful – a group on an ox-cart – but when I enquired further, it wasn't you at all. A Celtic girl called Kennis and her family – that was the only name the landlord could recall.'

I laughed aloud. 'I'll tell you all about it on the way back to the farm. I'd better drive the ox-cart – why don't you ride with me and get the gig to follow? You can bring Julia back to the temple overnight. And we'll arrange the hiring-carriage while we are in the town – there's no time to get to Glevum anyway, today. But I'll send to Marcus, explaining the Varius affair – then he can make the public statement about Porteus if he likes.'

'No problem with the message!' Junio made a face. 'I think the centurion will burst himself to help! Though tomorrow you and I will have to go ourselves – whatever other arrangements have been made. I am under orders from the magistrates. But I'd be interested to hear what your message will contain – you have not explained the Varius affair to me!'

So I told him, as I called for bark-paper and ink and wrote Marcus a brief account of the affair. We gave it to the centurion-in-charge, who promised he would see that it was sent – 'by the first available military courier, naturally, citizen! And there will be no charge'. (I did not mention to my patron that I hadn't suspected Porteus earlier, of course. If the Fates throw you a lucky *aureus* you do not insult them by bite-testing the gold!)

After that I walked to Aquae Sulis with my son. On the way we passed the straggling marketplace where Minimus was still waiting on the ox-cart, patiently, and we quickly made the purchases that I had agreed. (Things were more expensive than in Glevum, to my mild surprise – but Junio pointed out that this was largely passing trade, most people only made the journey to the temple complex once, so there was no need for the stallholders to try to lure them back.)

I visited the temple. There was not really time, but I could not come so close and not have satisfied my curiosity. It might be the only chance I ever had. And I was glad I made the time.

The sacred place was everything that I'd heard of it, and more. There really was hot water springing from the earth, and not only a shrine to honour the goddess, but a splendid bath-house which is rumoured to have magic curing powers. I could have stayed for hours, but it was getting late, so I simply paid for a pigeon to be sacrificed, bought a prayer-plaque in honour of the newest Emperor, and drove the lumbering ox-cart, for the last time, to Eliana's farm.

TWENTY-SIX

Gwellia was more startled to see Junio than I had been myself, and a great deal of explanation – and rejoicing – was required. Somehow, in my absence, the women had contrived to make the villa a more comfortable place: Tenuis had even briefly lit the hypocaust, Julia had spread fresh reeds and herbs around, and Gwellia had cooked an egg-dish in the pan, which – drizzled with the honey and fresh pepper I had bought – made a sustaining meal. I was almost sorry that we were to leave the next day.

Julia, however, was tearful with relief. She was anxious for her children and delighted at the prospect of seeing them so soon and returning to her normal comfortable life. That would begin this evening, I explained, with accommodation in the temple complex overnight, and I'd brought home a simple ready-made stola from the market-place – nothing of her usual standard, and a bit too big for her, but once she put it on, she looked much more like herself.

Tomorrow she and Gwellia would travel back in comfort with the slaves – with accommodation at a military mansio if required. I gave Julia the letter under seal, which would guarantee the army's help. I no longer needed it. It had already worked its charms again, and a splendid carriage had been easily arranged for her, and even a skilled driver who would take the ox-cart home. I was oddly reluctant to say goodbye to it – I had become quite attached to the awkward animal, and Minimus clearly felt the same, though he brightened when I appointed him in charge of Arlina. 'You can ride her back,' I told him, 'when the women's party have collected her and the children from the tanner's house.'

After we had eaten (and Gwellia had fed the driver of the gig) I took Junio out and showed him what we had discovered in the cave. Once he had seen it for himself, and heard what facts I'd gleaned, he hardly needed me to tell him what my conclusions were.

'It must have been the mother,' he said, thoughtfully, as we walked back towards the villa – carrying a new oil lamp, this time full of fuel, though we did not need the light once we had left the cave; it was not dusk as yet. 'And just before she left. Imagine finding that! Poor woman, what a dreadful shock for her. And clearly she believed that Varius murdered them. But what do you suppose he can have hoped to gain? Surely it can only be the villa and the land? That is what would come to him eventually, when the presumptive heirs were dead. We heard that he did not value the estate, but that is the only motive I can see.' He frowned at me. 'Do you think there really was a treasure after all – and he forced the boys to lead him to the hiding-place, and killed them so they could not tell their father what he'd done?'

I shook my head. 'I'm sure the treasure was the motive,' I replied. 'And you may be right about them showing him the hiding-place. But I'm fairly sure the gold – if it exists – was never found. Otherwise, why would he go on urging Eliana to come and live with him? He did that even when the father was alive. I thought it was unnaturally kind, when I first heard of it. But obviously it would ensure him the running of the estate and give him the freedom to search anywhere he chose.'

'So you think the treasure is still somewhere on the farm?' Junio stopped and looked around the tangled fields as if he hoped to see some evidence of it.

'Eliana clearly did,' I said. 'She only ceased to look for it the very day she left, but she'd only recently decided it was there – according to Hebestus, and that would make good sense. If there was money buried anywhere, obviously she would not want to leave it here. It would have ensured her independence – there was no legal will, so the lands defaulted to her great-nephew, but there was no record of the gold, so if she could find it she could carry it away and claim it as her own.'

'But in the end she had to cease to search and agree to come to Glevum?' We had reached the old orchard by this time, and he stopped to pick a half-formed apple from an ancient bough. 'It's still productive land. This must have been a splendid villa at one time. It must have saddened her to go. Still more to see it falling to ruin. It had been her home for years. And imagine leaving, if you thought there might be treasure here . . .' He threw the apple and it disappeared into a clump of weeds. 'I suppose there was treasure?'

'Only the gods know that,' I said. 'These things are often rumoured – and not often true, and usually exaggerated even so. But if there is a cache, her husband found a splendid hiding-place. Eliana went on searching and she did not find a thing. Probably she did not know about the secret opening into the inner cave – it's not a thing a woman is likely to be told – and if she'd known of it, she would have looked there first. But the place had been abandoned as a wine-store long ago, and nobody had been there since the roof caved in. She must have gone there as a last resort, and found the bodies rather than the gold – but realized who was responsible and vowed to have revenge.'

'So she went to stay with Varius and poisoned what he ate? And his whole household with him?'

'What they drank, I think. I'm sure we'll find she sent some wine ahead – and Varius was very slightly ill – so she came and nursed him better, earned his gratitude and then put a bigger fatal dose into the household wine and watched him suffering. Who would be suspicious? I certainly was not – even though I knew that she was eating separately and refusing even to drink the water in the house.'

'Fearful that she would poison herself by accident?'

I shook my head. 'More likely fearful that he was going to try to poison her! She was the one remaining person with claims to the estate. I suspect he hoped to kill the husband too – we'll never know exactly what happened in that fire – though the poor man was so damaged he could no longer speak, so he could make no accusation. Normally, with injuries like that, a man would not survive for long. But Eliana nursed him valiantly and he lingered on for years. Varius must have fumed!'

Junio walked in sombre silence for a little while. 'It's difficult not to feel some sympathy for her,' he remarked, at last.

'She was responsible for several very nasty deaths – most of them people who were wholly innocent – but there is something heroic about her determination to avenge her family. A pity that she was not born a man – no judge would find against a paterfamilias who took revenge on someone who had killed his sons, crippled his marriage partner and burned down his estate. He could have pleaded insupportable injury to honour and escaped all punishment. The law is likely to be harsh on Eliana though – and rule that for a woman these were unnatural acts.'

'We'll find her the best advocate there is to speak for her,' I said. 'That is, supposing that she lives so long. She is devising her own execution as we speak – "she has outlived her usefulness", she said, meaning that she had accomplished what she meant to do, and is refusing nourishment. Hebestus said she blamed herself for Varius's death. With good reason, as I now realize.' I could not repress a rueful smile. 'I only hope that she is still alive when we get back. There is one thing that we can do for her. See that Hebestus gets the freedom he deserves.'

'But he must have helped her?'

'I don't believe he did. I think she kept this secret from him very carefully – partly for his own protection and largely out of pride. This was personal and within the family – something that she wouldn't delegate to slaves. He struck me as very honest when I spoke to him – I'm sure he had no inkling of the truth. He's devoted to his mistress but he spoke quite openly, even about her choices concerning food and drink, which he would not have done if he'd realized that it was significant. And he did not believe the rumour of the hidden gold, he said as much to Esa and to me but, if he knew it was the background to a feud, surely for one thing he would never have mentioned it at all, and secondly he would have given more credence to the tale?'

'You may be right!' Junio pushed open a broken gate which now swung from a single rusty hinge. 'It would be nice to see him freed. What will happen to the rest of the estate? It is such a pity to see it fall to ruin.'

'If Varius is proved to be a murderer, then even if he left a will, his goods are forfeited. I imagine it will fall into the

imperial purse – so the magistrates will either try to sell the
place, or put a steward in to make repairs.' I grinned at Junio.
'And I might know someone who would be glad of such a
task . . .'

'Are you two coming?' That was Gwellia's voice, calling
from the villa, just a field away. 'The gig-driver is waiting.
He says that if he doesn't leave here soon, you won't get Julia
to the temple in time to find your rooms.' She shot a look at
me. 'And he'll be back tomorrow for you shortly after dawn.
I suppose the raeda has directions as to how to come for us?'

Junio nodded. 'Father drew a little map for him. He'll pick
up Julia first and then come here for you. About mid-morning,
third or fourth hour he suggests. But there is no special hurry
– you can stop at any inn, and the driver is prepared to take
a day or two. The ox-cart will travel at its own speed, later
on. But now, I suppose it is time for me to go. Is Julia ready?'

Gwellia gave him a peculiar look. 'She's already in the gig.
And while you've been away, we've taken down the gate, so
it's possible to drive in to the front court properly.' She gestured
to the vehicle which was drawn up outside the door.

Junio climbed up beside the driver on the seat. It was a
tightish fit for three – but there was room enough, which was
fortunate as I would have to go to Glevum in that fashion very
soon. We watched as it whisked off down the lane, and disappeared from view, quickly now that it wasn't following the
cart.

Gwellia caught my arm. 'So our little adventure has turned
out well. Everyone is safe, and we can go back home. And
tonight we'll sleep more easily. We've tapers and to spare.
This time we'll have the box-bed, and leave the boys the reeds.'

I grinned back at her. 'That sounds very satisfactory,' I said.

EPILOGUE

'So! Porteus has left me a portion in his will, provided that I take his ugly daughter as a ward and find a husband for her!' Marcus roared with laughter and clapped me on the back, meaning that lots of people turned and stared at me. We were standing on the top step of the basilica in Glevum, where the will had just been read, in the presence of the seven witnesses who had seen it sealed. It was a concession that I was here beside my patron, in my Roman best, instead of mingling with the crowds below. 'I shall decline the honour.' Marcus laughed again. 'The girl looks like a mule and by the time that all his debts are paid, there won't be much left for heirs!'

I murmured some conventional assent, though privately thinking that it must be pleasant to be rich enough to forego an inheritance, whatever size it was.

Marcus read my thoughts. 'I shan't go empty-handed, my old friend,' he said. 'The curia has ruled that – although issuing threats against a magistrate is always serious – on this occasion no real harm was done and his offence is better punished by a compensation fine, which comes to me as the offended citizen, of course. And is deducted before other creditors are paid.' He thumped my back again. 'I have you to thank for that. If you hadn't made your declaration before the magistrates, they would have convicted Porteus post-mortem of killing Varius, and everything would have been forfeited to the brand-new Emperor.'

He gestured to a corner the jostling scene below, where a group of slaves were putting up a statue of Septimius Severus (hastily commissioned and not very well produced) to the entertainment of a crowd of spectators. It was being hauled up on pulleys to an empty plinth, which had now held the image of four Emperors this year.

I nodded. 'I confess I did not like the man – but I would

not have his family honour compromised by having him condemned for a crime that he did not commit.' Marcus was walking down the steps by now, through a pathway cleared by his attendant slaves and I found myself trotting politely after him, at a distance appropriate for my rank.

When we reached the bottom, Marcus stopped and turned a beaming smile on me. 'You know, until you came and told your story to the assembled councillors, I was not wholly satisfied that he'd confessed at all.' He gestured to a slave to find a carrying-chair. 'After I'd sent to fetch you back, I had a dreadful thought. I was afraid that the unknown threatener had struck, and simply put the letter in Porteus's hand to make it appear to be a suicide, especially since I recognized the style of writing-block. I was still wondering if I would be next – that is why I would not let the curia announce it publicly, or give the body burial until I'd heard from you. But of course you convinced us all that the note was genuine. Largely because you had Eliana's admission by that time, of course. Ah – here is my attendant coming with the chair. Shall you come and join me at the baths? We can take some refreshment, if you do not wish to plunge.'

I nodded, though a bathhouse visit did not interest me. I have never shared the Roman passion for being half-cooked in steam, scraped down with a strigil-wielding slave and plunged into cold water. But an invitation from my patron could not be refused – to be asked to join him bathing was the highest compliment. 'I'll join you there as soon as possible,' I said, glad of the excuse that I was following on foot.

My route there took me very close to the apartment block where Varius had lived, and I could not help recalling the last time I was there – the day I'd appeared before the curia. I had insisted on visiting Eliana first, before I gave my formal evidence, and I am glad I did – though the memory of that visit will live with me for years.

The old woman was reclining, propped by pillows, on a couch, alone in the echoing apartment, attended only by Hebestus and a couple of sickly looking maidservants who had clearly once belonged to Varius, and still looked very ill. But Eliana was the frailest of them all. She had been a living skeleton before but she had faded to a shadow of herself, weak and shrunken and as pale as death – which was clearly very close – and the wispy hair hung round her face in thin dishevelled strands. Her eyes, though, were as shrewd as ever, and her mind as sharp. She knew me from the moment I was admitted to the room.

'Ah, the pavement-maker with the mule. What brings you visiting? Come to see an ancient lady die of grief?'

'Come to see a brave old mother who avenged her sons.'

A strange expression crossed the withered face. 'Bring a stool, Hebestus, and leave us for a while. This man and I have matters to discuss.'

It was easy, after that. I had rather feared she would deny it all, but quite the contrary. She readily confessed to everything, including the murder of Varius and most of the others in the house. She was anxious to tell me exactly what she'd done, and begged me to make it public after she had died.

'The world should know what kind of person Varius was,' she said. 'I should have suspected earlier that he had set the fire – it broke out while he was in the house – but he volunteered to fight it and went off with my sons. And that was the last I ever saw of them. Then later he went out to help my husband fight the blaze. Foolishly I was grateful at the time. I now think that Varius tried to kill him too, by pushing him into the centre of the flames.'

'So your husband liked him?'

'Not especially. He always said that Varius was ruthless. But he tried to act as paterfamilias when the father died, and certainly he took my nephew into his confidence. I've even wondered if there might have been a will, and Varius destroyed it in the fire, but of course I'll never know. My poor beloved never spoke again – though I knew by his reactions that he distrusted Varius ever afterwards. That's why I would never come to Glevum while he lived. But then he died and I no longer cared . . .' She tailed off. 'And then I went into the wine-cave . . . one last attempt to find the gold that wasn't there . . . and you know what I found.'

I nodded. She had confirmed my deductions in every detail. 'But I need to tell the curia that you killed Varius,' I said. 'Or someone else is likely to be blamed. I'm talking about Porteus, the man who called on you the day that Varius died.'

'The man who would not give up his litter until I told him to? Why should I care what happens to a man like that.'

Grief and horror had turned her mind, I thought. But I persisted, gently. 'He's dead, but people are sincerely mourning Varius, thinking him the honourable victim of a foolish man – and surely that can't satisfy your purposes? You want the world to know what kind of man he really was.'

She sighed. A massive sigh that shook her ancient frame. 'You're quite right, citizen. That would not do at all. It's only a pity that it cannot wait a day or two – I cannot last much longer. And I do not care. But tell them what you wish. Write it on that tablet and read it back to me – I'll seal it with my seal. Take Hebestus with you, he can swear on my behalf that I gave it to you freely. Though I would be grateful if he did not have to know what it contained. A woman should be respected by her servants – even when she's dead.'

I did as she requested and we called the old slave in to watch her seal the writing-block. 'Now go and leave me!' She waved us both away. 'I am going to sleep. Hebestus, bring me one last glass of wine. You will find it in the jug beneath my bed.' And I did not prevent him, though I guessed what it was. The old slave was stricken, later, when he learned what he had done, but the curia had freed him – at Marcus's request.

I looked up at the building once again. The flat was empty now – like everything that Varius and Eliana had once owned, it was forfeit to the state. I wondered idly who would take it next – and whether its sad history would make it hard to sell.

But there was no time to linger, Marcus would await. I hurried quickly to the main door of the baths, where I had to fumble for the entrance price. I evaded the slave-boys who would have helped me to disrobe and guarded my garments – for a fee – while I immersed, and instead went directly to the vestibule, where Marcus was seated on a marble bench, selecting tidbits from a vendor's tray. He looked up and saw me and signalled me to come and take a seat at his right hand.

He selected two goblets of cheap watered wine and offered one to me. 'Now,' he said expansively, 'I've brought you here on purpose, as no doubt you've guessed. I want to talk to you where we will not be overheard.'

I glanced around, astonished. The atrium was full of customers – playing ballgames, doing exercise, or simply promenading where they could be seen before proceeding to the bathing areas. But, I realized, Marcus was quite right. Nobody was likely to be listening to us.

I took a sip of warm, unpleasant wine, and nodded. 'There is some secret that you wanted to impart? You found the gold, perhaps?'

'We did!' The handsome face had darkened to a frown. 'Did I not tell you that? Exactly where you told us it might be – though I don't know how you knew. Who would have thought of moving the wine press and digging underneath? But there it was, indeed. Not a fortune, but a considerable sum, enough to pay for much of the repairs. And employing your tanner has been a good idea – he has caught a lot of pests – vermin, birds and foxes that had made lairs in the field and were eating what was left of any crops. I offered him a post as land-steward, but he rejected it – said he had his freedom, and was content with that. Though I was glad to help his little family and buy his slave-son back. Julia tells me that without their help the baby would have died.'

There was nothing useful I could say to that. The whole episode had shaken Julia to the core, and – though she had always been casually generous to us – she had become so kindly to the local poor that she was in danger of encouraging mendicants. Marcus was talking of closing up the house and moving to Corinium for a little while – making Cilla positively envious. She had enjoyed the most luxurious few days of her young life in the town house there, welcomed by the servants and treated as a guest, and she had been almost reluctant to come back.

'But finding the gold was not the reason that you asked me here?' I said.

Marcus shook his head. From a cone of twisted bark he shook out a handful of roasted fava beans and tossed them down his throat. 'You were impressive when you spoke before the curia,' he said. 'Several people have remarked on it to me.' He looked at me, as if expecting a response.

I couldn't think of one. I was uneasy now. Marcus is not given to such compliments. 'Go on,' I said, at last.

'You realize that the curia has lost two councillors?'

'Varius and Porteus,' I said. 'But there will be elections soon. And no dearth of candidates. Lots of people want to be on the curia – some men spend a fortune building public works and bribing sponsors. The rank brings influence.'

Marcus fiddled with his goblet. 'That is true, of course. But it's nice to know the posts are held by people you can trust. People who would vote as you would vote, and – if you were not there yourself – keep you informed of what was happening, not just the big events, but who was supporting whom and who had argued with his friends.' I still said nothing, and finally he said what he'd been hinting at. 'The thing is Libertus, I've been asked to ask you if you'd be prepared to stand. I would put you forward as a candidate, and several of my colleagues would speak in your support. By my calculation we would win the vote.'

I should have seen it coming, but I was so surprised that I upset my wine. 'Me? Stand as councillor? But I'm of Celtic blood – and I'm a tradesman and was once a slave. They would not want a man like me to be a councillor.'

'They do. You have impressed them by your intellect, and by the way you gave your evidence. And by the fact that you seem an honest man. What is to prevent it? You're a Roman citizen, you are more than old enough and you can read and write. Besides you were born a nobleman in your tribe, I think.'

'But I don't have the property requirement,' I said, seizing on the obvious objection to this absurd idea. I had not the slightest interest in seeking civic power. 'A councillor must have a residence within the town, and of a certain size.'

'We had considered that. Porteus's apartment will shortly be for sale – in order to satisfy his creditors. That could easily be obtained for you – we could buy it, for example, and install you there – on the written understanding that we will have it back when you cease to be a councillor. That satisfies the regulations. What do you say to that?'

But I don't want to be a councillor! I was screaming inwardly, but I dared not voice that thought aloud. Marcus's patronage was a valuable thing, and he did not care for people thwarting him, especially when he was offering something flattering. 'I have a workshop,' I said feebly, 'and important customers. In fact I have a big commission which I should be working on. Replacing all the pavements in the Egidius house, as you may remember? I made a formal contract and, as a man of honour, I cannot break my word.'

I had hit on a telling argument, in fact. Breaking a contract was a criminal offence – enough to debar one from the curia. Marcus conceded with a rueful nod. 'Well, I suppose there is no help for it – this time. And since you have refused the dignity, I suppose I'll have to tell you that you're due for a reward. If you had been a councillor, you'd be disqualified, but as it is the curia have ruled it should be paid.'

'Reward?' People of my status do not expect rewards.

'Something Porteus advertised before he died. Had them make a proclamation in the marketplace offering two gold pieces to anyone who could prove, to the satisfaction of the magistrates, who it was that poisoned Varius. He lodged the money with the curia at the time, so it did not form part of his estate. I'll see it comes to you.'

He swallowed the remainder of the beans, and rose. The conference was over. I stood up too, as courtesy demands, and bowed – discreetly tipping the wine into a drain.

'I'm invited to have *cena* with the other councillors,' my patron said, extending his ringed hand for me to kiss. 'I'll tell them your decision, which I'm sure that they'll regret – though they'll accept your reasons. I will see to that.' He chuckled. 'In the meantime, think of ways to spend your *aurei*.'

But I was already toying with a wild idea. The farmland around my roundhouse was not very large, but it stretched to several fields. Surely a man could find good uses for an ox? How much would persuade Jummilius to part with one I knew?